The Goddess Affair

The Raggedy Man

Lockout

Used to Kill

Pushover

A Private Crime

A Wreath for the Bride

A Good Night to Kill

The Other Side of the Door

Casual Affairs

Ladykiller

Cop Without a Shield

The Children's Zoo

Wicked Designs

Falling Star

No Business Being a Cop

Aftershock

Leisure Dying

The Baby Merchants

Dial 577 R-A-P-E

Don't Wear Your Wedding Ring

The Phone Calls

Dive into Darkness

The Face of Crime

The Tachi Tree

The Sleeping Beauty Murders

The Babes in the Woods

Death of a Player

Murder Under the Sun

Death Schuss

Death Blanks the Screen

Death on the Grass

G. P. PUTNAM'S SONS/NEW YORK

The Goddess Affair

LILLIAN O'DONNELL

G. P. PUTNAM'S SONS
Publishers Since 1838
200 Madison Avenue
New York, NY 10016

Library of Congress Cataloging-in-Publication Data

O'Donnell, Lillian.
The goddess affair / by Lillian O'Donnell.
p.   cm.
ISBN 0-399-14183-9
I. Title.
PS3565.D59G63   1997   96-9806 CIP
813'.54—dc20

Printed in the United States of America

1   3   5   7   9   10   8   6   4   2

Book design by Gretchen Achilles

The
Goddess
Affair

Prologue

The front pew on the left-hand side of the center aisle was occupied by the family of the deceased: Lewis Aldrich, her husband; and her daughters, Diana, Juno, and Minerva. Directly behind them were Vicente Chávez, husband of Juno, and Paul Racine, fiancé of Diana. Minerva was thus far unattached. The church was barely half full.

At the funeral two years ago the magnificent French Gothic revival edifice had been packed. It was a media event. Admission was by invitation only and was the hottest ticket in town. Inside, the mourners were all celebrities, high achievers in their fields. In the street, crowds strained against police barricades and shivered in the cold January drizzle waiting for the arrival of the hearse. They watched in solemn awe as the casket was removed and lifted to the shoulders of professional pallbearers who had the responsibility of maneuvering it safely up the steep, narrow steps into the church vestibule. There it was transferred to the honorary pallbearers who solemnly bore it beneath the soaring arches to the front of the altar.

A gasp of horror went up from the congregation as it slipped from their hands as they set it down. A ripple of relief followed as they caught it just in time.

At the same time, the drizzle outside changed to soaking rain and the service began. The crowds were not discouraged. They stayed till the service was completed and the casket bearing the remains of Valerie Horvath Aldrich, now safely back in the care of professionals, was returned to the hearse for the short trip to the cemetery. The crowd's patience was an indication of both admiration and respect. Valerie Aldrich's life was a true American success story known to all.

Born in Hungary at the time of the Communist coup after World War II, Valerie was only a schoolgirl when she began to run errands for the Resistance. In her teens, she married András Horvath, a freedom fighter. When it became apparent that the anti-Communist revolution in 1956 was doomed and Russian tanks were about to enter the city of Budapest to inflict a bloody retaliation on its loyal defenders, András urged his young wife to flee, but she refused to leave him. During the ensuing years, while he continued to work for the underground, Valerie gave birth to two girls, Diana and Juno. Ironically, when the situation had eased and the attitude of the Soviet-supported government became more tolerant, András, betrayed by one of his own men, was arrested, tried, and sentenced to death. Valerie waited till the sentence was carried out, and then, at last, left the country.

She arrived in New York in 1970 with five hundred dollars in her pocket, a child in each hand—Diana, five, and Juno, three—and a letter of introduction to the Hungarian expatriate community in Yorkville.

She took what work she could get. She was a domestic, a waitress, a cook, but she was not physically strong enough for those jobs. A neighbor who looked after the girls while Valerie was at work observed the refugee as she sat up late into the night mending her own and her children's clothing, nodding and almost falling asleep at the sewing machine. She sewed so beautifully, the neighbor told her. Skilled seamstresses were hard to find. She suggested sewing might be a more suitable and more lucrative occupation.

With the help of other refugees, Valerie Horvath started a modest dressmaking business. She had a flair for style, and by means of sharp wits and hard work, she expanded from the sewing machine in a back bedroom to a small store on Second Avenue to a trendy boutique on Fifth Avenue. At first she copied pictures cut out of magazines brought to her by her uptown customers. But her real strength lay in original creations. Soon she began to turn out exclusive, custom-designed dresses and gowns. It wasn't long before she was discovered by New York society, whose patronage made her a trendsetter. Later, through her marriage to Lewis Aldrich, scion of the Virginia Aldriches of racing fame, Valerie Horvath became a member of the elite to whom she had once catered.

Though she no longer needed money, Valerie Aldrich continued with her career. She was killed in a skiing accident, a sport she had recently taken up which she neither liked nor was suited to, but which she was determined to conquer because her husband and his friends set such store by it.

DIANA

How quickly people forget, Diana Aldrich thought, watching the stragglers come in.

She was thirty-two, tall, thin to the point of being gaunt. Hers was a frame on which to display the latest fashions. She achieved this by dint of rigorous dieting which left her chronically hungry and irritable, though she stopped short of becoming anorexic. Everything Diana Aldrich did was predicated on fashion, on being up-to-date. She wore her skirts short and tight or long and loose. Her dark hair was restyled every three months; at present it was chin-length with bangs that nearly covered her eyes. Even the color of her eyes, now gray, was susceptible to change by means of tinted contact lenses. From beneath the wide brim of her black hat, Diana Aldrich took note that most of those present were employees of Goddess Designs. They had come because they had been told to come and had been given the morning off in which to do it. As before, police barricades had been set up outside the church on Lexington Avenue to hold back the crowds. There were none.

It had been Valerie Aldrich's wish to have a memorial service two years after her death. It was almost as though she had foreseen the turmoil her demise would cause within the family, and that it would have reached the danger point at precisely this time. Maybe she thought the memorial would be a means of healing the rift. As a prudent businesswoman and a loving mother, Valerie had made a new will immediately upon the occasion of her second marriage; the codicil regarding the memorial had been added only weeks before her accident. As the eldest and president of her mother's company, Diana undertook to organize the event.

Her mother had specified a small and private service and reception for family and close friends. Somehow, it had turned out neither small and intimate nor large and impressive. It was merely embarrassing. Though she hid under the wide-brimmed hat and dark glasses, Diana Horvath Aldrich was very much aware of the looks being cast at her. The fiasco, she was sure, was being laid at her door. Her stepfather, an easygoing man, had said nothing, but she could sense his displeasure. Of the three daughters, Diana most resembled their mother in appearance and manner, though she had neither her creative talent nor her understanding.

At the majestic chords of the organ, the congregation rose and Diana rose with them, relieved to have attention shift away from her to the altar.

But her stepfather could no longer contain himself. "If you had let me know you weren't getting a response, I could have filled the place. And not with company employees either," he said in a low voice.

"We sent out a thousand invitations."

"You should have sent two thousand. How many telephone calls did you make?"

"Gloria called at least two hundred people."

"I didn't ask how many calls your secretary made, I asked how many you made yourself, personally. How many people did you talk to and issue a personal invitation?"

"You know how busy I've been. I just didn't have the time."

"Then you should have called me. I would have found the time."

Tears sprang into Diana Aldrich's eyes, and her bony shoulders quivered.

Behind her, Paul Racine heard the exchange. He reached for her hand and squeezed it.

LEWIS ALDRICH

Whereas his stepdaughter was humiliated by the poor turnout, Lewis Aldrich was angered. His face was austerely set as he noted, not those who were present, but those who were not. He regarded their absence as a personal affront. He would remember, and he was not a forgiving man.

At sixty-two, Aldrich had a body that was still lean and hard. Year-round exposure to the sun had made his skin like mahogany leather, which was a striking contrast to his snow-white hair. He took pride in being physically fit, particularly because he had achieved and maintained that condition not by use of machines in a gym but naturally, outdoors, in the saddle. Taking an active part in the running of his stables, he got up well before first light, rode out with his lads—as his British-born trainer called the hands—was present at the workouts, and familiar with the condition of each and every horse from the star of the stable on down to those enjoying honorable retirement.

Valerie was his second wife. His first wife, Eleanor Brady Aldrich, had been Valerie's customer early in Valerie's career when she'd had the boutique on Fifth Avenue. Lewis met her when she came to their townhouse one evening to oversee last-minute alterations on his wife's new ball gown. Eleanor Aldrich was an important customer and it was not the first time "Miss Valerie" had made a personal house call. Walking in on the fitting, Lewis Aldrich was immediately attracted by Valerie's exotic beauty. Her complexion was like lightly rose-tinted porcelain. Her hair was a lustrous blue black, worn in a soft coil at the nape of her neck—out-of-date, but that only called attention to it. No one who looked into Valerie Horvath's dark eyes could care about her hairstyle. Aldrich didn't realize at the time what a deep impression she had made on him. He had lingered to watch as his wife's couturier kept the gown from overwhelming the wearer with a deft tuck here, the removal of a lace ruffle there. He had never shown an interest in his wife's clothes before and Eleanor had been pleased and flattered.

After that, he took to dropping by the boutique when Eleanor had an appointment and taking her to lunch afterwards. On these occasions, his conversations with Miss Valerie were pleasant but unexceptional. Nevertheless, after a while Eleanor became suspicious. Her accusations, which he hotly denied, actually served to reveal his true feelings to himself. Even then, he might not have acted if Eleanor had not overplayed her hand.

The first he knew of what was going on was when Valerie presented herself at the townhouse and sent her name in asking if Mr. Aldrich could see her.

He came out immediately. He could see that she was upset, and though he knew it had to have something to do with his wife, his smile was filled with pleasure which he never thought to hide.

"Miss Valerie!"

"I'm sorry to disturb you, Mr. Aldrich. I've been trying to reach Mrs. Aldrich, but she won't take my calls. So I decided to come over and talk to her in person, but they say she's not in."

"No, she isn't," he assured her. "She's at a meeting of some committee or other."

"Then I thought . . . maybe you could help me. Would you?"

"Of course," he answered without hesitation, not even asking what she wanted. "Come this way." Though the headquarters of his Blue Hills Farms was in North Carolina, he kept one room of the New York townhouse as an office. He led Valerie there, pulled out a chair for her, made sure she was comfortable.

"Can I get you a drink? Coffee? Or something stronger?"

"No, thank you." Valerie's hands were clasped in her lap so tightly the knuckles showed white. "Mrs. Aldrich has canceled all her outstanding orders."

He didn't know what he had expected, but it wasn't that. He sat opposite her. "I'm so sorry. I admire your work, but I can't tell my wife where to have her clothes made."

"Oh no, I'm not asking you to do that. I wouldn't. The reason I'm here . . . The problem is . . . " Valerie paused. Her dark eyes filled. "Mrs. Aldrich thinks . . . She accused me . . . us . . . "

Lewis Aldrich's face darkened. "I *can* do something about that."

Valerie swallowed. "Mrs. Aldrich is . . . was . . . one of my best customers. Losing her business is a severe blow, but I'll ride it out. The real trouble is that she's warning off her friends. She's advising them to drop me or else keep a wary eye on their husbands."

He was shocked. "I will do something about that."

"In turn they will tell their friends, of course, and I'll be finished. I might as well close up shop right now. And what she says isn't true. We both know that."

Their eyes met and held. Lewis Aldrich was the first to turn away.

"You shouldn't be dependent on the whims of idle women and their gossip," he said. "You should branch out. Go for the mass market."

"Oh, I don't know. I don't think I'm suited . . . "

"Don't think. You're the artist. You create; I'll take care of selling and distribution." He stopped abruptly. "That is, if you want me to."

That was the beginning of Goddess Designs, which under Lewis Aldrich's guidance as CEO became the seventh-largest retailer nationwide and the parent company of Three Sisters Products as well as a dozen related, lower-priced chains in just four short years.

Inevitably, Eleanor Aldrich sued for divorce. Just as inevitably, the business partners married and Aldrich adopted Diana and Juno. Shortly thereafter, their own child was born; they named her Minerva. Thanks to Lewis's brilliant planning, he was able to continue operating his stables as Valerie served as businesswoman, mother, wife—the fulfillment of a dream. She shared her new husband's interests, attending the various meets at which Blue Hills Farms had entries. Already a good rider, she took up such elegant sports as sailing and skiing.

She even died elegantly, on the ski trail called the Whip in Manchester, Vermont, where the couple had a home.

Minerva had not been present at the time of her mother's death. She and her father were together at the stables. The news stunned them both. Minerva had felt as though the breath had been knocked out of her. Even now, two years later, that feeling could suddenly and for no apparent reason overcome her.

MINERVA

The reception held at the Aldrich townhouse after the memorial was a complete success. In the final codicil to her will, Valerie Aldrich had specified precisely who was to be invited. It was to be a happy occasion. They were to eat and drink and have a good time. They were to celebrate her life.

And there was indeed a great deal in her mother's life to celebrate, Minerva thought as she stood in the receiving line with her father and her two half sisters.

Born a scant nine months after her mother's second marriage, Minerva was twenty-two, ten years younger than Diana and eight years younger than Juno. Yet from the moment she learned to talk, Minerva was the leader. She decided what games they should play, chose the outfits they would wear, decided what stories were to be read aloud at bedtime. It was evident early on that she was blessed with both her mother's artistic flair and her father's business acumen. It was surprising her sisters didn't resent her; maybe it was because they never lost by following her lead.

With her delicate build, blond hair, and blue eyes, Minerva's appearance favored neither parent, but rather a man whom she had never seen and who was no relation—her mother's first husband, András Horvath. Since infancy she had been regaled with accounts of her mother and sisters' escape from Budapest. Privately she considered Horvath to blame for not having fled himself along with his wife and daughters. He might have saved his own life and saved Valerie and the girls their hard struggle. But then, who knows, she might never have been born.

She considered her father, Lewis Aldrich, the real hero. He had guided their mother to a brilliant career, to the fame and fortune they enjoyed even now. As the last guest filed past, Minerva Aldrich allowed herself to give in to the weakness that had pervaded her entire body. She swayed slightly and held out a hand for Juno to support.

JUNO

"Are you all right?" Juno's stolid face was all concern.

"I just need to sit down for a minute."

With an arm around Minerva's waist, Juno supported her younger sister and guided her to the empty library. She settled her on the sofa. "Can I get you something? A glass of wine? Cognac?"

"No, thanks. Don't worry. I'm tired from the excitement, that's all."

"Is that the truth?" Juno looked deep into her sister's eyes.

"Of course. I'm fine. Honestly."

"It will be good for you to get away. There's nothing like a cruise."

"I'm looking forward to it. I wish you could come."

"I wish I could too, but things are tough for us right now. I can't leave Vicente."

In fact, that was not true. Vicente had urged her to accept the invitation and take the trip with her sisters. It was Juno who hadn't wanted to go. There were many reasons. They had married a year and a half ago. The money Juno had inherited from her mother had paid off the mortgage on his home and his most outstanding debts. Vicente had been exuberantly enthusiastic about their future. He had restored and modernized the house, an authentic hacienda on a two-thousand-acre spread in the San Luis Valley of Colorado. He had increased the size of his herd—a major mistake, as he was to learn later.

When Vicente was a boy, his father had managed his holdings as he saw fit, without government interference. Things had changed. Having accepted government assistance, the ranchers had to accept government regulation; they were no longer masters of their own fate. It was Vicente's dream to return to the old ways, to restore the ranchers' independence. To that end he had begun to explore the possibilities of running for office, having the U.S. Senate in mind. He had the support of his fellow ranchers—moral support. They had no money, and politics is a rich man's game. Reluctantly, Chávez put his political ambitions aside, but he did not forget them.

Then he met Juno Aldrich. She encouraged him and was prepared to support him financially. She envisioned herself by his side—campaigning, graciously presiding at state functions, traveling to foreign lands. They both wanted a large family and Juno got pregnant almost immediately. For a brief period, they were happy.

Then she lost the baby. And nature, in the form of a killing drought, turned against them. Vast grazing areas were transformed into burnt stubble. The herds were thirsty and hungry. Vicente's credit, restored by injections of Juno's money, was running out again. The feed companies refused to make deliveries. He talked about selling. Ahead lay not only financial catastrophe but an emotional wipeout; the land had belonged to the Chávez family going back four generations. If he had to sell, where would they go? What would Vicente do? What could he do? There was no life for Vicente away from the land of his fathers. Political ambitions belonged with lost dreams.

Despite the odds, Juno was prepared to stand beside him, but she was not prepared to defend failure in the face of her success-oriented family. Nor was she prepared to be the poor relation.

Of the three sisters, Minerva was the only natural beauty, while Juno and Diana had to work for their looks. Diana's frenetic activity, her life in the center of the fashion world, demanded she present herself at her best. Juno had no such incentive. Over the past year and a half, she had allowed herself to become comfortable. She stopped coloring her hair and let it revert to its natural drab brown. While she thought about dieting, the weight accumulated—first five pounds, then ten; then she no longer got on the scale. When she couldn't get into her clothes, she replaced them, not with the custom-designed styles from Goddess, but with whatever the local shops stocked in her new size. She convinced herself that her neighbors didn't know the difference and that Vicente didn't care. But back East, everybody noticed and everybody knew the difference, and Juno was ashamed. She wished she hadn't come. She was glad to be leaving.

"I understand," Minerva said.

But she didn't, Juno thought.

"If I can help . . . "

Juno gasped. Minerva was known to be tight with her money, yet here she was actually offering . . . Then Juno saw the pity in her sister's eyes. She stiffened. She wasn't here to beg. "Thanks, but we'll be okay."

There was a tap at the door and Diana entered with Vicente Chávez, who was carrying his wife's coat.

"We've been looking everywhere for you," Diana complained.

"Minnie wasn't feeling well, so we ducked in here," Juno explained.

"Are you all right?" Vicente asked his sister-in-law. He was an imposing figure—a massive man with dark hair, a full beard, and blue eyes buried deep. "Is there anything we can do?"

"No, no, I'm fine. Just a little tired. I think I'll go up to my room and rest for a while. Will I see you before you leave?"

Vicente shook his head. "I came to say goodbye. I've just called for a taxi—it should be here any minute." He held out Juno's coat and helped her into it.

"I wish you were coming on the cruise," Minerva said after she and Juno had kissed each other goodbye.

"Another time." Vicente planted a brotherly kiss on Minerva's and Diana's cheeks.

"Safe trip," Minerva said, and started for the door.

"I'll come with you," Diana offered.

"If you don't mind, I'd rather be alone." Minerva gave them all a wan smile and left. Between the opening and closing of the door sounds of revelry gushed like an open faucet.

"She looked so well when we first got here," Juno remarked. "Now, suddenly, she looks terrible. What does the doctor say?"

"He doesn't say. He can't. We have to take it day by day," Diana replied cautiously. "She could last for a year or go in a week. It's totally unpredictable."

"Poor Minnie." Never before had Juno been in the position to pity her younger sister. "How much does she know?"

"She's been taken off her medication. She feels almost like her old self. So . . . she's full of optimism. You know Minnie; she's a fighter."

"What about Lewis?" Vicente asked. "He must be beside himself."

"He is. He watches her like a hawk, notes every change in her condition—emotional and physical—and analyzes it. Actually, the trip was his idea."

"I'm sorry. I wish I could go, but I can't."

"That's what I wanted to talk to you about, both of you."

Here it comes! Juno thought. *Here comes the pressure.* This time she was not going to let herself be swayed. She was tired of being the ugly duckling among the swans, the failure in the midst of success. "You can't expect me to jump every time you or Minnie punch my button."

"You're always so quick to say no," Diana complained. "Just listen, will you? And for once keep an open mind."

Juno gnawed at her lower lip; she prided herself on doing just that. "I can't go, period. You should have consulted me before making the arrangements."

"It's a nice trip. A free vacation. I thought you'd jump at it."

"Well, you were wrong. I'm tired of being treated like a poor relation. You're not exactly a roaring success yourself."

"Don't fight, girls," Chávez interrupted. "Maybe you *should* go," he said to his wife.

Juno was surprised by both their reactions. Diana never acknowledged her mistakes. Vicente rarely backed off from a decision. Whatever was bothering Diana must be very bad. Apparently, Vicente had an idea of what it was. Rumors of trouble in the company had reached all the way to the Valley, though Juno had paid little attention.

"If Minnie is that sick, you should go," Vicente said.

Diana sat down directly opposite Juno. "A group of shareholders has brought a class action suit against me and the board and the internal audit committee. I'm charged with reckless neglect in management and audit negligence with regard to committing fraud."

No, Juno thought, and slowly shook her head. Diana might not be qualified to run a company like Goddess, but she was not dishonest.

"The controller has admitted that he falsified corporate books since 1993 to inflate sales and profits. The company subsequently reported a total net loss of forty-two point two million for 1993 and 1994, wiping out the seventy-two million in previously reported net income for those years."

"That's since Mama died," Juno noted. Obviously the controller had taken advantage of Diana's inexperience. "It's not your fault."

"They also claim I pocketed two million which was supposed to serve as a bonus in luring Paul away from Elizabeth Troy, Inc. They say I enticed him by deceiving him about the company's assets."

"Did you?"

"Lure him? Entice him? Why not? That's not illegal, not the last I heard anyway."

"What does Paul say?"

"He says I offered him full artistic control—which I did and which was what he wanted."

"What does Paul say about the money?"

"It doesn't matter what he says; he can't produce it or account for it."

"What does Lewis say?" Juno asked. Though they had no memory of their real father and Aldrich had been everything a real father could have been, they didn't call him Dad. Nevertheless, the relationship was close and loving.

"He doesn't know."

"How can that be?" Vicente gasped. "He's chairman of the board."

"He's been tied up in Blue Hills most of the time."

"But the media . . . "

"We've managed to keep it quiet."

"He's bound to find out. Wouldn't it be better if he heard it from you?" Vicente asked.

"I'll tell him," Diana snapped. "He'll probably be called as a witness anyway."

"He should hear it from you." Juno echoed her husband.

"All right, yes, he will. Meantime, I need your help. Obviously, I can't go on the cruise. Just as obviously, Minnie can't go alone. Can't the two of you go with her?"

"Please," Juno cut her sister off. "I told you when we arrived that it was only for the service. I promised Vicente we'd go right back afterwards. We have problems too, you know. And commitments. There's a chance Vicente might be appointed to fill out the late Senator Clements's term in the state senate—"

"That's confidential," Vicente jumped in.

"All right. I understand he has to get back, but you don't."

Juno looked to her husband.

His blue eyes were full of compassion. "You must do whatever your heart tells you, *querida.*"

Juno wavered.

"Don't do it for me," Diana said. "Do it for Minnie. She's the one who's dying."

JANUARY 13, 1995

DAY 1

EMBARKATION

The airport bus from Fort Lauderdale pulled up at the Port Ever-
glades dock and unloaded its passengers. Through loudspeakers
they were instructed to enter the enclosed waiting area, where their
papers would be validated for boarding. Gwenn Ramadge was one
of the first to pass through the control gates and emerge into the
open on the other side. She stopped short, looked up, and caught
her breath. The MS *Dante Alighieri* towered above her.

Built in Venice, of Bahamian registry, the *Dante* carried 1,266
passengers. She was 50,000 gross tons, 720 feet long, and had 10
passenger decks, 8 passenger elevators, 15 public rooms. And that
was just an indication of the delights that lay ahead, Gwenn
thought. Flagship of Tri-Color Cruise Lines, the ship was dazzling
white. A light wind ruffled a row of flags on the dock. A limpid
blue sky completed the picture. For several moments, Gwenn
didn't move. New York, with its January sleet and snow, just a few
short hours away by air, was another world.

"Excuse me." A man behind Gwenn stepped around her. Someone else nudged her in the side.

"Sorry," she murmured. She was holding up the line.

Clutching her boarding papers, Gwenn hurried to the gangplank, where two sailors in impeccable uniforms waited to assist her. As she approached, each placed a hand beneath her elbows and literally lifted her to the ramp. Crossing over open water, she stepped up and onto the Main deck of the ship.

A string quartet was playing show tunes. An officer in white with gold epaulets needed no more than one practiced glance to check her credentials.

"Welcome aboard, Miss Ramadge."

A steward stepped forward and relieved her of her hand luggage. "This way, miss." He led her to one of a bank of elevators, and they rode up to the Promenade deck and walked along a narrow corridor to cabin 070.

Gwenn was not prepared for the large size of the cabin or its luxurious appointments. There was a queen-sized bed, a sofa and cocktail table, and a twenty-inch television set. The bathroom boasted a full-sized tub. Most wonderful, her luggage had arrived ahead of her. The steward showed her the controls for the air-conditioning and the television, and handed her what he called her electronic access card. He also gave her her dining room seating assignment, a notice of a lifeboat drill, and finally, a cream-colored envelope of rich bond with her name on the front written in a flowing script. It contained a stiff card:

Captain Niccolò Nicolletti requests the pleasure of your company
in the DaVinci Lounge tonight at seven-fifteen
for cocktails.

Aware that the steward was watching her with more than ordinary curiosity, she put the card aside casually and sat at the dressing table.

"I am Sergio," the steward said. "If you need anything, just push that button."

"Thank you."

In Vancouver, during the interview with the president of public relations for Tri-Color Cruise Lines, it had been agreed she should board ship and travel as an ordinary passenger. Nevertheless, she was a hired hand and as such she had expected modest accommodations—an inside cabin down in the bowels. As soon as the steward was gone, Gwenn kicked off her shoes, flung out her arms, and gleefully flopped down, spread-eagled on the big bed. *This is going to be great!* She had left her apartment on the Upper East Side of Manhattan at seven that morning, caught the nine-thirty flight from La Guardia to Fort Lauderdale, and it was now just after three. The ship was scheduled to sail at five. There was plenty of time for a nap before departure and even time for a bath before the captain's reception.

She closed her eyes, but opened them again almost immediately. She was too excited to sleep. There was so much to do and the time in which to do it strictly limited. She swung her legs over the side of the bed and sat up.

Gwenn Ramadge was thirty-two, blond, and petite, with large green eyes. Because she was so small and full of energy, and because her eyes seemed to reveal her feelings so openly, she seemed ingenuous and much younger than she was. Gwenn was aware of the impression she made, and didn't mind. In fact, she found it useful, but was careful not to rely on it. She dressed simply, usually in pants and a blazer, particularly when in the field. For the trip today, she'd chosen a beige suit of a lightweight, wrinkle-resistant knit, but the journey thus far had left her looking and feeling worn. Changing the top would help, she thought, and she searched through her suitcase for a silk shell in a glowing bronze. Before putting it on, she went into the bathroom to splash cold water on her face, then patted it dry. She wore her hair in a stylish yet easy-care mop of curls: all she had to do was run a comb through her locks and she was ready to go. A touch of lipstick and some fresh eyeliner completed the job. Not too bad, she thought, looking herself over. For now. For the captain's party, of course, she'd have to do better.

Checking to make sure she had her access card, Gwenn stepped over the coaming and out the door into the companionway. Immediately caught up in the excitement of the ship's departure, she located the nearest elevator and pressed the button marked *Sky Deck,* assuming it would offer the best view. Plenty of others thought so too, for the rail was already lined with passengers. She found an empty deck chair and sat down to wait for an opening. She put her feet up, her head back, and closed her eyes.

She let her mind roam, recalling her early days at Hart Security and Investigation. She had been at a very low point in her life when she went to work there; she was pregnant and the baby's father had walked out on her. Cordelia Hart had taken a liking to her and taught her the business. At the time, Hart S and I restricted itself to corporate work—background checks of prospective employees, white-collar crimes, security installations. After three years as an apprentice, Gwenn qualified for her private investigator's license. Shortly thereafter, as though she'd been waiting for the moment, Cordelia Hart suffered a fatal heart attack. She left everything to Gwenn, including a condominium on the Upper East Side and, of course, the agency. As the agency was barely surviving, Cordelia had humbly requested that Gwenn keep it going. If it proved too difficult, the agency was hers and she could liquidate or sell it, as she wished. Gwenn took a silent oath to her dead friend that she would do her very best to keep the agency alive.

From the start, things had gone well under Gwenn's management. Just three years ago, Hart S and I had taken on its first homicide case. It concerned the disappearance of a honeymooning young bride from the *Conte Bianco,* one of Tri-Color's ships. Gwenn had been called in not by the cruise line but by the girl's mother, and had been able to prove that the bride had been swept overboard with no blame attached to the company. Jeffrey Farnsworth, president of public relations, had expressed his appreciation for her discretion.

When he called Gwenn on Monday night to tell her there was a job she might be interested in, Farnsworth had reminded her of their previous association. After that, things happened fast.

On Tuesday they flew her out to Tri-Color's head office in Vancouver for the consultation. Farnsworth was much as Gwenn remembered him from their one brief meeting—young for the position but capable, much like Gwenn herself. Undoubtedly he delivered or he wouldn't still be around. As for the president's opinion of Gwenn . . . well, he had sent for her and appeared to be satisfied with what he was getting. He wasted no time sketching out the situation.

On recent crossings from Fort Lauderdale, through the Panama Canal, to Acapulco, the *Dante Alighieri* had been plagued by thefts. On each of the last three trips, passengers had reported valuable jewelry missing. On each occasion, the crew quarters were searched, to no avail. The passenger cabins could not be searched without the permission of each occupant, so requests had not even been made. All that could be done was to issue a general warning urging passengers to keep their valuables locked up in the stateroom safes; to do more would sully the line's reputation. There had never been a crime of any kind before on the *Dante* or any other Tri-Color ship. The thefts could not continue.

When Cordelia Hart had befriended Gwenn and taught her everything about the business, she had instilled in her certain precepts, one of which was not to raise false hopes in the client. In other words, Gwenn knew never to promise more than she could reasonably hope to deliver.

So Gwenn's first instinct was to turn the job down. "How many passengers does the *Dante* carry?" she asked.

"Twelve hundred and sixty-six," Farnsworth replied promptly. "And six hundred crew."

"And the cruise lasts thirteen days, two of which are used up in embarking and debarking?"

"Yes," Farnsworth said.

"And you have no suspect in mind?"

He shook his head.

"Or any clue to the identity of the perpetrator? . . . Then I have to tell you that finding him is a matter of pure luck. You have as much of a chance as I do. You don't need me."

Farnsworth's face fell. "Put like that, it is a large order, but . . . Have you ever been on a cruise, Miss Ramadge?"

"No."

"Do you like the sea?"

She weighed her answer. During her pregnancy, Gwenn had gone swimming in the Rockaways; the sea was rough and the undertow unpredictable, and she had to fight desperately to avoid being carried away or crushed against the rocky groin. She had saved herself but lost the baby. As an experienced swimmer, she knew better than to go out alone in those conditions, and she always wondered whether she secretly wished for such a thing to happen. With Cordelia's help and the passing of time, she overcame her guilt and could finally answer honestly.

"I love the sea."

"Well then, take a cruise with us, acquaint yourself with the ship and the crew, get a feel for the kind of people that sail with us. Whether or not anything comes of it, you will have had a wonderful experience. I guarantee it."

"That's nice of you, but . . ."

"Are you married?"

"No."

"Perhaps you have a special friend you'd like to take along?"

She grinned. "You've just made me an offer I can't refuse."

But it turned out that NYPD Sergeant Ray Dixon, her "special friend," had recently transferred to the Internal Affairs Bureau and was in the midst of a big narcotics investigation. Still, Gwenn felt she had committed herself.

That was on the Tuesday, and the *Dante* was due to sail on the

Friday. She'd had to jet back to New York, clear up a few minor matters at the office, pack, and fly to Fort Lauderdale to board the ship. And here she was, stretched out on a deck chair and looking out past the shipyards to the open water, waiting to get under way. She was barely aware of the vibration of the engines under her. It seemed the ship was stationary and it was the land slowly sliding by in the soft Florida twilight.

"It's a magic moment, isn't it?"

Gwenn looked up to see the man who was standing beside her chair. He was tall, thin, gray-haired, and at least seventy years old, but very handsome. Even at sixty, he must have been devastating, Gwenn thought.

"Yes, it is," she replied. If only she could be sharing it with Ray . . .

"No matter how many times I experience it, I get a tingle of excitement," he confided as he lowered himself into the chair beside her.

No further comment required, she thought, and looked ahead. They were definitely moving, and starting to pick up speed.

"Is this your first cruise?"

"Yes."

"I'm sure it won't be your last."

"Who can say."

"Are you traveling alone?"

If he hadn't been as old as he was, Gwenn would have said he was trying to move in on her. She decided he was only being friendly, and so she responded in the same way. "Yes. Are you?"

He smiled broadly. "My name is Simon Kittridge. I work on the *Dante.*"

"You do?" He wasn't in uniform.

"I'm a host. Right now I'm off duty."

"What's a host?"

"A companion, a guide, a dancing partner for the ladies who are alone."

"Like me?"

"You won't be alone for long." His smile was benevolent; he could have been her kindly uncle.

"And Tri-Color Lines provides this service?"

"We're not gigolos," he retorted sharply, but recovered. "At my age, I couldn't qualify. Dancing is only part of the job. I also lecture on the various ports of call on our itinerary—their history, points of interest, and most importantly, the shopping bargains. I'm a retired schoolteacher and my pension doesn't permit me to travel, certainly not in this style."

"I'm sorry. I didn't mean to offend you."

"Hosts are chosen carefully. Applicants have to submit a detailed résumé, and a videocassette is made of the interview in which they demonstrate their dancing ability. Actually, this is a public relations job. Keeping the passengers happy is the duty of every member of the crew. We all double in brass. The difference is that as a host I have a more direct contact." He paused, swung his legs off the footrest, and stood up with the agility of a man in his fifties. "It's been a pleasure talking to you, Miss . . . ?"

"Ramadge. Gwenn Ramadge."

"I have to change for the captain's reception. I'll be on duty."

Gwenn's face lit up. "I'm going to that. Maybe I'll see you."

"Well, I don't mean to put a damper on your enthusiasm, Miss Ramadge, but so are precisely one half of the passengers. The other half will be invited tomorrow."

FIRST NIGHT OUT

When Gwenn arrived, the DaVinci lounge—part theater, part nightclub, the scene for bingo games and lectures and the entertainment center of the ship, a vast room decorated in rich red and glittering gold—was already nearly filled to capacity and the receiving line snaked all the way back to the elevators. It was a five-minute wait to reach Captain Nicolletti and his staff. The passengers, elegantly dressed in accordance with the invitation, were patient. The captain, resplendent in his summer whites, rewarded each one with a warm handshake and a genial smile before briskly passing him on to his First Officer.

Captain Niccolò Nicolletti, in his mid-forties, a robust five foot eleven, carried himself with the pride of his position. He had thick iron-gray hair and a trim beard which further distinguished him. His father had sailed as a captain's steward and his two uncles as navigators; his grandfather had been a ship's engineer, so it was not unexpected for him to choose the sea as his profession. He had started as an apprentice officer on cargo ships, and gradually made his way up to second officer until his company sold their ships to Tri-Color Lines. They in turn had offered Nicolletti a position as second officer on the *Dante*. Two years later he became its captain. It was a contrast to serving on cargo vessels, and Nicolletti particularly enjoyed these formal occasions on which he came into direct contact with the passengers.

At last it was Gwenn's turn to be introduced. Having been in this kind of situation before, she expected to be politely shuffled along. Instead, after his formal greeting, the captain handed her off, not to the next in line, but to an officer who appeared from somewhere in the back. "This is our hotel director, Eric Graf."

"This way, Miss Ramadge."

Placing a hand on her elbow, Graf gently but firmly steered Gwenn to one of several alcoves at the far reaches of the huge room. Surprisingly, it was empty, and Gwenn soon saw why—a steward was discreetly on guard to prevent anyone from entering. As soon as they were settled, another steward appeared to serve champagne and yet another to offer an assortment of hot and cold hors d'oeuvres.

"Captain Nicolletti regrets he cannot talk with you just now, Miss Ramadge. This is a very busy time for him, as you can imagine. So he has asked me to speak with you and to assist you in any way you may require."

In contrast to his captain, the hotel director was clean-shaven. He couldn't be past his early thirties, Gwenn judged. His hair was dark blond, straight, of traditional length. The color of his eyes was obscured by tinted glasses, and his pale skin indicated that his work kept him inside. He wore a white uniform with gold braid and navy and gold epaulets. There was probably a variation between officer rank and staff and crew, but Gwenn hadn't figured it out yet.

"As you know, I was up in your head office in Vancouver at the invitation of Mr. Farnsworth. He reviewed the situation for me in a general way. I took notes. I didn't expect this meeting, so I don't have them with me, but they're in the cabin and . . ."

"We thought having you go to the captain's office would attract attention, and we want to keep the reason for your presence on board hidden as long as possible, but you should have been notified of the meeting."

It seemed to Gwenn that plucking her out of the receiving line was much more likely to have caught the eye of the captain's staff. Unless, of course, they suspected someone on the staff. In that case, why didn't Graf just come out and say so?

"I apologize."

"No need. I can go and get my notes. Or, if you're willing to trust my memory . . ."

"More than willing, Miss Ramadge." Graf smiled. The ice melted. A little.

"Well, as I recall, there were three thefts, all on the *Dante*."

"That's correct."

"The first occurred during the transcanal voyage of last October twelfth. Specifically, the theft was committed after the *Dante* passed through the locks and emerged on the Pacific side and before you reached your first port of call, that being Puerto Caldera in Costa Rica. At least that was when the theft was reported."

"Very perceptive, Miss Ramadge."

"The missing item was an emerald pendant garnished with rubies. The owner is a Mrs. Huntley-Harris. She values it at approximately twelve thousand dollars. The insurance company, Metropolitan Indemnity, confirmed the valuation. I understand they conducted their own independent investigation and could find no fault with your security arrangements."

"Because there is no fault, Miss Ramadge."

So that was what the interview was all about! Gwenn thought. He was vetting her for the captain to make sure she wasn't looking to put the blame on them and pass it along to the head office.

"I would expect no less," Gwenn assured him.

He relaxed some more. "The pendant could have been lost or mislaid. It might have had a loose catch and dropped into the sea."

"A mysterious disappearance," Gwenn suggested.

"Exactly." He was beaming. "That's what Metropolitan labeled it."

"And they paid the claim?"

"That's right."

"Now the second . . . loss"—Gwenn chose the word carefully—"was a pair of diamond and pearl earrings. That occurred on the next crossing, which was in early November, and the third occurred during the New Year's cruise. On that occasion the missing item was a fifty-five-thousand-dollar diamond bracelet. The insurance company has not paid off on that yet and is not likely to do so anytime soon."

Eric Graf was deep in gloom again.

Gwenn continued. "According to the owner of the bracelet, Mrs. Sarah Truebridge, she decided not to wear the bracelet on New Year's Eve for fear of attracting too much attention to herself, so she left it in the cabin safe. Someone had apparently noticed it on a previous occasion, because when she returned from the party, she found her cabin ransacked and the bracelet gone. My guess is that while everyone was having a good time, the thief was roaming the ship, trying the cabin doors. When he found one open, he went in. I think he's a small-time operator who's found an easy way to score."

"You think one person is responsible for the three burglaries?" Graf asked.

"I think for a different person to have committed them would be too much of a coincidence. We must assume it was the same person and that it's not likely to have been a passenger. A passenger repeating the crossing three times, all one after the other, would run the risk of being spotted and recognized. He might change his appearance or book under a different name, but it would still be taking a big chance. He could more easily and simply travel on another ship. No. It's much more likely to be one of the crew."

"We reached that conclusion ourselves, Miss Ramadge."

"Of course." She was conciliatory. "Since there are no clues and no suspects—well, actually there are six hundred suspects, those being the number of the crew, yourself included." She smiled.

"What?"

"Sorry. An attempt at humor. Out of place." She cleared her throat. "We need to narrow down the field. Bear with me."

"Go on," he growled, not at all placated.

"Is there much turnover in the crew?" she asked.

"No. We sign them to one- and two-year contracts. By the end of the term, they can decide whether or not they want to renew and we can decide whether we want to keep them or not."

"And how does it usually work out?"

"There's little turnover. A few do leave, of course, and others take their place. Those who go have specific goals—to finish school or get married and start a family. Those who stay have fallen in love with the sea and want to make it their career."

"When did the most recent contingent sign on?"

"At the start of the fall-winter season; that would have been early October. We leave European waters, the Mediterranean, the Adriatic, the Baltic and so on, and cross over to the South Atlantic to prepare for the winter in the Caribbean. We have never had any reason to doubt the crew's honesty, Miss Ramadge."

"Now you do. You not only have a new group of employees, you also have a new category of employee."

He raised his eyebrows. "You mean the hosts, of course."

"I do. How long since you started this hosts program?"

"This is the first year. We're trying it out in anticipation of a pair of gala, round-the-world cruises on two of our newest ships, which are still under construction in Venice. Each cruise will take approximately thirty days. Many of our passengers will be single ladies. Thirty days is a long time to be alone on a ship; we thought some male companionship would add to the enjoyment of our elderly ladies. The men we selected were thoroughly investigated," he concluded. But he appeared troubled.

"How many hosts are there?"

"On the *Dante* . . . half a dozen."

"And when did they join the ship?"

"I'm well aware that was when the thefts started, but there were other crew that came on at the same time as well. I can't fire them all."

"If you'll give me a list, I'll start interviewing them in the morning."

"Then they'll know you're a private investigator."

Gwenn thought of Simon Kittridge and their conversation on the Sky deck. "I suspect they know already." She got up. "Unless there's something else, Mr. Graf, I'll go in to dinner and make it an early night."

Graf got to his feet. "Let me show you the way."

"Thank you. Your ship is very beautiful and very easy to get lost in."

He acknowledged the compliment with a slight bow and led her to a door at the other end of the lounge. Reaching forward, he opened it for her. It gave on a glass-enclosed section of the Lower Promenade. The sea was all around them, vast and empty. The moon glinted on choppy waters. Gwenn caught her breath.

"You're accustomed to all this magnificence." She gestured outward. "I don't suppose you even notice it anymore."

"You never get used to it," he replied. "Once the sea casts its spell, it never lets go."

"Are you married, Mr. Graf?"

"Yes, and my absences are very hard on my family. I've taken jobs on land but I get restless and irritable. I'm more of a burden to them than when I'm away."

He opened the next door for her and led her through the casino, which was in full swing, past the Miramar bar to the central core of elevators.

"I know where I am now."

"Are you sure?"

"Positive. Thank you."

"There is no captain's table on the *Dante*. We found it causes rivalry among the passengers, so the captain takes his meals in his quarters. There is, however, an officers' table. We haven't put you there because we thought you would be too much in the spotlight. But if the seating arrangement is not satisfactory, please don't hesitate to let me know."

He was trying to make amends for his earlier churlishness, Gwenn thought. "I'm sure everything will be fine."

After an excellent dinner, Gwenn returned to her cabin, finished unpacking, and went to bed. The engines, the throbbing heart of the ship, were barely discernible. They lulled her to sleep.

The next thing she knew, the phone beside her bed was ringing. She experienced no disorientation; she knew where she was and why. She looked out the large window opposite the bed and saw nothing but sea and sky, both misty gray. Dawn had broken and swept away the night, but the sun had not yet risen.

She picked up the receiver.

"Miss Ramadge? This is Eric Graf. I'm sorry to disturb you at this hour, but we have a passenger who reports her cabin was entered while she slept."

"What's her number?" Gwenn asked.

"It's 0016 on A deck."

"I'll be right there."

CHAPTER

2

It didn't take Gwenn long to pull on a pair of jeans, a red and white striped T-shirt, and a navy cardigan and be on her way. She hurried along the empty corridors to the escalators, which were running in eerie silence. Reaching A deck, she was guided along by small brass plaques, and located 0016 easily. It was all so quiet and deserted, she feared for a moment that she had the wrong cabin or was on the wrong deck. But when she tapped on the door, it was instantly opened. She stepped inside and it was closed behind her.

The cabin was considerably smaller than hers and crowded by the four people in it—the steward who had admitted her, Eric Graf, Captain Nicolletti, and a short, pudgy woman with gray hair in a fussy satin robe. Gwenn was immediately aware that the cabin lacked a window or even a porthole. Being claustrophobic, she took care to stay near the door.

Captain Nicolletti stepped forward and extended his hand. "Thank you for coming, Miss Ramadge." He continued cordially, as though they were still on the receiving line. "This is Mrs. Ida Sturgess. Mrs. Sturgess has had a very traumatic experience," he told Gwenn.

The captain's words and manner seemed to remind Ida Sturgess of just how bad it had been. The tears welled up in her already reddened eyes. With a soggy, rolled-up handkerchief, she dabbed at them ineffectually. The captain turned away to hide his exasperation.

Gwenn studied the complainant. As she was in her nightclothes, the dress and underwear piled haphazardly on a chair—an old-fashioned panty girdle, stockings, bra, and a long, flowered chiffon gown—must have been what she'd worn the previous night. Gwenn judged her to be in her sixties. Her gray hair was teased into a beehive style and sprayed to keep it rigidly erect. It was not consistent with the careless way she had left her clothes.

"Would you like some water?" Gwenn asked. At Mrs. Sturgess's nod, she turned to the steward, who immediately poured from a carafe on the bureau and handed the glass to Gwenn, who then passed it to Mrs. Sturgess.

Her hand shook as she took it.

"Where do you live, Mrs. Sturgess?" Gwenn asked.

"Florida. Lake Vista. It's a retirement community just outside Miami."

Gwenn could visualize her as the chairperson of a variety of committees. "Is this your first cruise?"

Mrs. Sturgess nodded. "I won it in a raffle."

"Did you? You're very lucky."

"I thought so. At first. I was so happy. Thrilled. I was so looking forward to it." Her face puckered as she got ready to wail.

"We'll make it right for you, Mrs. Sturgess. Won't we, Captain?"

"Certainly. We'll do our best." Nicolletti got up. "I must leave you now, as I'm needed on the bridge."

Ordinarily, Gwenn would have preferred to conduct the interview without supervision, but there was something here that wasn't right, and if her hunch paid off, she wanted both the captain and the hotel director to be witnesses. "If you could spare us a few minutes more of your time, Captain, I'd appreciate it."

Put like that, it left Nicolletti little choice but to agree. He sat down again, waving a hand for Gwenn to proceed.

"Thank you. Mrs. Sturgess, would you please tell us once more just exactly what happened tonight?"

Some witnesses balk at repetition. Not Ida Sturgess. She seemed actually pleased. Maybe it was because it kept her at the center of attention.

"I was sleeping," she began. "Then suddenly, I woke up. I don't know—"

"Just a minute," Gwenn interrupted. "You have no roommate? You're traveling alone?"

"That's right."

"I thought these prizes usually consisted of a pair of tickets."

"No. The prize was for one person. They offered a special rate for a companion, but it was too expensive for any of my friends."

"And your husband . . ."

"I lost my Harold twelve years ago."

"I'm sorry. Go on, please."

"Like I said, I don't know what woke me, but I sensed someone was in the room. I opened my eyes but stayed absolutely still otherwise. After I got accustomed to the dark, I could make out this figure standing by the bureau with his back to me. He was going through my jewel box. I was afraid to move or to scream. I was afraid he'd kill me before help came. So I just lay there and prayed for him to leave."

"You did the right thing, Mrs. Sturgess."

"He took my mother's brooch. It was the only nice piece I had." She pointed to the small imitation-leather box and got ready to cry some more.

"May I?" Without waiting for permission, Gwenn went through

the contents. It didn't take long. It was all costume jewelry and not particularly good. "How do you suppose the thief knew about the brooch?"

"I wore it to dinner. Everyone at the table remarked on it."

"Who precisely?"

"I don't like to accuse anybody."

"I won't consider it an accusation," Gwenn assured her.

"Well . . ." Mrs. Sturgess still hesitated. "There was that nice Simon Kittridge. He's on the staff and does the shore orientation lectures?"

"He was at your table?"

"No, he came later. I was sitting with some ladies in the Miramar bar after dinner. He joined us and asked me to dance. He didn't actually mention the brooch, but I thought he was looking at it very closely."

"Is it very valuable, Mrs. Sturgess? Describe it please and give me a rough estimate of its worth."

"It was bar-shaped, about three inches in length with a leaf design in platinum, and set with the finest cultured pearls. I had it appraised and they said it was worth from seven to nine thousand dollars."

"So it was insured?"

"I was considering dropping the insurance. Thank God I didn't."

Gwenn didn't comment. The captain was fidgeting; so was Eric Graf. "Just a couple more questions, bear with me," Gwenn said, less to Mrs. Sturgess than to the men.

"What time did you retire last night?"

"Right after the entertainment. Close to ten."

"You came back to this cabin alone? I mean—unescorted?"

"That's right."

"And went straight to bed? What did you do with the brooch?"

"I put it in the jewel case."

"Not in the cabin safe?"

"No. Why should I have bothered? I didn't expect anyone to break in while I slept. I thought I could rely on the ship's security."

Uh-oh! Gwenn thought. No wonder Nicolletti and Graf had been anxious to leave. Tri-Color Lines took care to display a disclaimer of responsibility in case of theft or loss of valuables, but it looked as though Ida Sturgess might try to show negligence. This lady was trouble, and trouble of this kind was Gwenn's business.

"As indeed you can, Mrs. Sturgess, with some prudent precautions on your part."

"Such as?"

"Locking your cabin door before you go to bed, for instance."

"Of course I locked the door."

"Then how did the intruder get in?"

"I suppose he had one of those access cards like we all do."

"Excuse me," Graf broke in. "If you mean a card that would correspond to a master key, there is no such thing. There are cards that fit banks of cabins, but the intruder would have to know which card fits which section."

"And how to get hold of it," Gwenn added. "That suggests an employee." She stared at Mrs. Sturgess.

The woman was sweating. "All I know is—I locked the door."

"When it was all over and the intruder had fled, you immediately sounded the alarm. That is, you picked up the telephone and called the cabin steward. How long before he came?"

"Minutes. He was very prompt."

A point in Tri-Color's favor, Gwenn thought. "How did he get in?"

"I don't understand. What do you mean?"

"Did you get up from your bed and open the door for him?"

"No. That is . . . the intruder must have left it open when he fled."

Gwenn addressed the steward, who was standing to one side. A name plaque pinned to his tunic read: *Alfonse.*

"How did you get in, Alfonse?" she asked. "Did Mrs. Sturgess admit you?"

"The door was unlocked."

Gwenn went over and tried opening and closing the door. "The lock is not automatic. I'm afraid, Mrs. Sturgess, that the only logical conclusion is that you forgot to engage it."

"I did not forget."

"There was all that champagne at the captain's reception, and you probably had wine with dinner. You're not a habitual drinker, are you, Mrs. Sturgess?"

The question was not formed to get a positive reply. Gwenn continued: "You'd had a long, exciting day filled with new experiences, new sights, and new people. You were tired. Your head was spinning. You took off your clothes and dropped them on this chair, right here."

The flowered chiffon gown, the panty girdle, the heavy boned bra designed to lift an old woman's breasts, the badly scuffed pumps under the chair, were mute testimony to Ida Sturgess's condition.

"When did you put on your nightgown?"

"As soon as I got in."

"And what did you do with your mother's brooch?"

"Nothing."

"Didn't you have it pinned to your dress?"

"Of course. I told you." Ida Sturgess's frown deepened as she grew more and more anxious.

"A moment ago you said the intruder took the brooch from your jewel box. Now you say you never unpinned the brooch from your dress. Which is it, Mrs. Sturgess?"

"You're confusing me."

"Am I? I'm sorry. It just seems odd that the intruder should look for the brooch on your dress."

"Not if he'd seen me wearing it. I don't understand why you're cross-examining me like this. I'm not the criminal."

"Of course not," Gwenn soothed. "I apologize. I only want to make sure my report is accurate so that you get the full value of your claim from the insurance company."

Ida Sturgess pouted, only partially mollified. "I don't care about the money. I just want my mother's brooch back."

"We'll do our best," Gwenn promised.

One by one, the captain, hotel director, and cabin steward filed out. Gwenn was the last.

"Would you like something to help you sleep?" she asked. "I'll send the nurse."

They repaired to the captain's private quarters.

"Coffee, Miss Ramadge?" Captain Nicolletti asked.

"I could use it," she said.

"Something to eat—eggs, waffles, French toast? The chef is famous for his French toast."

"Another time, Captain. For now just coffee."

Nicolletti passed the order on to his cabin steward. The hotel director pulled out a chair for Gwenn. The atmosphere definitely had changed.

"I don't think Mrs. Sturgess will make trouble for us. Thanks to you, Miss Ramadge." The captain indicated his satisfaction by slowly stroking his beard. "Is there something else? You seem worried."

"The timing is inconsistent. The previous burglaries were committed when the *Dante* was three or four days out. This is only our first night."

"Is that important?"

"To be honest, I don't know. It could be that the MO calls for the loot to be handed over to an accomplice on shore who, for some reason, won't be available later on on this particular occasion."

"I can cancel the crew's next round of shore leaves, but I can't do that for the entire trip."

Gwenn nodded. "Also, this is the first time the perpetrator has

entered a cabin while it was occupied. Very risky and uncharacteristic. Burglars are sneaks; they don't want a confrontation. It puts
the crime into a higher category. If he's caught, it means the perp is
subject to a stiffer penalty. This is not an ordinary burglary."

"So he's not an ordinary burglar." Graf waved off Gwenn's concern. "Maybe he made a play for Mrs. Sturgess. Got her drunk, escorted her to her cabin, and was invited in."

"We've met Mrs. Sturgess. Would a professional con man seek
her out?" Gwenn asked.

"Depends on the value of the brooch," Graf replied. "I say the
opportunity presented itself and he took it. That's why he moved
earlier than usual. It's no more complicated than that. The woman
was tanked and he took advantage of it. Later, she woke up, realized
what had happened, but was ashamed to admit her culpability."

"So she's trying to make up the loss as best she can." The captain made a sour face. "The main thing is that we're off the hook. If
you can get her to name the man . . ."

Gwenn shook her head. "In my opinion, Captain, the man who
filched that brooch was not the same one who has been plaguing
passengers on the *Dante*'s previous voyages."

The captain blanched. "Oh God! Are you telling me there are
two of them?"

DAY 2
AT SEA

Gwenn spent the rest of that day acquainting herself with the ship
and interviewing the other hosts as well as various members of the
crew who had served Ida Sturgess, beginning with the cabin steward, Alfonse.

Alfonse had signed on the *Dante* six years earlier for her maiden
voyage. His record was unblemished, as were the records of all who
had served Mrs. Sturgess in the Michelangelo dining room, the

Miramar bar, and poolside on the Lido deck. It was difficult to dig deep and still maintain the fiction that she was an ordinary passenger. She suspected that they knew who and what she was and why she was questioning them. They had been interrogated in connection with the previous burglaries and were pretty well inured to the routine and prepared with their answers. She did not suggest searching the crew quarters, reasoning that that had also already been done, and that there were too many places to hide the stolen articles—if they were on the ship at all.

Eric Graf was relieved. Though the hotel director followed Captain Nicolletti's acceptance of Gwenn's competence, he remained defensive.

"We made a thorough search of the quarters of the ladies who claimed the losses, just in case the missing items had somehow fallen behind a piece of furniture or wedged between sofa cushions, or had fallen into the toilet and might still be caught in the trap."

Gwenn nodded. It was always difficult to check on security without implying blame. "Of course, you advised the passengers to take all reasonable precautions to protect their valuables."

"We made a general announcement. We thought anything more specific might cause panic. Tri-Color is very much concerned about its reputation, Miss Ramadge."

"Which is why I'm here. I suppose that the victims—that is, the ladies who owned the jewelry—talked about their loss at poolside, over the dinner table, and so on. The word must have gotten around."

Graf sighed. "Ran through the ship like wildfire."

And was doing so again, Gwenn thought.

CHAPTER

3

DAY 3
GEORGE TOWN

As on the night before, Gwenn went to bed early, and this time her sleep was not interrupted. She awoke at her usual hour feeling well rested. As she lay in bed, she was first aware of the silence and then the absence of motion. The *Dante* swayed gently. *We must be at anchor,* she thought. Looking out the window, she saw a calm purple sea, the verdant shore of Grand Cayman Island, and a cluster of buildings in George Town whose whiteness was tinged rosy by the early sun. A variety of pleasure boats—sportfishermen, sailing ships large and small, glass-bottomed boats—plied the bay. In the midst of an assortment of yachts, one commanded attention. It flew the Union Jack.

By now, the local authorities must have cleared the *Dante,* because tenders were shuttling back and forth between the ship and the dock, carrying passengers booked for shore excursions. As Gwenn had suggested to Captain Nicolletti and Eric Graf, the perp was probably handing off his loot to an accomplice on shore. Nicolletti had canceled all shore leaves for the crew. Too little, too late, Gwenn thought. The order would not be well received, and once traced back to Gwenn's influence, would not make her popular.

Since no member of the crew could go ashore, the accomplice, if there was one, would have to come aboard. Gwenn intended to station herself where she could watch, not those who were going off the ship, but those who were coming on.

But first, breakfast.

Though many passengers had already gone to their shore activities, the elegant two-tiered dining room was far from empty. Nevertheless, the maitre d' found Gwenn a window table on the port side looking toward the town, and handed her a menu. Yesterday, Captain Nicolletti had extolled the French toast; Gwenn ordered it and found he had not exaggerated. Cruise ships were famed for their excellent and abundant cuisine. Gwenn decided to enjoy every mouthful and go on a diet later.

When she emerged on deck, she was surprised that so many passengers had opted to stay behind and enjoy the tranquillity of the ship in port. In fact, she noted that the activities program was almost as full as when they were at sea. Over coffee, she skimmed the printed schedule that had been slipped under her door that morning.

7:00 A.M.	Our fitness instructor is available in the gymnasium for personal programs.
8:00 A.M.	Walk-a-mile. Lower promenade deck.
8:30 A.M.	Low-impact aerobics in the Floating Spa.
9:00 A.M.–1:00 P.M.	Our port lecturer is available at the gangway for your questions.

Would that be Simon Kittridge? Gwenn wondered. Yesterday in her interrogation of the hosts she had purposely avoided Kittridge, wanting a better grasp of the situation before tackling him.

Now she felt she was ready. His version of the evening with Ida Sturgess and his evaluation of her brooch would be interesting.

Leaving the dining room by way of the upper level, Gwenn chose to walk down to the Main deck rather than wait for an elevator or walk forward to the escalator. At the gangway, she found a continuous stream of passengers waiting to board a tender. As when the ship set sail, two young sailors stood at either side to lend physical assistance. Two other handsome young men, a matched pair in dark red blazers over cream-colored slacks, were busy answering questions and giving directions. Gwenn approached them.

"I'm looking for Simon Kittridge."

"I'm sorry. He's not on duty. May I help you?"

"Do you know where I could find him?"

"Sorry."

"Maybe he went ashore?"

"Shore leaves have been canceled." He looked sour. "You might leave a message at the reservation desk. That's on the Promenade deck."

"Yes, I know where it is. Thanks."

But she didn't go there. Instead, Gwenn followed the neat brass wall plaques that pointed *Aft* to the pool area. It would be pleasant to join the sun worshipers and watch the comings and goings from there. She was dismayed to find every deck chair occupied, but she wasn't discouraged. The intensity of the near-tropic sun was more than these pale creatures from the North could tolerate for long; she knew they would eventually retreat into the shade. Not only was Gwenn a devotee of the sun, she had already prepared herself with a generous application of sunblock. All she had to do was wait. It wasn't long before she was settled in a prime location.

At eleven, a steward came by with a tray of iced tea, another with lemonade. The refreshment was welcome.

Gwenn took particular notice of a young woman at the end of her row. Whereas everyone else wore either bathing suit or shorts, she was completely covered by an off-white caftan of a lightweight fabric. A floppy hat with a wide brim and a rose at the front provided shade for her face. Long blond hair crimped in waves was tied at the nape of her neck. She accepted a lemonade from the steward, and as she raised it to her lips, Gwenn noticed that her hand shook. It continued to shake as she put the glass down on the deck beside her chair. Pushing the skirt of the caftan to one side, she swung long, slim, alabaster-white legs off the lounge chair and leaned forward to stand, only to fall back, twice.

Gwenn got up and went over. "Want some help?"

The young woman's first reaction was to repel the intrusion, but Gwenn's good intention was obvious. "I think I need to get out of the sun." Her light voice quavered.

"It can be pretty devastating if you're not used to it. Here." Gwenn offered her hand, which the young woman grasped. She had complained of the heat, but her skin felt cold and damp. Gwenn placed her other hand on her new acquaintance's elbow and, bending her own knees, helped pull her to her feet. She noticed the metal cane beside the chair. "Do you want that?"

"Yes, please."

"Can you stand while I move your chair into the shade? Or would you like to go inside where it's air-conditioned?"

"I'd like to stay here in the shade, please."

"Good."

As she bent over to move the chair, Gwenn was able to look under the wide-brimmed hat. The eyes that looked back at her were large and gentle—and pained. She was also younger than Gwenn had thought. Her complexion was the palest ivory, smooth and translucent, her features exquisitely chiseled. Despite Gwenn's assistance in getting resettled, she had beads of sweat on her brow and upper lip.

"Okay?" Gwenn asked.

"Thank you. You're very kind. I'm all right now." She closed her eyes.

That meant go away. Ordinarily, Gwenn would have honored the unspoken request, but the girl was not well and shouldn't be alone. "Is there anything else I can do for you?"

"I'm fine. It was just a dizzy spell."

"Are you traveling alone?"

"No, I'm traveling with my sister. She went ashore, but I wasn't up to it."

"My name is Gwenn Ramadge. I'm from New York."

"I'm Minerva Aldrich." Minerva paused, waiting for a reaction. When there was none, she continued. "My oldest sister, Diana, was supposed to come too. This was supposed to be a very special trip for us, a kind of reconciliation, you might say. We've had misunderstandings, as all families do at one time or another."

Gwenn's face lit up. "Minerva Aldrich, of course! And Diana. And the sister who is with you . . . ?"

"Juno."

"Right!" Gwenn exclaimed. "Goddess Designs and Three Sisters Products. I'm one of your most enthusiastic customers, when I can afford it."

"Thank you. That's nice to hear."

All at once Gwenn felt awkward. Minerva Aldrich was no abandoned waif. To continue to force assistance on her when it was neither wanted nor needed would be rude. She prepared to excuse herself.

"You've been very kind, Miss Ramadge." Minerva spoke before Gwenn could. "I think I feel a bit nauseous from the sun. May I ask you one more favor? Would you accompany me to my stateroom? I think I should lie down for a while after all—in the air-conditioning."

"I'd be glad to."

As she went around to help Minerva once again, Gwenn saw a man and woman headed their way. They were smiling and waving, calling: "Minnie! Minnie!"

The woman, who approached slightly ahead of the man, was

stolid, shapeless, and reminded Gwenn of a pillar at Stonehenge. Gwenn had a friend who had been a world-class athlete and who, when she married and settled to raising a family, had put on an extra thirty pounds. From the way this woman carried herself, Gwenn judged she had muscles under the flab. Her complexion was muddy and pitted. Her hair hung limp and oily. She wasn't trying, or maybe—judging by her outfit, which consisted of tomato-red Bermuda shorts and a scoop-necked blouse in yellow—she was trying too hard. Flushed and out of breath, she was not a good advertisement for Goddess Designs.

The man with her was slim and very handsome. He showed no signs of exertion.

"Minnie! Look who's here! Look who I found."

"Hello, Paul." Minerva's response was cool. As the man bent to kiss her cheek, her eyes were on her sister. "I thought you were going sightseeing."

"I was, but as I got out of the tender, there was Paul on the dock waiting to get on." She beamed.

"What are you doing here?" Minerva asked Racine. "What's happened?"

"Nothing's happened. Everything's under control. That's why I'm here. Lewis sent me. He thought the two of you should have an escort. So here I am. Aren't you pleased?"

"I'm surprised." Suddenly, she turned to Gwenn. "I'm sorry, Miss Ramadge. This is my sister, Juno—Mrs. Chávez. And this is Paul Racine, my sister Diana's fiancé. Miss Ramadge was about to accompany me to my stateroom," she explained.

Instant concern showed on the faces of Juno and Racine.

Juno exclaimed, "Minnie, darling! Are you in pain?"

"No, not at all. Don't fuss. I'm fine."

The contrast between the two sisters was striking, and not limited to weight, Gwenn thought. Juno Chávez was built on a big frame, her features were thick; drawn on paper, her profile would appear to have been done by a clumsy hand. Minerva was all grace and delicacy; she was a watercolor painted on china. Yet if one looked hard enough, there were similarities. Money had bred them. They were both accustomed to being served. A wish amounted to a command. Paul Racine, though holding himself apart, nevertheless stood ready to implement the command.

Gwenn judged Racine to be in his early forties. He had black hair, which he wore slicked back from his high forehead and glistening with hair gel. His pinched-waist, custom-made Italian suit was not suitable to either the climate or the occasion, yet he wore it with a supreme confidence that made it acceptable.

"It was kind of you to assist my sister, Miss Ramadge." Juno Chávez's smile was patronizing. "We'll take over now."

"Goodbye, Miss Aldrich." Gwenn smiled warmly at Minerva. "Nice to have met you," she said to the other two, and left them. She walked across the open section of the Lido deck, past the pool, and went inside. There, she turned to look.

Racine had taken a position on one side of Minerva Aldrich and Juno on the other. They were preparing to help her. Minerva, however, shook them off. Head up, shoulders squared, she got to her feet and stepped out on her own while they trailed behind.

That evening before dinner, Gwenn saw the three of them having drinks at the Miramar bar. They seemed relaxed, even congenial. Minerva was elegantly turned out. She wore a slinky gown of pale beige charmeuse with plenty of gold jewelry. Her makeup was minimal but a work of art. Her blond hair was pulled back to the crown of her head and allowed to fall in a cascade of tight curls. She looked stunning, Gwenn thought, but what impressed her most and pleased her was Minerva Aldrich's energy, her exhilaration, which seemed entirely natural.

No doubt Juno had done her best, but she continued to rely on bright clashing colors that didn't work for her. Racine, in black tie, sat between them scrupulously dividing his attention. As Gwenn passed their table, Minerva smiled warmly. Juno raised a limp hand in salute. Racine somehow managed to calibrate the warmth of his greeting somewhere in between.

The threesome had attracted every eye in the room. Obviously, they had been identified, and word that the Goddess sisters were aboard had spread. Simon Kittridge was eyeing them speculatively from the bar, but didn't approach. If he had been considering it, he would have been too late, for as soon as they became aware they were being observed, the three rose and left. Soon after, the gong sounded for the second dinner seating.

By that time, Kittridge had selected another companion. She was within his age group, dressed with elegance and restraint, and bejeweled. He went in to dinner with her and afterwards they watched the show in the DaVinci lounge and danced, as the brochures promised, under the stars till the wee hours. Rather than trying to tail them, Gwenn got the woman's cabin number from the office and settled herself in one of the service bays to keep watch. It was just two A.M. when Kittridge brought her home.

He opened the cabin door for her, handed back her access card, bowed and kissed her hand in a most chivalrous manner, and left.

To her dismay, Gwenn found she was relieved.

CHAPTER

4

DAY 4

AT SEA

Many passengers truly enjoyed the time at sea, and Gwenn found
that she was one of them. The routine of shipboard life was soothing. Using the daily activities bulletin as a guide, she could plan
the next day's schedule. In that way she joined a variety of groups.
For the young, there were sports—paddle tennis, Ping-Pong, vol-
leyball, golf putting, deck quoits, horseshoe throwing. For the not
so young, there was a library, board games, bridge, and that classic
of cruise life for all ages—shuffleboard. For those neither young nor
old but just lazy, there was wine tasting, a demonstration of ice
carving, tea with pastries served to the accompaniment of the Lombardo Strings, or just plain dozing on the protected side of the
Promenade deck.

Having spent an active morning during which she had met a
large number of passengers, none of whom she had any reason to
suspect were anything other than what they appeared to be, Gwenn

decided she had earned a siesta after lunch, and an afternoon of relaxation.

It was the thief's turn to move.

DAY 5
CARTAGENA

Before anyone had time to get bored, the *Dante* put in at Cartagena, Colombia, one of the oldest cities in the New World. Captain Nicolletti informed Gwenn he would lift the ban on crew shore leaves. She agreed that no purpose was being served and it was only causing resentment. For herself, Gwenn decided to remain on board, as she had at George Town. She wondered what the Aldrich party would do. She had been keeping an eye on Minerva, but the beautiful young woman never appeared alone, so she never got the opportunity to speak privately with her again. It seemed to Gwenn that Racine served almost as a bodyguard for Minerva, his presence a constant reminder to other passengers to keep their distance. And they did. Nor did it seem the trip was benefiting the younger sister very much. Despite the sun and the sea air, her color was not good. She moved with difficulty and depended more and more on the cane.

Checking the reservations for shore excursions, Gwenn found nothing booked for the Aldrich party. However, there was a reservation for a sightseeing tour for Mrs. Christine Fleming, the lady on whom Simon Kittridge had been bestowing his attentions since the second night out. By wary questioning, Gwenn learned that Simon had gone ashore on his own. The ship was due to depart Cartagena at five P.M. He barely made it back.

Christine was on deck waiting for him.

That night Gwenn watched as Simon Kittridge addressed himself to soothing the lady's feelings. He was good at his job, Gwenn thought. He did not devote himself solely to Mrs. Fleming, excluding all the other unattended women. He made sure that he and Mrs. Fleming joined a large group, and then he invited every woman to dance. But somehow he managed to dance the longest set with Christine, to hold her a little closer than he held the others. Somehow, she would be the one in his arms at the end of the evening.

But the lady was not responding to these attentions; she seemed preoccupied. As Kittridge bent solicitously close to whisper in her ear, Christine Fleming's eyes wandered. Kittridge was not accustomed to that kind of treatment. He redoubled his efforts.

Meanwhile, Gwenn was attracting her own share of attention. There were few single men among the passengers, none of them under sixty. But the staff officers sought her out and she was on the dance floor almost continuously. The group at her table grew larger and larger. Finally, Kittridge detached himself from his group and presented himself.

"May I have this dance?"

Gwenn glanced over her shoulder at Mrs. Fleming. "Won't your friend mind?"

"She knows it's my job."

"I see." Gwenn got up and walked ahead of Kittridge to the edge of the dance floor and waited for him to put his arm around her.

"I told you you wouldn't be alone for long," he reminded her as they glided out.

"That's true, you did."

"Are you having a good time?"

"Yes. Yes, I am." Gwenn surprised herself when she realized it was true.

The music was slow and seductive. He held her close. "And your young man, the one you left behind—do you miss him?"

"How do you know about my young man?"

"A girl like you is bound to have a young man." He shrugged.

"And how about the job? How's that coming? A pretty girl like you doesn't take a trip like this alone without a purpose."

Before she could answer, an officer from Gwenn's table tapped Kittridge's shoulder and cut in.

Kittridge's reminder of Ray had turned the night bittersweet for Gwenn. She continued to dance, in part to show the host that his words hadn't touched her, but she also knew that if she turned in now, she wouldn't be able to sleep. Ray was now a palpable presence; his face was superimposed on every one of her partners. She was glad when the band finally played "Goodnight, Ladies" and the group broke up, but she wasn't ready to go back to the cabin.

All the various bands had packed up; the Karaoke in the Eagle's Nest was over; even the casino had shut down. Gwenn decided to take a turn around the deck. Leaning against the door, she stepped over the coaming and emerged into the sultry tropical air. Above, only a sprinkling of stars poked through the overcast sky. She hoped that didn't mean bad weather ahead. The *Dante*'s running lights were on and colored spotlights illuminated the pool. Everything else was dark. Gwenn took a deep breath and flung her arms wide as though she could embrace it all. It was all and more than she had expected, and the desire to have Ray there with her was stronger than ever.

It wasn't his fault he hadn't been able to join her, she thought. It was just bad luck that they couldn't ever seem to accommodate each other's schedule. Her mother was right, she and Ray had not had the opportunity to know each other except under the fast-paced and stressful conditions of their jobs. Ray was particularly affected now that he was working for Internal Affairs. How would they react under normal circumstances? Could they adjust to a quiet, domestic routine? They needed to find out. She felt an urge to call Ray just to hear his voice, just to tell him she missed him and be told he missed her. But it was nearly three in the morning, and he was in the midst of a big narcotics investigation and needed his sleep. And anyhow, this wasn't something you discussed on the telephone. They would talk about it when she got back. First thing. Now it was time to get some sleep.

Below, on the Lido deck, a door was flung open and a rectangle of light spilled out. A voice, a young girl's voice filled with delicious fear, squealed.

"Oooh . . . ! It's so dark out here. And cold. It's too cold to swim."

"The water's warm. Once you get in you'll be fine."

"No, I don't want to. I've changed my mind."

"Oh, come on, Sandy. It'll be fun."

"Suppose somebody catches us and tells our parents?"

"Nobody's going to catch us. You said you would. Be a sport." The voice was that of a young male.

"No, I don't want to. Give me back my suit, Humphrey!"

"Come and get it!"

A figure stepped out of the shadows into the pool lights and Gwenn saw he was naked.

"I want my suit, Humphrey." The girl emerged and she was naked too. "Don't be so mean. Give it to me."

"Come and get it! Come on." Waving the suit over his head like a flag, the boy started to run, laughing, while the girl, frustrated and near tears, chased him. Still twirling the suit, the boy took a flying leap into the water. The girl jumped in after him. Neither one realized there was somebody already in the pool, a shadowy figure tethered by her long, fair hair to the grill over one of the drains at the deep end. As their playful antics agitated the water, the tangled hair came loose and she rose—slowly, majestically, breaking the surface between them. At the touch of her, both turned and tried frantically to swim away. It was Sandy who realized that the flesh that had touched her own was cold.

She screamed, and went on screaming.

By then, Gwenn was running down the stairs. At the pool's edge, she pulled off her pumps and lowered herself into the water.

"Stop howling," she told the girl even as she reached out for the victim. "There are towels in the cupboard on the right—cover yourself and then find a phone and get some help." Gwenn now concentrated on towing the inert body to the nearest pool ladder.

"You—give me a hand," she ordered the boy.

He worked from above and Gwenn from below, but even between the two of them it wasn't easy to hoist her out of the water. She was dead weight, literally. Also, she was fully dressed and the long, water-soaked garment added to the difficulty of raising her. At last, they managed to get her over the lip of the pool, turned her over, and laid her faceup on the deck.

"Do you know CPR?" Gwenn asked Humphrey.

"Yes, ma'am."

"Good. Let's get to it."

CHAPTER

5

It was, of course, Minerva Aldrich. Gwenn knew it the moment she saw the inert form rising slowly, with an eerie fatalism, the long blond hair streaming behind her. She also knew that CPR was useless; Minerva Aldrich was already past the point of resuscitation. Yet she and the boy, Humphrey, persisted while the girl, Sandy, went to call for help.

Eric Graf arrived first. Asking no questions, he got down on his knees to relieve Gwenn. After a brief rest, she nudged Humphrey to one side and took his place in forcing the breath of life into Minerva. As a team they continued to work in silence until the doctor arrived and pronounced Minerva Aldrich dead.

After that, everything remained in suspension while Captain Nicolletti was informed.

"Can't we go back to our cabins?" Humphrey Taggart appealed to Gwenn. "We don't know this lady, we don't even know her name."

"Please, oh please! I'm so cold," Sandy pleaded. Both had their bathing suits on by now, and Sandy Nash had wrapped herself in an oversized beach towel. They were cold and frightened. They would have wanted to give each other comfort and warmth by hugging, but that might have been a tacit admission of intimacy.

"The captain will want to see you both."

"But we don't know anything," Humphrey repeated with a touch of frustration. "You know as much as we do, probably more."

In contrast to Gwenn's experience of other crime scenes dominated by noise and confusion, this one was quiet and even orderly. Voices were kept low instinctively so as not to wake sleeping passengers. At Captain Nicolletti's arrival, the voice level dropped but the intensity increased. The ship's doctor and the hotel director immediately stepped to his side. Gwenn waited to be summoned. She didn't have to wait long.

"You are the one who found . . . That is, you were present when she rose to the surface . . ."

"The children found her." She waved them over and introduced Humphrey Taggart and Sandy Nash. "They went for a late-night swim and literally bumped into her."

Nicolletti groaned. "You saw it?"

"Yes." She waited, but the captain only shook his head and groaned. "It was a traumatic experience for them. They're cold, and they'd like to go back to their cabins. If need be, you can talk to them in the morning."

"Very well."

But they didn't go.

"Are you going to tell our parents?" Humphrey wanted to know.

"We'll see," Nicolletti replied.

"Not unless we have to." Gwenn spoke at the same time.

"All right." The captain sighed and gave in.

Gwenn shooed them away.

"Have the members of Miss Aldrich's party been informed of . . . the accident?" Nicolletti asked his hotel director.

"Not yet," Graf replied. "Dr. Halliday and I thought that to bring her sister and Mr. Racine here to the scene would be a terrible shock to them. And since Miss Aldrich has to be moved anyway, seeing her later in a neutral environment might cushion the shock."

Nicolletti scowled. "They might not appreciate your good intentions. Call and then escort them personally."

"Captain." Gwenn stepped forward once again. "I think we should call the ship's photographer before we disturb the scene."

"The scene has already been *disturbed* by your actions, Miss Ramadge," Graf reminded her.

"The boy and I pulled her out of the pool in the hope that she was still alive, or could be saved."

"And you were right to do that," Nicolletti said.

"Thank you. We'll need photographs of the scene and of Miss Aldrich." It was protocol at the ME's office to refer to the victim by name till after the autopsy was completed, at which time the dead person might be referred to as "the body." "The photos can't serve as official evidence, but they will at least provide a guide for the investigation."

The captain stiffened visibly. "What kind of investigation did you have in mind, Miss Ramadge?"

"Whatever may be necessary."

"It looks absolutely straightforward to me. However, I agree we should have photographs."

So Brian Bates was summoned.

Brian Bates was a young man with a pleasant, open face, light red hair, and a generous number of freckles. Confronted by the inert form of Minerva Aldrich lying on the deck in a puddle of water, he stopped short. It was his job to photograph merrymaking revelers eating and drinking, wearing funny hats, sunning themselves around the very pool at which he now was faced with the grim task of recording tragedy. He turned green at what he saw. He swallowed hard and prayed he wouldn't throw up in front of everybody.

Juno Chávez arrived while Bates was still shooting. Her face was swollen by sleep. She was dressed in an assortment of clothes—metallic silver tights topped by a black cable-knit sweater, and tennis shoes. Apparently, she'd put on whatever came to hand. She didn't see Minerva right away; there were too many people between them. As Bates set off another flash, Juno jumped.

"What are you doing?" she demanded, and pushed him to one side. Then for a long moment she stood transfixed in the presence of her dead sister. "Minnie," she murmured. "'Darling Minnie." She knelt and lightly brushed the cold blue lips with hers.

Nicolletti went to her. "I'm so sorry, Mrs. Chávez."

In his usual role of shadow, Paul Racine had followed, and now stood at the grieving woman's shoulder. He wore a silk robe over silk pajamas. Despite the situation, he managed to look elegant. He spoke quietly to the captain.

"What happened?"

"It appears there was an accident." Nicolletti tried to make sense of what little Gwenn had told him and what he knew. "She fell into the pool. She must have tripped . . . somehow. Over the hem of her pants, probably—they're very wide at the bottom." He pointed. "She pitched forward and fell into the water. Then either the pants or her hair caught in the grill of one of the drains and she was not able to free herself." He threw a quick look at Gwenn Ramadge. "A tragic accident," he pronounced.

In this brief summation, Captain Nicolletti had both anticipated and answered the objections Gwenn had been about to make.

"We tried CPR," Gwenn told Juno Chávez and Paul Racine.

Juno bowed her head.

"I'm very sorry to trouble you at this time," she continued, "but could you clear up a couple of things that might be important later on?"

"I'll do my best."

"Thank you. Did you and your sister turn in at the same time last night?"

"Yes. We turned in right after the entertainment; Minerva tired easily. We went straight to the stateroom."

"Both of you? You shared the room?"

"Yes. I was supposed to keep an eye on Minnie. She was my responsibility." Tears welled up again.

"Your sister didn't mention she might go out again?"

"No."

"She got undressed and went to bed?"

"We both did."

"You didn't hear her get up? She would have had to turn on the light to dress, wouldn't she?"

"My sister was very sick. She might have had trouble sleeping and decided to come up on deck for some fresh air. She wouldn't have wanted to disturb me, so she probably went into the sitting room to put on her clothes. She was very considerate."

"Palazzo pants with a gold mesh top seem somewhat elaborate for a stroll around the deck," Gwenn remarked. "Jeans and a sweater would have been more suitable."

"Actually, Minerva was very casual about clothes—despite the business we're in. She would have put on the first thing that came to hand. That would also be in keeping with her wish not to wake me."

Gwenn stared hard at Juno Chávez, at her stolid face, her tight jaw, her eyes that gave nothing away. "Just how sick was your sister, Mrs. Chávez?"

She hesitated. "That's no business of yours."

"If you recall, I was with Miss Aldrich when you and Mr. Racine came aboard at George Town. I got the impression she was a lot sicker than she wanted anyone to know. You and Mr. Racine in particular. You tried to support her but she pushed you away."

Juno Chávez's glare softened. "That's true. Minnie, poor darling, did try to keep it secret from us. She didn't want to cause us pain. But we knew. We talked to the doctors. It was terminal." She sighed. "Maybe this was her way of sparing us."

"And herself?" Gwenn asked.

A great sob convulsed Juno Chávez and at last she cried.

Racine put his arm around her and held her for several moments. "There will be no more questions," he declared. "Mrs. Chávez has suffered a severe shock. She needs to rest. Doctor?" He appealed to Halliday.

"Certainly."

Racine nodded. "I'll take her back . . . No, actually, she shouldn't go back to the suite. She should have other accommodations."

"We have no other accommodations," Eric Graf protested.

"You must have."

"I was going to say, we have nothing in the type of accommodation Mrs. Chávez is accustomed to."

"She can have my cabin," Gwenn offered. "I'll take whatever else is available. I'm not in the cabin much anyway."

Racine hesitated. "It's very kind of you, Miss . . . ?"

"Ramadge."

"It's very kind of you, Miss Ramadge," echoed Juno, for the first time really looking at Gwenn.

Racine took the access card Gwenn offered. "She'll need something to make her sleep." Again he looked at the doctor.

Halliday nodded. "I'll send the nurse."

As Racine led Juno away, she stopped. "What are you going to do with Minnie?"

It was a problem no one had thought of.

"We can't just leave her. Somebody has to stay with her."

"We have medical facilities. There will be someone in attendance," Nicolletti assured her.

With that, Juno allowed herself to be led away.

Everyone, including Gwenn, breathed easier. Once again, Gwenn knelt beside Minerva Aldrich and studied her. "I can't believe this was an accident, Captain. In order to fall into the pool facedown, she would have had to trip and pitch forward as you suggested, but there's nothing here to trip over except the hem of her palazzo pants." She paused and examined the cuffs of the wide pants. "I don't see a rip and the stitching is in perfect order. However, assuming that she did trip—would the force with which she hit the water knock her unconscious? I doubt it."

"What do you suggest?" Nicolletti asked.

"She might have been hit from behind."

Halliday got down beside Gwenn and probed. "I don't feel anything." Carefully, he parted the long blond hair into sections and examined the scalp, and again probed with his fingertips. "Nothing."

"Mrs. Chávez thought it might have been suicide," the captain recalled.

"I'm sorry, I didn't know Miss Aldrich, so I can't offer an opinion. If she had cancer, and I assume that's what we're talking about here, she might have had an attack. The disease is unpredictable. Or it might even have been a small stroke. There's no way of knowing. Her own doctors, perhaps . . . but I doubt even they would be able to say positively."

Halliday had been traveling the seas a fugitive from reality. As a young doctor starting his career, he had joined an HMO. Influenced perhaps by a need for economy, he had failed to order certain tests for a patient; the condition had gone undetected till it was too late and the patient died. He had resigned and found a place in a world of other people's fantasies, where he would never again have to take on hard responsibility.

"Jumping into the pool is not an effective means by which to commit suicide," Gwenn told him. "The instinct for self-preservation is too strong. It would not have allowed her to die," Gwenn pointed out, for a moment losing herself in the memories of her own close call off the shore of the Rockaways.

"Anyway, why choose the pool when the great wide ocean is all around us? If she'd jumped over the side, the impact might have been enough to render her unconscious; she might have been sucked so far down that she couldn't come up again; she might have been caught in the ship's propellers, or carried by the current—"

"We're well aware of the possibilities, Miss Ramadge," Graf cut in.

"We should search the suite for a suicide note," Gwenn said, "though I don't think we'll find one. She wasn't the type to give up. She was a fighter."

"So? What is your theory, Miss Ramadge?" the captain asked. "I assume you have one."

"I think leaving the suite furtively, as she did, suggests she was going to meet somebody and she didn't want her sister to know about it. Why the meeting had to be secret, I don't know, but something went wrong. There was a quarrel, maybe even a struggle. Minerva either slipped and fell or was pushed into the water. The person she had come to meet jumped in after her and held her under till she stopped breathing."

"A clandestine meeting would account for the elaborate outfit," Graf said.

"How about time of death?" Nicolletti asked the doctor.

Halliday shook his head. "There are so many variables, particularly in this situation, where the temperature of the water is a factor. The stomach contents might tell us, if we could find out when she had her last meal."

"Actually, we can get a pretty good fix on the time without that, Doc," Graf interjected. "Nothing could have happened earlier than two A.M., which is when the various lounges and the casino shut down. The children bumped into her . . . Sorry . . . they found her at close to three A.M. Miss Ramadge was a witness to that. Did you have any reason to take particular note of the time?" the hotel director asked her.

"As a matter of fact, I did. I was considering calling a friend in New York and I looked at my watch to see whether or not it was too late. It was ten to three," Gwenn told him.

"Good. Thank you." Graf continued: "Do you have any idea who Miss Aldrich might have been expecting to meet at that late hour?"

"No, I don't, but . . ."

"There's no indication she knew anyone on board," Graf overrode her. "I'm told Miss Aldrich and her sister and Mr. Racine kept very much to themselves."

"They did."

"Miss Aldrich was not well. She couldn't sleep so she decided to go up on deck for some air. Somehow, she tripped and fell into the pool. Her hair got caught in one of the grills at either the bottom or side of the pool. She couldn't free herself. What we have here is a tragic accident," Graf concluded.

"That part of it was an accident, yes," Gwenn agreed, "but what led up to it was not."

Graf looked to the captain.

"Shouldn't there be an autopsy?" Gwenn appealed to Nicolletti.

"Doctor?" He appealed to Halliday for a response.

"The cause of death is obvious—drowning. There don't appear to be any marks on the body. I've probed the skull. I will take a closer look. I lack the equipment or the expertise to do more. I do not believe anything more is called for."

"Thank you, Doctor."

Gwenn was embarrassed. She didn't want to show the doctor up, but she couldn't let it go. "Skin scrapings under her fingernails would indicate a struggle. And water in the lungs . . ."

Halliday flushed. "Are you a pathologist, Miss Ramadge?"

"In the process of CPR I noticed there was an inordinate amount of blood in her mouth."

"She might have bitten her tongue."

Nicolletti came to Halliday's rescue. "I appreciate your insights in this matter, Miss Ramadge," Nicolletti said. "But you need not concern yourself further. In the morning we'll talk about your other responsibilities."

Clearly that marked the end of the discussion. Nevertheless, Gwenn waited till Minerva Aldrich was strapped to the gurney and wheeled away before leaving.

By "other responsibilities" Captain Nicolletti meant solving the series of thefts, doing the job she had been hired to do, Gwenn thought. On the way to her cabin, she realized suddenly that she had offered it to Juno Chávez and had nowhere to go. While she pondered what to do, a cabin steward approached her.

"Miss Ramadge? Your cabin is ready for you. This way."

An inside cabin, it was down in the ship's bowels. Being claustrophobic, Gwenn felt uncomfortable at the mere thought of it. She had no choice but to bear it. It would teach her to think twice before being so helpful. And what about her clothes? She'd have to make arrangements to go and get them.

The steward opened the door for her and she saw her luggage neatly stacked to one side. "We unpacked for you, Miss Ramadge. We may not have put everything in the right place."

"I'm sure everything is perfect. Thank you."

Gwenn looked around. The cabin was cramped. There was barely enough space to pass between the twin beds.

The steward sensed her disappointment. "The cabins in this section were originally intended for the crew. Lately, there has been such a demand for accommodations that they were upgraded."

With plenty of chintz and wall-to-wall carpeting—nothing structural, Gwenn thought.

"There's no bolt on the door," he warned. "But there's a good Segal lock." He showed her how it worked. "But if you wish I can send someone to install a bolt or a chain."

"Don't go to any trouble, not tonight anyway. In the morning, we'll see." Nobody was going to steal from her, Gwenn thought, since she had nothing worth stealing.

"Well then, goodnight, Miss Ramadge."

"Goodnight," she repeated. By now it was morning. There was no way of knowing what kind of morning, since there was neither window nor porthole to show her. Never mind, she thought. It would be easier to sleep. She went to the door and turned the lock as the steward had shown her.

CHAPTER

6

DAY 6
AT SEA

Gwenn slept late and missed breakfast both in the Michelangelo dining room and the Lido restaurant, which served until half an hour before lunch. However, like all cruise ships, the *Dante Alighieri* prided itself on providing food at any hour of the day or night. In a small coffee bar near the Cine Verdi theater, Gwenn was able to get coffee and a pastry. Sitting at a corner banquette, watching the passengers stroll by, she mulled over the captain's remarks to her earlier. Obviously, he wanted her to play down Minerva Aldrich's death. Mysterious deaths on cruise ships were not good for business. The captain wanted to write off the drowning as an accident. She, on the other hand, had made it clear that she believed it was neither accident nor suicide. If she insisted on sticking to that position, Nicolletti would find a way to get rid of her.

As captain, Niccolò Nicolletti was the sole arbiter of everything that happened on board, but Gwenn sensed that Nicolletti had a touch of the devious in his makeup. He would not act unilaterally. The home office had sought Gwenn out and hired her and would not be pleased if she was fired out of hand. Nicolletti would consult with them first. So she had a period of grace, and she meant to put it to good use. She had never before been fired from a job and she wasn't going to be this time either.

Unfortunately, she still lacked direction. Interrogation was her principal tool, but there were no suspects to interrogate. Shipboard alliances were being formed: like seeking like, couples gravitating to couples with similar interests, singles joining just because they were single, and all of these according to age. Gwenn also noticed that certain of the service staff sought out favored passengers, memorized their names and preferences. Since Ida Sturgess had reported the disappearance of her brooch and mentioned Simon Kittridge in connection with it, Gwenn had been looking for an opportunity to talk to him.

It seemed to Gwenn that the hosts were a link between passengers and staff and that Kittridge was the leader of the hosts. While dancing with him the night before, she had been about to bring up the subject of the thefts and Mrs. Sturgess's brooch in particular, but one of the officers in her group had chosen that moment to cut in. Scanning the daily activities program, Gwenn noticed that Kittridge would be speaking as port lecturer in the DaVinci lounge at one-thirty that afternoon. His subject: the Panama Canal, through which they would be passing tomorrow. She decided to go in early and get a good seat.

She was lucky to get any seat at all. It was only one P.M. and the big red and gold room was filled to near capacity.

Kittridge took the lectern promptly at the appointed time. He started by setting out the topics he would cover and those he would not. He would speak only briefly about the history of the canal; the film to be shown at three-thirty in the Cine Verdi would cover that in detail. He would deal with their passage through the canal by means of the various locks, identify what points of interest there were and what to look for. He spoke for precisely twenty minutes without interruption and then invited questions. He answered questions for the next fifteen minutes, then announced the end of the session, though people were still lining up to consult him. Gwenn made sure to be the last one.

"You did a very thorough and very interesting job, Mr. Kittridge."

"Miss Ramadge! I thought I spotted you in the balcony." He glanced up to the spot where she had, in fact, been sitting. "What would you like to ask?"

"Many things. Is there somewhere we can go to talk for a few minutes?"

"I don't know." He looked at his watch. "I've got to give this same speech in fifteen minutes for those who missed it the first time."

"I won't keep you that long. I promise."

"All right. We can go to one of the dressing rooms. This way."

He led her backstage to a narrow room with a metal shelf running its full length on one side and on the other a pair of clothes racks. Mirrors were set in the wall over the shelf . Five chairs were lined up to face the mirrors, and at each chair an array of makeup was like a place setting. Gwenn wasted no time.

"Did you know that on our first night out as we were approaching George Town, there was a theft on board?"

Kittridge sighed heavily. "So you are the private investigator the company hired. I figured it must be you."

"How?"

"We knew they'd hired somebody; they had to. But you're not exactly standard issue, and you're not credible as a passenger either. You're young and single and you're alone. Usually, young singles travel in pairs; it's cheaper. Also, you don't hang around the pool or the cocktail bars. You keep to yourself. And you haven't been asking questions. Until now."

"So you knew that the woman you danced with Friday night lost a valuable antique brooch."

He hesitated. "I understood Mrs. Sturgess was robbed."

"How did you find out? Did she tell you?"

"She didn't have to. The word got around, the way it will get around about you whether I say anything or not."

He had forestalled her neatly, Gwenn thought, and waited in case he should volunteer anything about Minerva Aldrich. But either the news of her drowning had not been passed along the grapevine or he was waiting for her to open the subject—which she was not about to do, yet.

"Tell me about Mrs. Sturgess and the events of that evening."

He shrugged. "There's not much to tell. She was in a group of eight ladies. I danced with each one. I make a point of showing no preference."

"But you did leave with Mrs. Sturgess."

"She asked me to escort her to her cabin. She'd had a little too much champagne and she was feeling dizzy. So I took her to her door, opened it for her, and left."

"You didn't go inside?"

He sighed. "No, Miss Ramadge, I didn't go inside."

"What did you think of the brooch?"

"I'm no expert."

"Give me a ballpark figure."

"Two thousand, because of its antiquity."

"She says seven to nine."

"Never. At least, I don't think so."

"She said you admired it greatly."

"She called my attention to it and asked what I thought of it. What could I say? I said I thought it was very beautiful."

"Was the brooch the subject of conversation at any other time during the evening?"

"It wasn't that remarkable a piece," Kittridge responded.

"Did Mrs. Sturgess dance with anyone else?"

"Yes. A couple of the other hosts joined the party. As I mentioned, there were eight ladies—a handful even for me."

Gwenn didn't share in his attempt at humor. "Assuming she did remark on the brooch to one of her other partners, is it possible that he waited till everyone turned in and then went to her cabin?"

Kittridge raised his shaggy eyebrows. "Anything is possible, but in my opinion the piece was not worth the risk—particularly as it entailed entering the lady's cabin while she was in it."

"I assume you know about the other burglaries that took place during the *Dante*'s three previous crossings."

"I do, and so does every member of the crew," Kittridge replied tersely. "After the first passenger reported that an emerald pendant was missing from her cabin safe, the ship was searched from stem to stern, every inch of it. That is to say, every inch of the public rooms and the crew quarters. All crew shore leaves were canceled until the search was completed. Nothing was found, of course, so shore leaves were reinstated, but before going ashore each crewman had to go through a metal detector."

To make sure he didn't carry the loot ashore and dispose of it or pass it to an accomplice, Gwenn thought.

"It was humiliating," Kittridge told her, "and brought no result, so finally it was dropped. I'm surprised the captain tried it again in George Town."

Gwenn made no comment.

"We've accepted that until the culprit or perpetrator or whatever you want to call him is apprehended, we are all under suspicion—the crew, that is, not the passengers. The passengers aren't searched; their word is not challenged. Our jobs are in danger; the entire host program is at risk and may be canceled. So we're very glad to see you, Miss Ramadge, and we wish you success. I think you'll find all of us cooperative. Whatever you want, you have only to ask."

"Thank you."

"You might try talking to the waitress who served us that night. Nancy Castel." He looked at his watch. "Sorry. I'm on."

She made no attempt to detain him. She knew one thing—if Captain Nicolletti had ideas about running his metal detector again, this time he'd better make sure the passengers were required to pass through as well as the crew.

One good thing about investigating a crime at sea: neither suspect nor witness could run away.

Captain Nicolletti had ordered Gwenn to keep hands off anything pertaining to Minerva Aldrich's death. He had urged her to get on with the investigation of the jewel thefts. What goodwill she had managed to build up by discovering Ida Sturgess's duplicity was dissipated when she took a position opposed to his and Eric Graf's regarding the drowning. She could get back into favor by joining the party line, but that was not Gwenn's way. Nor would she actively try to prove she was right. No, she would bide her time and let the natural aftershocks of the death have their effects. Meanwhile, she would follow the captain's orders.

The Miramar bar served from just before lunch to three P.M. There was barely time for Gwenn to make it in before closing.

When she arrived, only a few passengers still dawdled over their drinks, and the band, a jazz combo, was packing up. The waitresses were clustered around the service bar waiting for the closing gong. Gwenn sat at a nearby table and signaled for service. There was some uncertainty about who should respond.

Finally a young, pretty girl came over. "Yes, ma'am. What can I get you?"

She was slight and delicate. Her eyes were large and dark. Her hair was nearly black and hung down her back in a curtain as lustrous as satin. Her complexion was creamy, without blemish. She moved lightly, with the fluid grace of a dancer. Her long, narrow skirt was slit to the thigh and revealed long, slim legs that Gwenn suspected were strong as well as seductive. In contrast, the tailored, long-sleeved white blouse was modest. All the girls were similarly attired; it was the uniform, but on this girl it was very special. The plaque pinned to her breast pocket spelled out her name: *Nancy.*

Gwenn ordered a Perrier and gave her name and cabin number. Nancy had trouble spelling Gwenn's name. "Are you enjoying the cruise so far, Miss Ramadge?" She pronounced the name carefully.

"Yes, very much."

"Do you come from Florida?"

"No, New York." Gwenn noticed that at another table a waitress was also engaged in conversation with passengers, an elderly couple. Were these people genuinely friendly, or was it part of the job?

"I was in New York once!" Nancy's aspect brightened. "We were in Baltimore with the *Dante* while she was being refurbished between seasons. A group of us took the train to New York and went to see the Statue of Liberty. It was wonderful."

She should leave now and go to fill the order, Gwenn thought, but she hung back as though waiting for something, as though expecting Gwenn to make some move. Had Kittridge primed her? "I'm a private investigator, Nancy. Do you know what that is?"

The girl's dark eyes sparkled. "I've seen them on television."

"Do you remember serving a group of eight ladies, mostly elderly, on the first night out? They were joined by Simon Kittridge. Do you know who he is?"

"Yes, ma'am. He's one of the hosts."

"That's right. Well, I'd like to talk to you about what happened that night. When are you off duty?"

"From four to six."

"Shall we meet in my cabin?"

"I'm not supposed to be in that section of the ship."

Kittridge had warned her that the grapevine was active. "I'll come to yours, then."

Nancy Castel hesitated.

"Don't worry," Gwenn told her. "I know how to get around without being noticed."

Nancy Castel didn't seem to be either reassured or amused. She sighed. "All right. I'm on B deck, number 2201. At four."

Gwenn was pleased that she was able to find the cabin without having to ask for directions. It was just as well that the news they were meeting didn't get around. Gwenn arrived promptly at four and knocked lightly. There was no answer. She didn't want to be seen loitering, so she went up to the main deck to wait. After fifteen minutes she went down again. Getting no response to her knock this time either, she stayed where she was. At four-thirty, as Nancy had still not shown up, Gwenn took the elevator up to the promenade deck and entered the management office.

"You're overreacting, Miss Ramadge," Eric Graf told her. "She probably took a little nap and didn't hear you. I'll send somebody."

"Can't you just call her on the telephone?"

"There are no telephones in the crew quarters."

"Well then, let's go."

"Has it occurred to you, Miss Ramadge, that Nancy might just have decided she doesn't want to speak with you?"

"It has. In that case, I want to know why. I also want to make sure she's all right."

Graf grunted and pushed his chair away from the desk. "I'll go. You wait here."

"If you're afraid that if I'm seen with you, the crew will know who I am and why I'm here . . . they know already."

Without further argument, Graf rose and led the way. He took a shortcut, passing through the working section of the ship. Nothing was there for adornment; everything was functional, and transmitted a sense of power. No attempt had been made to muffle the throbbing engines, which imparted a sense of the stored energy that could be unleashed at any moment. At the door of Nancy's cabin, Graf knocked, loudly.

He had no better luck than Gwenn. He sent for the cabin steward. Passing crewmen eyed them curiously while they waited for him to return with the access card, but a scowl from the hotel director sent them scurrying. It didn't take long for the steward to arrive and, with the skill of long practice, slip the card into the appropriate slot, turn the handle, and open the door. Gwenn started forward, but Graf put out a hand to block her way.

"Let me," he said.

The cabin was cramped. It contained a two-tiered bunk bed, two wardrobes, two chairs, and a single dresser. A washbasin stood in a far corner. There was barely room to move. Nancy Castel, lying on the floor between the lower berth and the bureau, took up most of it. The door was in the way, so Gwenn could see only a partial reflection in the bureau mirror.

"You'd better not come in," Graf warned.

"I'm all right," Gwenn said, and stepped over the coaming.

Nancy Castel lay on her right side, knees slightly bent, head turned, arms up to shield her face. No wonder, Gwenn thought as she knelt beside her. Blows must have rained on her. Her pretty face was swollen and discolored. She looked like a blowfish washed to the shore. Welts and bruises ran into each other. Some wounds still oozed; others were already caked dry.

"Nancy?" Gwenn called softly. "Nancy!" Getting no response, she placed the tips of her fingers under the jaw to feel for the carotid pulse.

"She's alive!" Gwenn's eyes filled with relief. "Can you hear me, Nancy? Everything's going to be all right. You're with friends." She looked up to Graf. "Please, call the doctor."

Graf's nod to the steward was an order for him to take care of it. "Maybe we should get her up on the bed."

"I don't think so—in case anything's broken. We should cover her though. Keep her warm."

Together they stripped the blanket from the lower bunk and covered the unconscious girl. Gwenn sat on the floor beside her and held her hand. She was very still, Gwenn thought. Her breathing was shallow but regular. *Thank God.* Gwenn couldn't think past that, couldn't speculate; right now she couldn't even attempt to reconstruct what had happened. It didn't matter; as soon as Nancy regained consciousness she'd tell them. Meantime, where was Halliday? Why didn't he come?

In fact, he came very quickly and went right to work. His examination was brief. He felt for her pulse as Gwenn had. He flashed a beam of light into Nancy's eyes, and got no reaction. He examined the back of her skull. Then he got up.

"As you can see, she suffered a series of blows to the head, none of them fatal, in fact superficial. There is no indication she put up any resistance. Her arms are raised to shield her face; that's instinctive. There's no indication she tried to get away by crawling or pulling herself erect. She was hit from behind, went down, and the facial injuries were inflicted while she was prone."

"When will she regain consciousness?" Gwenn asked.

"I can't say. We'll take her to the infirmary. I'll dress her wounds and we'll see."

"But will she be all right?" Graf insisted on reassurance.

"As far as I can tell . . . as of now . . . yes. I think so."

Gwenn had questions for the doctor but decided to keep them for later, for a private moment. She waited till Nancy was carried out with the doctor in attendance. Graf waited also.

"It seems your instincts were right," he observed.

"I wish they hadn't been."

"Are you through here?"

"Not quite. I'd like to make a thorough examination of the premises. To that end I'd like to keep the cabin locked and off limits. I assume there's a roommate. Could she be moved?"

He nodded. "Sofia Rossi. We'll move her in with somebody. First, I'd like to know what's going on."

"You know as much as I do. More, probably."

"You'll have to do better than that, Miss Ramadge. The captain won't be pleased."

"I cautioned Mr. Farnsworth when I was in Vancouver and the captain when I came on board not to expect too much."

"Are you saying that what happened here this afternoon is in some way connected to the burglaries?"

"Nancy served Mrs. Sturgess on the night of the robbery."

"That's not much to go on."

"Never underestimate the power of the subconscious, Mr. Graf."

"You don't seem to follow any set procedure," he complained. "You stir things up."

"I don't intend to."

He sighed lugubriously. "How do you explain what happened here?"

"I talked to Nancy at the Miramar bar this afternoon. We made a date to continue our talk in her cabin at four o'clock."

"To talk about what?"

"About the burglaries, of course. She was anxious that nobody should know about our meeting. Somehow, somebody found out. The way I see it, this person gained access to the cabin and lay in wait for her. I notice the door opens inward, as most outside doors do. He stood behind it as she entered, and struck her on the back of the head." Gwenn looked around, frowning. "I don't see anything here that would have been handy. Maybe he brought it with him . . . Anyway, one blow brought her down, unconscious but not dead. He hit her some more, but according to the doctor, not hard. I think he wanted to throw a scare into her, make sure she didn't talk to me or anyone else."

Graf's face darkened. "She'll talk to me."

"How are you going to make her?" Gwenn demanded. "Do you think you can frighten her more than she's been frightened already? Or do you think you can reassure her enough, make her feel safe enough so that she'll confide in you? You could end up reinforcing her determination to keep silent. The best thing to do is to leave her alone—for now anyway. In fact, I insist you leave her alone. I'm in charge of this case," she reminded him.

"Not for long."

Gwenn's reply was to turn her back and begin to study the condition of the cabin, searching for traces of the attack. According to Dr. Halliday, Nancy had not put up any resistance. She just lay there and absorbed the blows that were inflicted. With what—his bare hands? Yes, once she was down, but what had the perp used initially to knock her out? Visualizing the scene, Gwenn again felt a wave of pity. Nancy might not have been able to put a mark on her assailant, but it was possible he had inadvertently left some trace of his presence and actions.

"I'll need a small vacuum to collect dust and hairs," she told Graf.

"No problem." He was watching her every move.

"About the roommate . . . I'd like to talk to her."

"I assumed you would. She's on her way."

"Thank you." Graf surprised her, not for the first time.

"I am here to help you, Miss Ramadge."

"I appreciate that."

"Both Captain Nicolletti and I are on your side. We want you to solve this problem."

Before Gwenn could come up with a reasonably honest comment, there was a knock at the door and Sofia Rossi presented herself. Graf made the introductions and then sat down. Obviously he intended to be present for the interview. Gwenn was not in a position to ask him to leave. She turned her attention to the roommate.

Sofia Rossi was a little older than Nancy, Gwenn judged, say twenty-six or -seven. She was also a bit taller, but otherwise very similar. She had the same clear complexion, dark hair, and dark eyes. All the crew, male and female, were attractive, Gwenn thought.

"Have you heard about what happened to Nancy?" Gwenn began.

Sofia cast an anxious glance at Graf.

"Answer the question, Miss Rossi."

"She was attacked," she said softly, almost in a whisper.

So word had spread. You could hardly expect otherwise in a

closed community, Gwenn thought. "That's right. Have you any idea why?"

Sofia cast her luminous eyes down. She shook her head.

"From what we can deduce, the assailant was in the cabin, here, waiting. How could he have gotten in? Are there any extra access cards?"

"There have to be, in case of emergency." Graf was loath to admit it. "But they're not easy to get hold of."

"Have you any idea how he got in?" Gwenn continued.

"No, ma'am."

"Could Nancy have given her card to anyone?"

Sofia flushed. "We're not permitted to have men in our cabin. Anyway, Nancy doesn't have a boyfriend. She's not interested in men. Her only interest is in her children."

"Nancy has children?" Gwenn exclaimed. *She's only a child herself,* she thought.

"Three. They're all she lives for. They're with her mother in Naples. Nancy supports them all."

"What about the husband?"

Sofia shrugged. "She never mentions him."

"She didn't mention on her application that she was married or that she had children," Graf remarked.

"Maybe she isn't married," Gwenn suggested.

"I don't care whether or not she's married or whether she has children. I do care that she kept it hidden, that in essence she lied." He turned on Sofia. "You should have reported it."

"I didn't know what she put on her application. Besides, it was none of my business."

"What's the problem?" Gwenn asked. "Is it company policy not to hire anyone with children?"

"No, of course not!" The hotel director flushed. He was appalled at the thought of the furor the mere suggestion, made public, would cause. "Of course not," he repeated.

"Have you any cause to complain about Miss Castel's job performance?"

"None. You're off the track, Miss Ramadge."

"Maybe. Maybe not. You never know where a path may lead till you get to the end."

Exasperated, Graf addressed Sofia again. "Are you holding back anything else?"

"I haven't been holding anything back," she retorted with new-found courage.

"Do you know anything about the recent thefts on this ship?" Gwenn asked.

"No."

"I have to point out to you that your friend Nancy took a serious beating today. She could have been killed. If you want to see how close she came, go up to the infirmary. You may think you're helping her by keeping silent, but you're not, you're only putting yourself in danger along with her. I don't think she would want you to do that."

"May I go now?" Sofia asked.

"Of course."

Graf waited till she closed the door behind her. "So?"

"I don't think I got through to her."

"What's next?"

"I'm going up to the infirmary to sit with Nancy. I want to be the first one she sees when she regains consciousness." *If she regains consciousness,* she thought.

Gwenn was surprised to find Dr. Halliday's waiting room filled. It had not occurred to her that he was not there to treat only the passengers but that the crew might need his services too. In fact, several, in uniform, were lined up. A sign on the desk indicated evening consulting hours were from five to seven P.M. The clock on the wall showed the time to be nearly seven.

No one was at the desk. Probably the nurse did double duty and was inside with the doctor and a patient. Gwenn proceeded past everyone and peered down a long corridor which she assumed led to the doctor's office and examining room. She entered. No one challenged her right to do so.

She heard voices and traced them to Dr. Halliday's office. Then, turning the corner, she discovered two bedrooms, doors open, and approached on tiptoe. But there was no need for silence. The person in the first room would not hear her. It was Minerva Aldrich; at least, Gwenn assumed that's who it was. She had been lifted off the gurney and laid on top of the bed with the sheet still covering her from head to toe.

The room was filled with flowers, most likely upon the request of the victim's sister, Gwenn thought. Probably more order than request. It was a vast array which must have been created by using the arrangements in every public room. The scent was heavy and sweet. Gwenn was about to go in, when she heard voices at the far end of the corridor—porters with more flowers. She slipped into the next room.

It was small and bare with the standard hospital equipment, nothing more. Nancy lay on the bed hooked up to various monitors and the usual IV drip. Her face had been cleaned and her wounds treated, but she still looked terrible. She was breathing on her own and that was certainly encouraging, but it wasn't a medical emergency that Gwenn feared. She pulled a chair up to the bed and sat down. She leaned forward and spoke softly.

"Nancy. Wake up, Nancy. You're safe. Nobody's going to hurt you anymore. I'm going to take your hand, Nancy. I'm going to squeeze it just to let you know you're safe. If you understand, I want you to squeeze back."

Gwenn did as she had said, and waited. Nothing. She shouldn't expect results on the first attempt. She would try again and keep trying through the night. If Nancy didn't wake by morning, Captain Nicolletti would probably put her ashore where there would be access to better facilities. There was only one problem—they were about to enter the Panama Canal and no one, with the exception of the pilot, was permitted to get on or off a ship in transit. Awake or not, Nancy would be better off on shore, Gwenn thought, and squeezed the girl's hand a second time.

Gwenn came to with a start. She was still in the infirmary, still sitting beside Nancy Castel's bed, but no longer holding her hand. Though she knew where she was and why, Gwenn had no idea at first what had awakened her. It wasn't either a loud noise or a sudden movement; it was the lack of sound and movement. The ship's engines were idling; the ship rocked gently in response to the ocean currents but it wasn't going anywhere. Whatever had happened, it hadn't affected Nancy; she seemed to be resting comfortably, breathing evenly. Gwenn made a careful check of the electrical outlets to make sure all the monitors were properly connected.

Next she went to the window, expecting to see open water; instead, she saw a few lonely lights on a sparsely inhabited coast. Special notification in the form of a flyer slipped under every cabin door earlier that day had informed the passengers that the *Dante* would make an unscheduled stop at the San Blas Islands to take on certain additional passengers. The pilot who was to guide them through the canal would board with them, thus making up some of the lost time. Gwenn saw the distinctive shape of the pilot's craft silhouetted in the moonlight, riding lights on, chugging toward them.

An inordinate number of persons were lined up along the railing of the Promenade deck to watch what was, in Gwenn's opinion, an ordinary event. She recognized Eric Graf and Captain Nicolletti somewhat apart but also waiting. They didn't turn out like this for just anybody.

The gangway was lowered and the pilot boat drew up alongside the wooden landing platform. Two persons, a man and a woman, stepped from the boat to the platform and were assisted up the stairs to the deck of the *Dante*. The captain stepped forward to greet them and then they were whisked away. Gwenn saw no more than the backs of their heads. Almost immediately the ship's engines engaged and the *Dante,* throbbing, continued on its course. The crowd of passengers dispersed.

Gwenn was still at the window wondering exactly what she had witnessed, when a light tap sounded on the door behind her. Nurse Giorgina Kent looked in.

"Well, you're awake! How are you feeling?"

"Me? I'm fine. How's the patient?"

"She's stable."

Gwenn felt the woman's eyes studying her. "I didn't mean to fall asleep. I meant to keep watch."

"That's my job," Nurse Kent said.

Nevertheless, Gwenn was disappointed in her failure to keep watch. Anybody could have walked in while she slept. She changed the subject.

"Who was it that just came aboard?"

"Lewis Aldrich, Miss Minerva's father, and Diana Aldrich, her half sister. They've come to take her body home."

CHAPTER

7

Lewis and Diana Aldrich boarded the *Dante Alighieri* in the soft tropical night in the waters off the San Blas Islands. Captain Nicolletti and Eric Graf stood to one side of the landing stair, and Juno Chávez and Paul Racine to the other. Nicolletti stepped forward to greet them and to offer condolences. It was formal and muted. Next, the sisters embraced. After that, stiffly, like figures on the lid of a music box, the sisters changed partners.

"I'm so sorry, Lewis," Juno murmured to her stepfather. "I don't understand what happened."

Racine embraced Diana silently and placed a kiss as dry as a dead leaf upon his fiancée's lips.

"Would you like to go to your quarters? Or perhaps you'd like to eat something?" Captain Nicolletti asked.

"Thank you, but I want to see my child. Where is she?"

"We put her in the infirmary."

Lewis Aldrich's lips were pressed tight. There was no doubt he was displeased. "She'd booked a suite, hadn't she?"

"We felt there should be someone in attendance." Graf spoke for the captain. "It was easier to arrange if we put her in the infirmary."

Aldrich looked from Juno to Paul Racine. "Couldn't either of you . . ." he began. His shoulders sagged; he was close to exhaustion. "I suppose it doesn't matter."

"Perhaps you and Miss Diana would care to use the suite? Miss Minerva's room can be closed off, if you wish."

"It doesn't matter. We'll sleep anywhere. We'll be leaving in a few hours anyway."

Nicolletti was taken aback. "I'm afraid that's not possible. We are scheduled to go through the canal tomorrow morning. Reservations for passage are made months in advance and cannot be changed. Once we enter the locks, no one may get on or off. The passage takes nine hours."

"I plan to leave the ship before she enters the locks. I've already made the arrangements with the local authorities."

Nicolletti turned to Eric Graf. "Why wasn't I informed?"

"No one's told me anything, sir."

"I told *you*, Captain, that I would take care of all the details," Aldrich reminded the captain.

"And I told you, Mr. Aldrich, that the arrangements would be subject to my approval. That was not a formality, sir."

"I want my daughter's remains to be treated with dignity. I want her to make this final trip in a seemly manner. But if necessary, I can take her off this ship within the next hour."

Nicolletti clenched his jaw. Beads of sweat appeared along his upper lip and trickled into his beard. All at once, he relaxed. "I apologize, Mr. Aldrich. We are both under stress; you have the greater cause. I'm sure we can work this out. Meantime, may I once again suggest something to eat and then a rest?"

"I don't want to rest or eat. I want to see my daughter. If someone will just, at last, show me the way . . ."

It had been Giorgina Kent's responsibility to prepare the body for viewing. The first thing she'd done was turn the air-conditioning in one of the patient rooms up as high as it would go—this would slow the rate of decomposition. Next, she had the dead girl taken out of the body bag and placed on the bed. In an effort to be kind and to lessen the shock for the family, she now folded the sheet back to show her face. She had combed Minerva Aldrich's long blond hair and spread it out on the pillow. Minerva had not been in the water long enough to be bloated or discolored, so Nurse Kent put some lipstick on her and tried a little rouge for her cheeks. She did such a good job that at first it seemed as though the girl might only be sleeping. Seeing his daughter so nearly normal was the greater shock. Lewis Aldrich stood stock-still just inside the door.

"My child. My little girl."

Slowly, he drew closer while the two sisters hung back with Racine. Having reached Minerva's side, her father leaned over and kissed her. Her lips were an unearthly cold, and he was forced to face the reality that she was gone. He turned and regarded Juno.

"How could you let this happen?"

"She sneaked out in the middle of the night while I was sleeping. I couldn't watch her day and night. How could I stop her?"

"Sneak? What do you mean she sneaked out? Why should she sneak out? She must have had a reason."

"I don't know what it was. Maybe she couldn't sleep. Maybe she was taking a walk in the cool night air. Maybe it wasn't anything more than that. I don't know." Juno's unpainted lips quivered. She was a stolid woman and tears were not her style. Besides, she knew they would only serve to irritate her stepfather.

"You're asking me to accept that Minnie got up at two in the morning and was taking a stroll when she accidentally fell into the pool and drowned? No, I don't buy that. How about it, Paul? What do you think Minnie was doing out on deck, alone, at that hour?"

"I don't know."

"Well, think! Try to think, for God's sake. Make an effort."

Racine cast a look at Diana. "You don't want to know what I think."

"Try me."

"You already know what I'm going to say."

"Then go ahead and say it, if you have the guts," Aldrich challenged. "You're going to say Minnie used drugs. She did, but she was no addict. She was sick. She needed the drugs to ease the pain of dying. That's not being an addict. Anyhow, she'd quit. She didn't need the stuff anymore, not since she went into remission." He turned back to Juno. "I told you to watch her. I warned you."

"What could I have done?"

"You could have slipped her a couple of sleeping pills before the two of you went to bed."

"I didn't think there was any need," Juno moaned.

"You mean like putting something in her drink? Come on, Lewis. Minnie was too smart for that." Racine defended Juno. "And how could Juno know when Minnie was getting ready to prowl? How could she even know she was coming out of remission? Just looking at her, well, it was hard to tell, believe me. If she'd confided in me, I would have gotten her whatever she needed. The thing is, she didn't want us to know." He paused. "She wanted to spare us."

Racine joined his future father-in-law at the bedside. He clapped a hand on Aldrich's shoulder. "Minnie was making an intense effort to behave normally so that we could have happy memories of this trip. I could see something was wrong, but I didn't want to admit it; I told myself she was just tired from the trip and the excitement. I would never have let Minnie roam this ship in search of a connection."

"I was uneasy too," Juno admitted. "Her condition varied. She had good days and bad days."

"You should have called me," Aldrich said, but he was calmer.

"Juno didn't want to cause you needless worry." Diana supported her sister. "She couldn't possibly anticipate anything like this."

"No, of course not." He drew Juno to him in a gentle hug. "Don't worry. We'll find out what happened."

"How?"

"You don't mean an autopsy!" Racine was shocked.

Aldrich looked down at his beautiful daughter for a long time.

"I'll never let them do that to my girl." His voice was a soft caress. "No, a simple blood test will tell us everything we need to know."

"Is the ship's doctor competent . . ." Diana let the question trail off.

"We'll get someone who is." Aldrich became brisk, authoritative. "If she tests positive, meaning she was back on drugs, then that's it: the drugs were responsible. They caused a dizzy spell or a blackout; she fell into the pool and could do nothing to save herself."

"Suppose the test shows she was clean?" Juno asked. "Then what?"

"We'll never know," Diana said.

"Oh yes we will," Aldrich snapped. "Count on it." He leaned down and placed a last kiss on his daughter's cold lips, lingering as though he could transmit the warmth of his body to hers. At last he rose, apparently energized, squared his shoulders, and strode to the door. Opening it, he called into the corridor.

"Mr. Graf? Please inform Captain Nicolletti that I've decided to stay on board during the passage through the canal and perhaps on to the final destination. If that's agreeable to him, of course. That will give me extra time to make suitable arrangements to transport my daughter."

The next time Gwenn Ramadge woke, room B of the infirmary was gray with the light of dawn. She was still sitting beside Nancy Castel's bed but in a different chair, which she must have drawn up in the night. Looking up, she found Nancy's eyes watching her.

Gwenn smiled. "Good morning."

"Good morning."

"How are you?" Gwenn asked.

"My face feels stiff and I ache all over."

"That's not surprising. Do you remember what happened?"

"No." Nancy started to shake her head, but it hurt too much.

"You were attacked and badly beaten. We think whoever did it was in your cabin lying in wait. You opened the door and when you stepped inside, he jumped you."

"We had a date at four," the waitress recalled.

"That's right. Did you tell anybody about it?"

"No."

"Could someone have overheard us in the Miramar bar?"

"I don't see how."

"Does anyone besides Sofia have an access card to your cabin?"

"No."

"Well, he got in somehow." Gwenn sighed. "After we parted, did you go directly to your cabin?"

"I stopped at the laundry machine, but it was in use so I didn't wait."

"Apparently it was long enough for him to get to the cabin before you. You must have some idea who it might have been," Gwenn almost pleaded, but still got no answer. "He knocked you unconscious and after you were down, he went on hitting you—always in the face. He cut and bruised your face. You want to see what he did?" Gwenn took the hand mirror from the bureau and handed it to her, but she refused to take it. "Who did it, Nancy?"

"I don't know. I didn't see him. He was behind the door."

"How did he get into the cabin?"

"Please . . ."

"Why did he do it? Why doesn't he want us to talk together? What is he afraid you'll tell me?"

"I don't know."

"Why are you protecting him?" Gwenn's voice reached the peak of an accelerating scale. At this stage, she didn't expect an answer. She believed she already had it, and that it connected to Nancy's mother and the three children back in Naples. Its tentacles reached beyond casual thefts aboard a cruise ship, past anything Gwenn had suspected when she took the job. She would not press the young mother. She would not force her to put herself and those she loved so dearly into further jeopardy. She leaned forward and kissed Nancy's forehead, which was damp with perspiration.

"I'll send the nurse in."

Nurse Giorgina Kent was alone in the reception room. She sat near the table lamp, knitting something blue and fluffy.

"She's awake," Gwenn informed her.

"Thank God." The nurse set her knitting aside right away, rose, and went into room B. Gwenn waited to make sure everything was all right. She listened but heard nothing to cause alarm. Turning to go, she noticed a line of light under the door of room A, in which Minerva Aldrich reposed. She went over, listened, and tapped lightly. Getting no response, she edged the door open cautiously. When she'd looked in earlier, Minerva Aldrich's body had been covered head to toe by a sheet. That sheet was now folded back to show her face. Her eyes were shut in a gruesome imitation of sleep. A man sat at her side, silver head bowed, hands clasped in prayer. It was a private moment and Gwenn was about to withdraw when he looked up.

"I'm sorry to disturb you," she apologized. "I saw the light under the door. I didn't know . . . Is there anything I can do for you?"

"No, thank you." Lewis Aldrich turned away.

But she had already seen the stain of tears on his raddled cheeks.

CHAPTER

8

By the time Gwenn returned to her newly assigned cabin, it was seven A.M.

In fact and fiction, private eyes were universally credited with being able to function brilliantly on little or no sleep. Not so Gwenn Ramadge; she needed every minute of her eight hours. She looked longingly at the narrow twin bed; she could afford to sleep for a couple of hours. She could set the alarm, but she knew that once she laid her head on the pillow, she'd probably sleep right through it. There was too much going on, and she couldn't risk missing any of it. So she took a shower, starting with the water set at lukewarm and adjusting it carefully down to cold till her teeth chattered and she broke out in goose bumps and she couldn't bear it any longer. She rubbed herself dry with a thick, thirsty towel until her whole body tingled. She put on jeans and a white shirt. Coffee at the coffee bar adjacent to the Cine Verdi, the best to be had anywhere on the *Dante,* completed the job of restoration.

Today was regarded as the high spot of the cruise, the day everyone had been looking forward to. While Gwenn sat on a leather-covered banquette and sipped her coffee, the ship came awake around her.

At eight-thirty, the pilot took command of the *Dante Alighieri* from her captain and assumed the responsibility for her safe transit from the Atlantic to the Pacific. She began her nine-hour journey entering the channel from Limón Bay at the Cristobal breakwater. A representative of the Canal Orientation Service had come aboard with the pilot, and his comments were broadcast over loudspeakers throughout the ship. Gwenn gulped down what was left of her coffee and raced up to the Sports deck to get a good view. The best spots were already taken and people stood three deep waiting for vacancies. The weather was glorious, as it had been from the start of the trip; the water was calm, the sun hot. People recorded the event with expensive video and still cameras. They shot the scene and each other: a once-in-a-lifetime event, the eighth wonder of the world!

Yet Gwenn sensed an underlying unease. It was over twenty-four hours since the discovery of Minerva Aldrich's body. Surely by now the word had spread. It was inevitable. It was also inevitable that there should be discussion, assumption passed on as fact; an edifice of whispers and insinuations based on false foundation. Gwenn knew that Captain Nicolletti had talked to the parents of the two teenagers whose highjinks culminated in the gruesome discovery. She had no doubt that Sandy and Humphrey had made a clean breast of it. Very probably their parents had confided in friends, who in turn told their friends.

Usually the pool area was very popular in the morning. People sunbathed, swam, lounged in the whirlpool, read, or simply caught up on their sleep. Today, they stayed away. Arguably, that was because of the excitement of going through the locks. After a while that wore off and they came back. They found chairs, placed them in the usual favored locations, ordered drinks, and talked.

Captain Nicolletti, observing from the bridge, was not deceived. Under the calm, there was an almost feverish activity. The affair was being discussed, he thought, and everyone had an opinion. The situation could not be allowed to continue. He sent Graf to invite Lewis Aldrich and his party for lunch, to be served in the captain's private dining room.

The invitation was accepted.

The occasion began in a most civilized manner with drinks being served first.

"I'm told that you and your party wish to continue with the *Dante*, perhaps as far as Acapulco. You are, of course, welcome," the captain said. "But you may find it awkward."

"How so?"

"The passengers know that something out of the ordinary has happened. By now, imaginations are running wild. An explanation is the best way to bring them under control."

"I agree. I want to know what caused my daughter's death. I mean to find out. I mean to offer a reward."

Not a muscle in Nicolletti's face twitched.

"I have in mind a sizable reward. Say, ten thousand dollars for information leading to the discovery of who was responsible for my daughter's death."

The reaction, or rather the lack of it, surprised Aldrich. He looked around the room at the captain and the hotel director, at his own family. "You don't think it's enough."

"Oh, it's enough," Paul Racine remarked wryly.

"It's too much, Lewis," Diana told him. "People are going to make up stories just to get the money."

"That did occur to me," her stepfather replied. "The informant will have to offer proof of his allegations. We'll get somebody to check. Perhaps your staff might help, Captain."

"The staff and the crew are fully occupied in sailing this ship, Mr. Aldrich. We have no time for games."

"Finding out how my daughter died is no game to me."

"I'm sorry. I apologize, but I cannot allow you to turn this ship into a scene for a 'murder weekend.'"

"You can't stop me."

"I can confine you to quarters."

"I don't advise you to do that."

The two men glared at each other. In the tense silence, Eric Graf leaned forward and whispered something in Nicolletti's ear. As he listened, the captain's black look gradually disappeared. He came close to smiling.

"I am reminded that we have a private investigator aboard. She happens to be on a case for us, but I'm willing to let her set that work aside to assist you."

Aldrich frowned. "What kind of case?"

"I can't say, but I can tell you that she has worked for Tri-Color Lines before and was successful in solving a homicide."

"She's a professional? She has a license?"

"Of course. I wouldn't recommend her otherwise. As it happens, she was present when Miss Aldrich was discovered in the pool. She can tell you exactly what happened. Let me send for her. You can talk to her and make up your own mind."

"I don't think we want to drag any more strangers into this, do we, Lewis?" Diana asked.

"Miss Ramadge also administered CPR to your daughter in an attempt to save her," Nicolletti told Aldrich.

He made up his mind. "I'll see her."

End of discussion.

Before the next round of drinks was served, a steward was sent for Gwenn Ramadge. She arrived as they sat down at the table.

"Sorry to interrupt your activities, Miss Ramadge. Thank you for responding so promptly."

"You're welcome." The charm meant the captain wanted something, she thought.

"This is Miss Diana Aldrich, Miss Minerva's sister, and Mr.

Aldrich, her father. You already know Mrs. Chávez and Mr. Racine, of course." Completing the introduction, he nodded to the others. "This is Miss Ramadge, the private investigator I told you about."

Lewis Aldrich looked her over. His eyes narrowed. "We met earlier this morning in the infirmary."

"Yes."

"You asked me if there was anything you could do for me. It seems there is."

There was instant empathy between the elderly millionaire and the young investigator, and the others sensed it.

"Thank you for trying to save my daughter."

"I wish we could have been successful."

"I want you to do one more thing, for her and for me. Find out how and why she died." Aldrich held up a hand forestalling Gwenn as she was about to speak. "Obviously, she drowned. But how did it come about? Did she slip and fall? Did someone push her?"

"In other words, was it an accident, or was it murder?"

Gwenn's plain, blunt question sent a chill through everyone present. "Have you any reason to think it might have been murder?"

No one replied.

Gwenn continued. "On our second day out, when we were anchored off George Town, the Grand Caymans, Miss Aldrich and I were sunbathing on the Lido deck. The sun was very hot; she couldn't tolerate it and asked me to help move her chair into the shade. She didn't look well at all. I was concerned, but she played it down. She said it was just an upset stomach, but I had the impression there was a lot more to it. I didn't persist; I didn't want to pry. I wish now that I had."

Lewis Aldrich took a deep breath. "My daughter had cancer, Miss Ramadge. It was judged terminal, but when she boarded this ship, she was in remission, or so we believed." He spoke with sad dignity. "We believed, we hoped, she would remain in remission for a long time, maybe even years. I've heard of such cases. Evidently, it was not God's will for Minnie. There were signs the disease was taking hold again. She couldn't keep food in her stomach. She tired easily." He paused and finally summed it all up. "She didn't laugh anymore."

"I'm sorry," Gwenn murmured. "So it's possible that Minerva had an attack which resulted in her blacking out and falling into the pool. Was she taking painkillers or medication of any kind?"

Aldrich shook his head. "She had taken marijuana for the pain when it was very bad, but once she was in remission, she stopped."

"She might have started again," Gwenn mused aloud. "It would be interesting to find out where she might have gotten drugs while on the ship."

"Miss Ramadge!" Captain Nicolletti snapped. He had given her free rein up to now, but he couldn't let her go any farther. "There are no drugs on my ship. Drugs are available at every port of call, but not on my ship. She might even have brought a supply on board with her."

"Of course."

"She did not bring any drugs with her," Juno assured them. "I checked her luggage to make sure, and she didn't go ashore in either George Town or Cartagena."

"She might have had someone go ashore for her," Gwenn suggested. "Well, let's set that possibility aside for now."

There was a murmur of relief, except from Lewis Aldrich.

"No! On the contrary, it must be looked into immediately!" His mild eyes flashed. "I mentioned earlier that I'm prepared to offer a generous reward for information and I suggested ten thousand dollars. I'm prepared to go higher if necessary."

"It's already too high, Mr. Aldrich," Gwenn said, and felt the family's instant support. "We're not trying to flush a major player here. We want somebody small-time who happened to see something he shouldn't have seen or who didn't realize the importance of what he saw. Ten thousand dollars would arouse his suspicions and his greed. One thousand dollars is more in the range of what he can understand."

"Whatever you say, Miss Ramadge."

"Also, I was thinking that as there is usually a minister aboard, we might arrange for a prayer service for Miss Aldrich. Would that be all right, Captain?"

"I don't see why not."

"An announcement could be printed and slipped under the door of the cabins in the same way the daily bulletin is distributed. People will come, if not out of piety then out of curiosity. At the conclusion of the service, Mr. Aldrich might speak briefly." She addressed him directly. "You might just say you are looking for information relating to Miss Minerva's death and are offering one thousand dollars; no questions asked."

"But there will be questions," Aldrich insisted.

"Of course. And by adding to the bait, I'm sure you'll get answers."

When the meeting broke up, the *Dante* was in the Miraflores lake and approaching the Miraflores locks.

PORT OF BALBOA
BRIDGE OF THE AMERICAS

The prayer service was set for five-thirty. It didn't leave much time for preparation, but once the Reverend Horatio Kirk agreed to conduct it, everything moved fast. It was almost as though Captain Nicolletti, having given his backing, was showing off the efficiency of his staff. The announcements were printed and distributed. At four, a discreet reminder of the upcoming event was broadcast over the PA system into the public rooms and, contrary to the usual respect for the passengers' privacy, into the cabins. The ship buzzed with excitement and speculation. This was better than any *whodunit* weekend; this was the real thing! An office had been made available for Lewis Aldrich's use. Gwenn waited there, but by five no one had attempted to make contact. She decided she could safely go and change into something more suitable for the service.

Gwenn had brought only a limited wardrobe, though she did have her black charmeuse pants and an assortment of tops for evening. She chose one of black lace with a scoop neck and long sleeves, put it on, and looked at herself in the mirror. Not bad, she thought. In view of the circumstances, she decided to forgo the usual assortment of gold chains. Punctually at five-fifteen, she was back at the entrance of the Cine Verdi to observe the people as they lined up.

They were subdued, respectful in manner and in dress. Though this was a short holiday cruise, it was surprising, Gwenn thought, how many of the women had brought along something dark and formal, and how many of the men who wandered around in garishly colored shorts and shirts during the day now appeared in somber business suits. It soon became apparent that the crowd would fill the theater to capacity, as well as the adjoining Mariner's Cave, which was opened and set up with folding chairs.

On the dot of five-thirty, the Aldrich family, including Paul Racine, lined up at the rear. As the familiar strains of "Amazing Grace" filled the room, they walked solemnly down the aisle to take their places at the front on the left side. Faces set, they stared straight ahead, well aware of the interest they caused.

"That's Diana Aldrich," someone whispered.

"Her makeup must be an inch thick," commented a woman who had a good layer on herself.

"She's not nearly as good-looking as her mother. Valerie was a beautiful woman."

Gwenn listened as the comments were hissed around her. It was the first chance she'd had to stand apart and observe the Aldriches.

Juno Chávez, walking beside Diana, attracted almost no inter-est. To start with, she'd been aboard the ship but had made a point of rebuffing overtures and was resented. Gwenn wondered whether it was being overweight or a low achiever in a family of high achievers that made her reclusive.

The men drew their share of attention too. Lewis Aldrich, scion of the Virginia Aldriches, presently of Southern Pines, North Carolina, was a prominent figure in the racing world, appeared regularly in the society pages, and was acclaimed for his financial acumen. Tired by the rigors of the sudden trip, bowed by sorrow, he still cut a dashing figure.

"He's gorgeous!" a secretary in her twenties gushed, comparing Aldrich at sixty to her fat, bald, forty-year-old boss back in Rochester.

Paul Racine was paired with his father-in-law-to-be. Aggressively handsome and meticulously groomed, his hands well tended, his black hair slicked back as usual—though a little too heavy on the gel for Gwenn's taste—he moved on the balls of his feet like a dancer. He would age well, Gwenn thought.

In front of Gwenn, a woman well into her seventies mooned over him. "Handsome devil. He reminds me of Ramon Novarro."

Studying the faces, Gwenn thought there were more than a few in that room who knew who Ramon Novarro was.

The Reverend Horatio Kirk, a large pear-shaped man, brought up the rear of the modest procession. Balancing his weight carefully, he stepped up to the shallow platform to take his place at the lectern. Waiting for a ponderous moment as the final strains of the hymn died away, the minister addressed the people.

"My friends, we are gathered here to bid farewell to a young spirit taken from our midst suddenly and without warning. I do not say 'before her time' because only God knows when that time is to be for any of us, and no act of man can change it. Young as she was, Minerva Aldrich had already suffered greatly. It was her destiny to die alone amid strangers. We are those strangers. We who were not called upon to help her before her tragic end are now called upon to honor her memory and to clear up the obscure circumstances surrounding her death. We are called upon to clear her name and to ease her family's pain, to offer solace to them in their loss.

"At each armrest you will find a copy of the Order of Remembrance. I invite you to recite with me:

> *The Lord is my shepherd; there is nothing I shall want.*
> *In verdant pastures he gives me repose.*
> *Beside restful waters he leads me; he refreshes my soul.*
> *He guides me in right paths for his name's sake."*

The minister had been well coached, Gwenn thought. By Aldrich, of course.

Next, Kirk led the assemblage in a series of responses to the litany and finished with a chorus of "Christ the Lord is risen today!"

Before anyone could leave, Lewis Aldrich mounted the platform.

"May I have your attention for just one moment, please." He waited until they resumed their seats. "My name is Lewis Aldrich. Minerva Aldrich was my daughter. I want to thank you for attending this service and for praying for her. I also want to thank Reverend Kirk for his touching tribute." He paused to collect himself. "The reverend appealed to you for help, but he didn't specify what kind of help. He is too sensitive a man and too kind to add to our family's already nearly overwhelming burden of grief, so he didn't put into words what we suspect, what we fear—which is that Minerva, my Minnie, did not die accidentally. That she was murdered."

There was a gasp and then a stunned silence.

He sure knows how to get the attention of the crowd, Gwenn thought.

"When Reverend Kirk said we need your help, he meant we need your cooperation in solving the crime. We need information, clues, anything you may know about how my daughter died."

It seemed as though everyone had stopped breathing.

The captain definitely isn't going to like this, Gwenn thought.

Aldrich continued. "For example: Maybe you saw Minnie in the early hours of Wednesday morning; she died at approximately two-thirty. Maybe you observed her at some other time in circumstances that might have struck you as odd—either alone or with someone, it doesn't matter. Exclude no one. And do not be concerned about how you happened to get this information. I said no questions would be asked and I will keep that promise."

He was taking a dangerous path. Gwenn was nevertheless impressed.

"You will notice that at the bottom of the announcement of this service I offered a reward of one thousand dollars for any information relating to my daughter's death. I now raise that to ten thousand dollars."

Stunned silence was followed by nervous chatter.

"I offer ten thousand dollars," he repeated. "Please note that I don't say I offer ten thousand dollars for information leading to an arrest and conviction, but simply for *any* information no matter where it leads or if it leads anywhere. You can contact me in my cabin or you can contact Miss Gwenn Ramadge in her office on the Upper Promenade." He gestured, indicating he wanted Gwenn to stand up and be identified. He didn't specify what her connection to the case might be. His wave in her direction was enough to authorize her.

"Thank you for your attention," he concluded, and swept out of the theater followed by his two daughters and Racine.

Definitely, the captain is not going to be happy, Gwenn thought.

CHAPTER

9

The office allocated for Lewis Aldrich's use which he had turned over to Gwenn Ramadge was in a row of cramped cubicles as alike as paper cutouts. It barely accommodated a desk, two chairs, and a filing cabinet. She didn't mind the lack of space, but she didn't like being without natural daylight. As opposed to her cabin, the cubicle was at least well over the ship's waterline, which made it less oppressive. She knew that a short sprint would get her to an open deck.

As she sat at the desk waiting for someone to call or to walk in, it struck Gwenn that this office was not well suited for its purpose. If anyone should summon up the courage to come forward, he would have to pass all the other offices in the row, all with open doors. Privacy, or secrecy, if you will, should be offered a potential informant. Ten thousand dollars, however, should provide a certain amount of courage.

The dinner gong rang for the second sitting, and no one had

even passed her open door to look in out of sheer curiosity. She decided to order her meal from room service and go on waiting. Meantime, she would call her assistant in New York, Marge Pratt.

"Gwenn! Is that you, Gwenn?"

"Yes, it is." Gwenn smiled in response to the enthusiasm in Marge Pratt's voice. She could visualize the young woman's plain and sensitive face, her pale gray eyes lighting up.

It was four years since Marge Pratt had come to Hart S and I. She came with few skills, desperately needing a job. Marge was the single mother of a five-year-old boy named Bruce. Her situation was much like Gwenn's had been when she'd applied to Hart S and I and Cordelia Hart had befriended her. If she hadn't lost the baby, Gwenn's child would now be the same age as Bruce. Marge Pratt knew as little about the private investigation business as Gwenn had. The difference was that Gwenn readily admitted she didn't know, whereas Marge would set her thin lips in a tight line and try to bluff it out. Gwenn had hired her and put up with her mistakes and defensive attitude. Marge's stubbornness was frustrating and Gwenn had been on the verge of firing her at least three different times.

Then she found out that Marge was going to night school to improve her office skills. She knew Marge was hurting financially and she would have given her a raise, except that by now she knew Marge would look on it as charity and be offended.

So each woman doggedly continued to try to understand the other, and without knowing exactly how, they became friends.

"Where are you?" Marge asked excitedly. "You're not back yet?"

"I'm calling from the ship."

"That's marvelous! How do they do that?"

"I don't know. By satellite, I suppose."

"Are you having a great time?"

"Oh yes, absolutely. Listen, Marge, I need you to do some research for me."

"You've got a suspect? Great."

"No, no. This isn't about the thefts." Gwenn had almost for-gotten why she was on board. It seemed Captain Nicolletti had too. "This is something else. I want you to find out everything you can about the Aldrich family. You know—Goddess Designs and Three Sisters Products."

"You're on a case for Goddess Designs and Three Sisters Prod-ucts?" Marge sighed with satisfaction. "That's great. Congratula-tions."

"Not so fast." In fact, Gwenn wasn't certain how deeply in-volved she was, or how much Aldrich expected from her. "I need in-formation. One of the sisters, Minerva, the youngest, drowned in the ship's pool early yesterday morning. Have you heard about it? Has there been anything in the papers or on TV?"

"I haven't heard anything."

Marge was an ardent follower of the doings of the rich and fa-mous. If she didn't know, it meant Aldrich had clamped a lid on it. Tight. It was Gwenn's observation that once having achieved the limelight, most celebrities were obsessive about staying out of it.

"It may have been an accident, it very likely was, but Lewis Aldrich is offering a ten-thousand-dollar reward for information."

"Wow! Are you in line to collect?"

"I wish. No, I'm screening what comes in. So far, nothing has."

"Well, I can tell you one thing: The Three Sisters are only two and a half."

"What?"

"Minerva was the child of her mother's second marriage. Lewis Aldrich is her father and the stepfather of the other two, Diana and Juno. When he married their mother, Valerie Horvath, he legally adopted the two girls and they took his name. They say he has al-ways treated them like his own; the bond between the girls is equally strong."

No one had mentioned the relationship to Gwenn. Maybe they assumed she already knew, for apparently it was common knowledge. Maybe they thought it wasn't important. Maybe they were right.

"What else do *they* say?" she asked.

"There's trouble at Goddess—rumors of possible bankruptcy. I don't read the financial pages, but the story is finding its way into the gossip columns. The consensus is that Diana's to blame and that she's about to be sued by the stockholders. With what you tell me now, the story will explode."

It was a wonder it hadn't done so already, Gwenn thought. In view of the situation, she was impressed that Diana should absent herself to come and escort the body of her half sister home.

"Find out whatever else you can about the family and about a Paul Racine."

"The designer? He works for Goddess. His first line for them was a flop. The word is he would be long gone if he weren't engaged to Diana."

"You're a wonder, Marge. What else?"

"That's it."

"I need more. Do some digging and get back to me."

But Marge wasn't ready to hang up. "Aside from all that, are you having a good time? Is it like you imagined?"

Gwenn paused before answering. She realized suddenly that since watching in fascinated horror as Minerva Aldrich's body floated up from the bottom of the pool, she had thought of little else. It was not what Marge wanted to hear.

"Even better."

"Ah . . ." her assistant sighed in satisfaction. "I guess you didn't imagine you'd get involved in a big murder case."

When Gwenn first went to work for Hart S and I, the cases dealt with white-collar crimes. There was no contact with criminals. Certainly no violence. Even after she got her license and Cordelia Hart died, Gwenn still avoided what she thought of as "blood crimes." She had been drawn into that first homicide investigation on a Tri-Color ship reluctantly and in response to the desperate pleas of the victim's mother. She'd promised herself it would be the only time, but then Emma Trent, a battered wife, had asked for help. And recently a friend of Ray's, a policewoman, charged with dealing drugs, was killed. Gwenn had thrown herself into that investigation without any urging from anybody. It was getting easier and easier to find an excuse.

"Gwenn? Hello? Are you there?" Marge asked. "Gwenn?"

"Sorry. I was thinking. Call me as soon as you get anything."

"Like what?"

"You'll know when you find it."

Sergeant Ray Dixon was at his desk in the squad room of the Internal Affairs Bureau in Brooklyn. His handsome face was grave as he studied the sheaf of reports in front of him. He had lost weight in the months since his divorce from Patty Foley, his childhood sweetheart. A frown cut deep between his eyes; his features were sharpened, emphasizing his full lips. Almost overnight, gray salted his dark wavy hair.

Dixon had met Gwenn during still another homicide investigation, in which her client was the chief suspect. Though they were on opposite sides, he had been immediately attracted to her. The problem was that she was seeing his partner, Lew Sackler, at the time. Ray held back but didn't give up. His patience was rewarded when Lew had to resign from the force and relocate in Florida due to his father's illness. He gambled in counseling Lew to propose to Gwenn, and won when she turned Sackler down.

It was because of Gwenn that Dixon now found himself working out of IA. His friend, Jayne Harrow, had been charged with drug possession and temporarily suspended. On his recommendation, Gwenn gave her a job. When she was killed no one had to urge Gwenn to investigate. To the contrary, Ray warned her off. But she didn't listen and herself became a target of violence. Dixon believed that certain men on the Narco squad were responsible for a raid on

Gwenn's apartment and her office; the only way he could protect her was through Internal Affairs. He requested a temporary assignment, an unheard-of action and one which earned him the contempt of his fellow officers. When the Harrow case was finally solved, IA offered him a permanent job and promised a promotion. He wanted to turn it down, to get back to his old assignment and his old friends. But that wasn't possible; they didn't want him—they didn't trust him. There was nothing to do but take what was offered.

As time passed, Ray Dixon settled into the new job. He came to see that the code of honor to which police paid such fealty was a false concept. The IA job offered two options—to prove guilt but also to prove innocence. The case he was currently working concerned police rowdyism. There were times when the lid had to blow off, he thought. Unfortunately, no time or place was ever right for it.

Though the phone was at Ray's side, it rang three times before it broke his concentration.

"Hello? Ray?"

"Gwenn?" Ray was just as surprised as Marge had been. "Gwenn? Is that you? Where are you? Are you back already? Is something wrong?"

"No, no. Everything's fine. I'm calling from the ship."

"You are? That's terrific. How do they do that? By satellite, I suppose. So, how's the trip? Are you having a great time?"

"You bet."

"Miss me? I miss you. You have no idea how much. I think of you at all kinds of odd moments." As the words came tumbling out, Dixon realized that was exactly what he had been doing. Her absence had left an unexpected void. Dixon was quiet and reserved, but he was not solitary. Their relationship was on hold, at a stage that had suited them both. It was time to move on.

"I miss you too. I'll be back in a few days."

"Then we have to talk. Seriously. Okay, Gwenn? We can't keep putting it off."

"What's going on, Ray? What's the matter?"

"Nothing. Your being away has crystallized our situation for me. And for you, too, I guess, or you wouldn't be calling. Right?"

She was embarrassed. "Actually, I'm calling because I need some information."

There was a heavy silence at the other end.

She had been too abrupt; she tried to make it up. "Though I have been thinking about you, too. I have. Honestly."

"Forget it. What is it you want? Is it about the thefts?"

"No. Something else has come up."

His reaction was totally different from Marge Pratt's. He groaned. "What are you into now?"

"I shouldn't have bothered you. I'm sorry. If it's inconvenient . . ."

"It's not at all inconvenient. It's just that I didn't think you'd be getting into trouble on a cruise ship off the coast of Central America."

"I'm not in trouble, thank you very much."

"Let's start over, okay? What do you need?"

"Some information on the Aldrich family. You know who they are?"

"I know they're big in the fashion business. Also, they're high society."

"I'm particularly interested in their financial position."

"Why? Do you mind if I ask?"

"Minerva Aldrich, the youngest daughter, fell into the ship's pool and drowned." Gwenn paused. "She might have been pushed."

"God! I don't know how you get yourself into these things," Dixon marveled.

"I don't go looking."

"Well, I know that."

"Sometimes my friends even bring me cases."

"I haven't forgotten." He cleared his throat. "I'll get back to you as soon as I can." For another minute or so, both tried to make amends, but the parting was awkward.

Gwenn sat and stared at the phone for a while, expecting Ray to call back.

Ray sat and stared at the phone and wondered how to place the call. It rang as he was about to contact the operator. He grabbed it eagerly.

"Hello?"

It wasn't Gwenn.

After five minutes which seemed like ten, Gwenn jumped out of her chair. She needed air.

Half the passengers were still in the dining room; the other half were enjoying the live entertainment in the DaVinci lounge. On this night it consisted of an abbreviated version of the Broadway hit *Guys and Dolls*. She looked in but didn't stay. She took the elevator all the way up to the Sky deck. She had no idea someone had been watching outside her office and waiting for her to come out. He had observed her as she entered the elevator and noted where it took her.

The *Dante Alighieri* had long since passed beneath the Bridge of the Americas and was out in the Pacific heading toward the next port of call, Puerto Caldera, Costa Rica. No longer sheltered in the locks and lakes of the canal and well off shore, the wind was strong. In his daily announcement the captain had warned that as they neared the Gulf of Tehuantepec, the winds would gain in velocity. They probably wouldn't reach their peak for another day or so, Gwenn thought as she pushed the door to the deck open and stepped out. Even now the wind was a force to contend with; it smacked her in the chest and made her gasp for breath. She lurched across the deck and reached for the railing and clung to it. The waves were high, with plenty of whitecaps. The ship rolled and

Gwenn's stomach rolled with it. She was too preoccupied with her condition to be aware of the man who came and stood beside her.

"Rough sea," he commented. "Are you all right?"

She turned and looked up at him. "Mr. Kittridge."

"This is a very dangerous spot, Miss Ramadge. You shouldn't be out here by yourself."

A fresh gust was so strong that for a moment Gwenn feared she would be swept off her feet.

"Let me help you."

Gratefully, she took the arm he offered and clung to him as he led her back inside. Once the door was shut behind them, the sudden quiet made her head spin.

"Would you like to sit down?"

"Yes, please."

The library was nearby and empty. He settled her into the nearest chair. "Would you like a drink? I can order . . ."

"A glass of water, please."

He filled a paper cup from the fountain and handed it to her. When she had drunk, he took it from her. "Feel better?"

"I do. Thank you. I had no idea how easy . . ."

"How easy it is to go overboard? It's scary, all right."

"Lucky for me you were there."

"As a matter of fact, I was looking for you. I wondered . . . Has anyone come forward to claim Mr. Aldrich's reward?"

"Not yet."

"Suppose I tell you that I saw Paul Racine and a woman strolling on deck Tuesday morning while we were in Cartagena?"

"And?"

"And the woman looked very much like Diana Aldrich."

Gwenn considered carefully. "What time was it when you saw them?"

"Eleven or thereabouts."

"Let's see . . . Minerva died after we left Cartagena on Tuesday.

Actually, it was in the early-morning hours of Wednesday, the eighteenth. The news was relayed to Lewis Aldrich in New York by the captain almost immediately. He in turn contacted Diana and she was there. If what you say is true, then Diana would have had to leave the ship, get to an airport, have a jet waiting . . . I suppose it's possible."

"I'm telling you what I saw."

"What you think you saw," Gwenn corrected gently. "It's not enough. I'm sorry."

"You're going to dismiss this out of hand? You're not going to make any attempt to verify it?"

"Unless you can substantiate your allegation, no. Can you even make a positive identification? Are you well enough acquainted with Diana Aldrich or with Paul Racine, for that matter, to identify either one? How close to them were you? How well could you see them? Were they in sun or in shade?"

"I might mistake one, but not both."

"Missing one is all it takes. It's not enough, Mr. Kittridge."

"Suppose I tell you that while they were talking, Minerva joined them? I *can* make a positive identification of her," he added.

"All right. What is the significance of this furtive meeting supposed to be? Why was it held on deck instead of in the privacy of their quarters? Why was it held at all?"

"I have no idea. Isn't it your job to find out?"

"Possibly. Could you hear what they were saying?"

"I could tell they were arguing. After a short time, Minerva left. Diana and Racine talked awhile longer; then they separated and went their ways."

"Where?"

"He to his cabin and she back to New York, I suppose."

"Did you see her leave the ship?"

He shook his head.

"I can assume then that you didn't attempt to follow either of them? Precisely where were you when you made these observations?"

"I was on the Upper Promenade deck overlooking the small pool. I had placed a lounge chair in the lee of a stair housing. I could see them but they couldn't see me."

"You just happened to choose that spot."

"No, I go there regularly. It's private and sheltered from the sun and the wind. They just happened to pass by."

"And you expect Mr. Aldrich to pay you ten thousand dollars for . . . what?"

"He said any information."

"Pertaining to his daughter's death," she reminded him. "Your information is not relevant. It's all moot, anyway. It doesn't matter whether or not Diana Aldrich was on board the *Dante* Tuesday morning, because Minerva was still alive nearly fifteen hours later."

10

Despite what she'd said to Simon Kittridge, Gwenn had no intention of dropping the matter. She knew Kittridge didn't either.

Not that she could blame him; ten thousand dollars was a lot of money. Before she reported the host's claim to Aldrich, however, Gwenn wanted to know more about the alleged meeting. The easiest way to find out was to ask the people involved. She would start with Paul Racine.

The ship was alive with activity: dancing in the bars and lounges to the accompaniment of various styles of music, gambling in the casino, shopping in the stores along the arcade, card playing, movies. At eleven-thirty the crew would put on a talent show. At midnight, the festivities would culminate in the presentation of the renowned buffet reputed to be a feast as much for the eye as for the palate—there were as many snapshots taken as plates filled.

The Aldriches were not likely to be participating in any of the events. They would have retired early, but probably were not asleep. Gwenn dialed Racine's cabin. He answered promptly.

"Sorry to disturb you, Mr. Racine, but some puzzling information has come my way. Before going to Mr. Aldrich, I thought it might be wise to discuss it with you."

"Oh? What kind of information?"

"I don't think we should discuss it on the telephone."

"Well, we could meet . . . You could come to my cabin . . ." he floundered.

"How about the coffee bar? In ten minutes?"

She had purposely left him little time in which to think or prepare. As it turned out, she was short of time herself and arrived to find Racine waiting. He was sitting at one of the small pedestal tables in a corner of the semidark alcove. It was already closed, but that actually was an advantage. At her approach, he rose and extended a hand. She took it and allowed him to settle her in the chair opposite his—all with courtesy and charm.

"Can I get you something from next door? A drink?"

"Nothing, thank you."

As he sat down again, he held out a pack of cigarettes. She shook her head. "Do you mind?" he asked.

"Actually, I do."

He put the pack away. That took care of the preliminaries. "What's this all about, Miss Ramadge?"

"A member of the crew has stepped forward in response to Mr. Aldrich's offer of a reward. He states that when Mr. Aldrich and Miss Diana Aldrich boarded after midnight on Wednesday, it was not the first time Miss Diana had been on the ship. He claims to have seen her late Tuesday morning when we were docked in Cartagena. He says the two of you were together and that the meeting appeared to be clandestine."

"I would laugh, Miss Ramadge, if you didn't look so serious."

"I am very serious."

"First of all, as you may or may not know, Miss Aldrich is currently defending herself against charges of mismanagement. Also, she is preparing to answer a class action suit brought against her by some of the stockholders of Goddess. She's innocent, of course, but preparing a defense is not easy, particularly if she has to go before the grand jury. Under the circumstances, she would have come down here only in the event of a crisis. There was none, not insofar as I know."

"Why are you here, Mr. Racine?"

"That should be obvious." He sighed heavily. "By now it's common knowledge that Minerva was dying. This trip was planned with a view to giving the sisters the opportunity to be together one last time. Due to her business problems, Diana had to bow out. Mr. Aldrich didn't want Minerva and Juno traveling alone, so I came as escort—to make sure they'd be all right." He paused. "I didn't do much of a job."

"My source also tells me he saw Minerva join you and Miss Diana on the deck that morning. The three of you appeared to be having a long discussion. It grew heated before it broke up. Minerva left first; then you and Miss Aldrich talked awhile longer before you went separate ways."

"Did he also say what the argument was about?" Racine challenged.

"He wasn't close enough to hear."

"What precisely is he accusing us of then? Or, more accurately, what are you accusing us of?"

"No one has made any accusations, Mr. Racine. I'm merely trying to get the facts."

"The facts are that your informant is either mistaken or fabricating the story in order to get the reward. I have nothing more to say. That ends the interview, Miss Ramadge." He got up.

Gwenn didn't.

"I understand there's a great deal of controversy regarding the artistic direction Goddess Designs has taken recently and it centers on you and your fashion concept."

"A direction supported by the president of the company, yes. Last year, I was too avant-garde in my vision. The public wasn't ready. Adjustments will be made." He sounded very certain.

"Assuming Miss Diana is cleared of the charges against her."

"She'll be cleared."

"And the board votes to keep her on as president."

"They will."

He sounded absolutely certain. Gwenn was impressed. "Who controls Minerva Aldrich's votes? I assume she was on the board?"

"The whole family is on the board of directors. Minerva's father will now vote her shares."

No surprise there. "And who gets her money? I suppose she has independent means?"

Racine's response was more a bark than a laugh. "Minerva was a rich woman. She was richer than Juno, Diana, and Lewis put together. Minnie was smart, even smarter than her father. Actually, she had her mother's acumen, particularly in business matters. Valerie always gave Lewis credit for her success, but the fact is he did little more than introduce her to modern marketing techniques and the magic of advertising. The imagination and creativity were hers."

Early on, Gwenn had pegged Racine as a man who used women. It seemed she had been precipitous. With regard to his work at least, it seemed he had integrity. His admiration of the creator of Goddess Designs was sincere.

"People said that by marrying Lewis, Valerie was introduced to society and raised to his social level, which in turn contributed to her business success."

"Then it was a good marriage?" Gwenn asked.

"It was successful. I don't know if that's the same thing."

Again, Gwenn was impressed by the depth of his observation. Also, she wondered at his willingness to express his thoughts. Why confide in her? So far, no one in the Aldrich family had indicated any particular respect for her expertise. Even Lewis Aldrich had made it clear he had hired her because she happened to be available. Yes, there was that moment of grief they had shared in the infirmary, but that no longer counted for much.

"It's my opinion that Valerie would ultimately have been successful without Lewis Aldrich, though it would have taken longer," Racine went on. "I would say they had a partnership in the fullest sense. What counted most with Valerie, I believe, was Lewis's kindness to her girls. She was grateful to him for adopting Juno and Diana and giving them his name. Even after Minerva was born, he continued to treat the two like his own. He never showed preference."

"And the girls?" Gwenn asked. Underneath Racine's Gallic charm, she discerned a core of pragmatism. What she still didn't understand was his choosing to reveal it.

"Diana and Juno look to Lewis as their real father; they have no memory of anyone else."

"How did it come about that Diana took over Goddess? Was it because she's the oldest?"

"Not entirely. When the girls were through with their academic studies, Valerie insisted that each one serve an apprenticeship in the business; I guess now it's called an internship. She wanted them to get a taste of what it was like to produce and then sell an item. After that, if they wanted to do something else, that was all right. She gave them a stake and her blessing. That was while Valerie lived. When she died, her estate was divided into four equal parts for the girls and Lewis. There were no restrictions on how the money was to be used. However, Valerie did express the hope that neither Goddess nor its affiliate, Three Sisters Products, would be abandoned. To that end, she left an additional five million to whichever one of the family undertook to run it. That was Diana."

"There was no dissension over this?"

"None. Diana wanted it. Always had. She was anxious to follow in her mother's footsteps and beyond. Minnie, as I've indicated, had other, bigger ideas. She added her share of the inheritance to her original stake. Everything she touched prospered: securities, real estate. She even provided major backing for the production of a motion picture. She could have given Donald Trump lessons."

"What about Juno?"

Racine shrugged. "Juno got married and moved out to her husband's ancestral lands along the Rio Grande, intending to raise a family. She got pregnant but couldn't carry to term."

"What happened to her share of the inheritance?"

"Ask her husband, ask Vicente."

"Were there other bequests, say for trusted and loyal employees? Family retainers?"

"No. Only the immediate family."

"So it wasn't till after her mother died that Diana took over the company. Things haven't been going well. She made mistakes." Gwenn summed up: "Some say her biggest mistake was hiring you."

"They're jealous."

"They say she should fire you and go back to the more classic style Goddess is known for. But Miss Aldrich is determined to give you another chance."

"I told you the public wasn't ready for my concept. It was too extreme. I admit it. However, with a little modification . . ."

"You're going to try again." Gwenn fixed him with a cool and steady look.

"With the support of the president of the company."

"Who happens to be your fiancée," Gwenn pointed out.

"That is correct." He stepped around her, heading for the elevators.

"Mr. Racine . . ."

"No more questions."

"What was Diana Aldrich doing aboard the *Dante* on Tuesday?"

"I've told you she wasn't here."

"She was seen. I have a witness who saw the three of you together."

"Impossible. You can't see something that isn't there. Your witness is mistaken. Or lying."

"I want an explanation of what was apparently a clandestine meeting between the two of you and Minerva."

"There was no such meeting."

"What was so urgent that in the midst of all her difficulties Diana had to drop everything and fly down here and attend to it in person?"

"I keep telling you . . ."

"Was the purpose of the visit accomplished?"

Racine's voice rose, topping Gwenn's. "If you don't believe me, ask Diana, why don't you?"

"That's an excellent idea. I'll do that." Gwenn now made a move to leave.

"Where are you going?"

"To call Miss Aldrich."

"Now? You're going to call her now?"

"Certainly. I'm not going to give the two of you time to compare notes." She left him without so much as a backward glance, but she was aware that he trailed after her.

Gwenn dialed the Aldrich suite. She let the phone ring several times, but there was no answer. Next, she tried Juno Chávez, who was in the cabin formerly Gwenn's. She picked up on the second ring.

"This is Gwenn Ramadge, Mrs. Chávez. I'm sorry to disturb you, but I need to speak to Miss Aldrich."

"She's not here."

"Oh? Where is she?"

"In the casino, I suppose." There was a brief pause; then she added bitterly, "Where else?"

It was just past one A.M., and the action was at its height. The lights were soft, an amber-pink combination, kind to women's complexions. Conversation was at a minimum, dominated by the calls of the croupier at the roulette table and the dealers at the blackjack and craps games. Along the outer perimeter, ranks of slot machines were tended by tense players who pulled the handles and listened to the whirring motors, waiting for the ringing of the bell that would announce a jackpot. The players sitting side by side ignored each other, staring at the revolving cylinders as though hypnotized—which, Gwenn thought, taking in the scene, they most certainly were. Yet these were not your addicted gamblers or your high rollers, merely your recreational players. Then she caught sight of Diana Aldrich.

She was at the roulette wheel, seated on a high stool, slim, black-stockinged legs crossed, a champagne glass to one side, stacks of chips in front of her. She wore a slip of a dress completely covered in black sequins. Very short and cut low at the top, it was provocative. A crowd had gathered behind her chair three or four deep and growing as the word spread that she was having a winning run. Impulsively, Gwenn started forward toward Diana, but Racine put out a hand to stop her.

Gwenn watched fascinated as Diana Aldrich, frowning with concentration, placed her bets.

"Does she play a system?" she asked Racine, who stood at her shoulder but well behind her.

"Sometimes."

"No more bets, ladies and gentlemen. No more bets," the croupier intoned, and deftly spun the wheel with one hand while flicking the metal ball in the opposite direction with the other. The spectators held their breath as the wheel slowed and the ball bounced over the slots, seemed to settle on the number Diana had chosen, and then at the last moment jumped out.

The spectators breathed out in one long collective sigh. Diana Aldrich's expression never changed. She had lost a large amount—Gwenn had no idea how much those stacks of chips represented—yet she watched impassively as the croupier raked up what had been her winnings into the general pile and the crowd dispersed.

"Now," Racine said to Gwenn, and together they went over. "Too bad, sweetheart."

She swiveled around, stared at her fiancé, and ignored Gwenn. "How long have you been here?"

"Not long. A few minutes."

"I could sense it. I could sense a disturbing influence. I could feel it was going to go bad for me. I could feel the luck leaving me."

Racine neither argued nor apologized.

They've had this exchange before, Gwenn thought. "How much did you stand to win, Miss Aldrich?"

"I had a chance to break the bank." She shrugged.

So it was the power that attracted her, Gwenn thought. She pointed to the short stacks of chips that remained. "You didn't lose everything."

"I never lose everything, Miss Ramadge. I always leave myself enough to start over. My mother taught me that. Though in another context." She raised her chin, emphasizing her sharp, strong jawline, and with her fingers raked back the dark, glistening curtain of hair that had been hiding the determination glittering in her gray eyes.

"Your mother was a very capable woman."

"Yes."

"So was your sister."

"Minnie had luck on her side."

"And you don't?"

Suddenly, Diana Aldrich relaxed. "Not tonight anyway. Do you gamble, Miss Ramadge?"

"Very rarely."

"Ah well, then you wouldn't understand." With a sweeping gesture, Diana gathered up what was left of her stake. "We'll say goodnight, Miss Ramadge. It's been a long and much too eventful day. Paul?" Her look and her tone were an order.

"Please, could you spare me a few more minutes?" Gwenn asked. "I've received certain information which I need to corroborate before passing it on to Mr. Aldrich."

"What information?"

Standing a few feet from the roulette table, they were being jostled as streams of people tried to get by.

"It's in answer to your stepfather's offer of a reward."

Diana Aldrich groaned. "For God's sake! I need a drink. Let's get out of here," she said to her fiancé.

The Miramar bar had been turned into an intimate nightclub-style retreat by the simple expedient of restricting the lighting to flickering candles on the tiny tables. The band was packing up, but they were still serving. Leading the way, Diana selected a table in a far corner. Racine sat beside her and Gwenn opposite. They ordered but said nothing while they waited to be served.

Diana took a long, thirsty swallow of her rum punch. She set the glass down with a sigh of satisfaction. "Now. What's this all about? And make it short, if you can."

"Certainly. You were seen on this ship on Tuesday morning while we were docked in Cartagena."

"Wrong. I was in New York."

"Can you prove it?"

"Why do I have to?"

"You were seen in the company of Mr. Racine and your dead sister."

"By whom?"

"For the moment, I can't say."

"You expect me to defend myself against an unknown accuser? Anyway, suppose I was here? What's wrong with that?"

"If there's nothing wrong with it, why are you so determined to keep the reason hidden?"

"Because it's none of your damned business, Miss Ramadge." With that, Diana Aldrich rose and strode out of the bar with Racine trailing after.

In the candlelight, his look was one of utter and unmistakable relief.

CHAPTER

11

With this much leverage, Gwenn seldom failed to elicit the information she was after. But these two, Diana Aldrich and Paul Racine, were tough. Accustomed to the cutthroat competition of the fashion world, they weren't easily manipulated. But neither did Gwenn give up easily. She was far from finished with them. This round was theirs, but it wasn't the last round. She hadn't lost the fight.

In fact, Gwenn thought, she had gained new insights regarding the Aldriches and the family situation. It was not as serene as they would have the public believe. Envy and jealousy festered beneath the tranquil surface. Diana was not the capable businesswoman she presented herself to be, and, it seemed, neither was Minerva the frail and tragic figure.

The dim lights of the Miramar were turned up to bright and then flashed to indicate it was closing time. The music was cut off in the middle of a chorus. According to Gwenn's watch, it was not quite two A.M. She stayed where she was.

What about the middle sister? What about Juno?

Living on the ranch with her husband, Juno Chávez seemed removed from the stresses of the competition between Diana and Minerva, but by now Gwenn had learned to take nothing in this case for granted. When she'd telephoned earlier, Juno had answered. She'd told Gwenn to look for Diana in the casino. She hadn't asked why Gwenn wanted her. It was hard to believe she wasn't curious.

Gwenn went back to the telephone.

"Sorry to disturb you again, Mrs. Chávez. I need to talk to you."

"I wasn't sleeping."

Gwenn could sense her tension.

"I haven't slept since the night Minnie died. If I close my eyes . . . I see her. So I don't close my eyes."

"Would you mind answering a few questions?"

"I've already told the captain everything I know. You were there when I told him."

"He asked you specifically about the night she was drowned. I'm interested in the day before." A sudden thought struck Gwenn. "Are you alone? Has your sister come in?"

"No. Wasn't she in the casino? Didn't you find her?"

"Yes, but I thought she might have turned in since."

"No, and I doubt that she will."

It was not necessary to ask where Diana might spend the night. "Then may I come over for a few minutes?"

"Sure, why not?"

Juno opened the door almost at Gwenn's knock, as though she'd been standing and waiting for it. Once again Gwenn was struck by the difference between her and the other two. She must favor András Horvath, her and Diana's father. Her face was square, jowls heavy. She was fat; there was no kind way to put it. Whereas Cordelia Hart, founder of Hart S and I, had been overweight as well, a few moments after meeting her, people forgot what she looked like. She was intelligent and caring. She was capable. She "took charge." Juno Chávez, when she was with her family at least, kept in the background. She effaced herself. Gwenn had no idea what she was really like, whether she, like Cordelia, had talents hidden under the fat.

When she admitted Gwenn, Juno was wearing a black satin peignoir with black lace ruffles that somehow made her look blowsy. A half-unpacked suitcase lay open on the sofa; clothes were strewn everywhere. Gwenn could see that nothing had been hung up. The elegant cabin that had once been hers looked like a particularly messy teenager had moved in. She had to clear herself a place to sit.

"Would you like a drink?"

"No, thank you."

Before she replied, Juno was already at the drinks cabinet fixing herself what looked like a Scotch on the rocks, which she downed in a generous swig. Then she sat on the bed and leaned against the headboard.

"What are these questions you need to ask?"

"As you know, I met your sister Minerva when we were in port in George Town. She didn't look well; she seemed depressed. How was she that night?"

"She was going downhill."

"What time did she turn in?"

"I don't remember. We both went to bed early as a rule. I'm not used to late nights anymore. On the ranch we get up while it's still dark and go to bed while it's still light. My biological clock is out of order here. On this schedule I'm hardly able to keep my eyes open through dinner. That was before Minnie died, of course. Now I'm full of coffee and full of booze. I'm all mixed up." Her eyes filled.

"You and Minerva were close. Would you say you were closer to her than you are to Diana?"

"The three of us were close. We supported one another in everything. It was all for one and one for all."

"I have information that Diana came aboard on Tuesday morning when we were in Cartagena and that there was a meeting between Diana, Minerva, and Mr. Racine."

"Who told you that?"

"Someone who saw them."

"Who?"

"I'm not at liberty to say."

"Neither am I then."

"Why were you excluded?" Gwenn pressed.

Juno blushed. "Because it concerned Goddess and I have nothing to do with Goddess anymore. I sold out my interest long ago."

"So had Minerva. Isn't that right?"

"Yes."

"Well then?"

Juno sighed. "I suppose you know by now that the company is in bad trouble and Diana needs money. She came to hit Minnie up for a loan. She was desperate, and desperation doesn't transmit over the telephone. She came to make her pitch in person."

"So she *was* here! So what happened? Did she get the money?"

Juno shook her head slowly. "You'll have to ask Diana."

Diana's attitude earlier was all the answer Gwenn needed. "Have you any idea how much Diana was asking for?"

Juno pursed her lips. "I know that when things started going really bad—that was about a year ago—Diana made a public offering of her shares in Goddess. That took care of the most pressing obligations, but robbed her of autonomy. Tied her hands, she said. What it actually meant was that she couldn't keep Paul on as designer and CEO because the stockholders wouldn't have him. So now her idea is to buy back the shares and go private again."

"How much money are we talking about?" Gwenn asked.

"Considering the number of shares outstanding and their current value, which isn't easy to determine because it could and does change from one hour to the next . . . I'd say roughly twenty million."

Gwenn formed a silent whistle. "Minerva had that kind of money?"

"That's in liquid assets. She owned properties, made investments."

"So her death will affect . . ."

"Many. Individuals and corporations."

They were both silent for several moments.

"You should have come forward with this information," Gwenn said.

"To whom should I have offered it? You're not a police officer. You don't have official standing. You're employed by my stepfather and he knows all about the situation. In fact, he's the one who calculated how much money would be needed for the buyout."

Suddenly, Gwenn felt very much out of her depth. She really was in an untenable position. Should she tell Juno who the witness to her sister's presence on board was? Simon Kittridge was also entitled to know there was someone who could support his testimony—whether she would or not was another matter. He also had the right to know that what he had seen could turn out to be very important. What she must do, Gwenn decided, was inform Lewis Aldrich of these facts and then withdraw from the case.

The phone rang and Juno answered. "Yes, she's here." She held the receiver out to Gwenn.

"Miss Ramadge? I didn't hire you to investigate my daughters." Lewis Aldrich's voice was like an icicle dripping his displeasure.

"No, sir." So Diana had gone running to Daddy, Gwenn thought.

"You were supposed to find out whether my Minnie's death was an accident or foul play, not harass the girls."

"I'm not harassing—"

"If Diana says she wasn't on board on Tuesday in Cartagena,

then she wasn't. If she says she never set foot on this ship till she came with me to claim Minnie's remains, then she didn't."

"Maybe you should speak to your other daughter," Gwenn suggested.

Aldrich did not immediately snap out a reply. Instead, he asked a question. "Do you have any brothers and sisters, Miss Ramadge?"

"No, I don't."

"Let me tell you what it's like. They argue. They squabble. There's dissension, but it doesn't mean anything. When the chips are down, they stick together. Do you understand?"

He was telling her the family was off limits. Was he doing so to save her time and effort, or because he feared what she might discover?

"What happened Tuesday morning is irrelevant. It's what happened during the early hours on Wednesday that we're interested in."

It sounded as though Simon Kittridge had already gotten to him. He thought that as long as he was paying her, he controlled her. But that was not the way Gwenn worked, and this was the moment to tell him so. That would have one of two results: either he fired her or she quit. But Gwenn had knelt on the deck and straddled Minerva Aldrich's cold, inert, dripping-wet body. She had pressed her mouth to Minerva's icy lips, had forced her breath into Minerva's lungs. She hadn't given up till Dr. Halliday pronounced her dead. She was not going to give up till she found her killer. So she remained silent.

"Is that clear, Miss Ramadge?"

"Very clear."

"Good." He hung up.

Gwenn did the same, slowly, thoughtfully. "Maybe you should talk to your stepfather," she told Juno. "Tell him what you told me."

"It wouldn't do any good."

"Sleep on it," Gwenn suggested, and headed for the door. As she pulled it shut behind her, Juno Chávez was pouring herself another drink.

No more interviews tonight, Gwenn thought; she was bone tired and couldn't wait to fall into bed. But as she turned into the corridor that led to her cabin, she saw a woman waiting at her door.

"Miss Ramadge? Do you remember me? Sofia Rossi. Nancy's roommate."

"Of course. How are you?"

"I'm upset. You told me I should go and see Nancy, so as soon as I got off duty, I did, but they wouldn't let me in. She was sleeping, they said, and couldn't be disturbed."

"Oh? I suppose she needs as much sleep as she can get." Gwenn frowned. She opened her door and stood aside for Sofia to go in.

"Will she be all right?"

"Of course." Gwenn tried to reassure herself as well as her visitor.

"The nurse said they're keeping her under observation, but if she doesn't improve by the time we get to Acapulco she'll be put ashore."

"There'll be better facilities for treatment there."

"She'll be alone in a strange country."

"Why have you come to me?"

"You're the only one who seems to care what happens to her."

"I can't do anything unless you're straight with me. You have to tell me who might have had a motive for attacking Nancy."

"I don't know, honestly."

Gwenn was annoyed but she controlled it. "You must remember that this was not a random attack, that it was planned, that the attacker had access to your cabin. Also, never forget that the attacker was not satisfied with hitting her and knocking her out for a few minutes. He went on hitting her after she was down—over and over and over again. Her face was swollen out of shape, black-and-blue and bloody. It appears he intended to disfigure her, and went about the job methodically, without passion."

Sofia, eyes downcast, remained silent.

"Please listen to me, Sofia," Gwenn went on. "This attack on Nancy can be read only one way—as a warning. I talked to Nancy in the Miramar right after lunch and we made a date to meet in her cabin at four o'clock. Somebody didn't want that meeting to take place, that's obvious. Have you any idea why?"

"No."

"We had been discussing the recent thefts on the *Dante*. She indicated she might know something."

"She never said anything to me."

"But you do know about the thefts? You do know that valuable jewels have been reported stolen?"

"Of course. The whole crew knew. Every one of us was searched, and so were our quarters. It was humiliating. Nothing was found. We're not thieves."

The remark resonated in Gwenn's memory. Someone had said something similar to her lately. She couldn't remember who. "Everybody on board must have been talking about the thefts and you want me to believe you and your closest friend didn't discuss it?"

"We don't see that much of each other. We're on different shifts. We meet coming and going. We don't have time to talk, only to sleep."

Gwenn was openly disbelieving. She let natural frustration grow into indignation. "You must have some idea why your roommate was beaten. If she wasn't involved in the thefts, then what? Drugs? Was she using drugs? Selling drugs?"

"No, never! Nancy wouldn't have anything to do with drugs."

"And you say there's no man involved; she's not having an affair. What then? What's left?"

"If I could get in to see her, maybe I could find out," Sofia suggested.

"If I arrange it and she confides in you, will you tell me?" Gwenn asked.

"I promise."

Gwenn considered. "I'll set it up."

CHAPTER

12

DAY 8

AT SEA

Gwenn had forgotten to set the alarm clock. As a result, she over-slept and woke with a start and the familiar sense of having missed out on something, but without any idea what. The clock told her it was eleven; considering she had gone to bed at four, that wasn't so bad, she thought. But she didn't feel rested and the anxiety she'd felt on waking persisted and even grew. Could it have something to do with the last interview? It occurred to Gwenn as she snuggled under the covers that Sofia Rossi had undergone a marked change of attitude with regard to her roommate. What had caused it? Was it really true that Nancy was asleep when Sofia tried to visit her? If so, why was an excuse deemed necessary, and who had given the order for it?

She checked for the blinking red light at the base of her bedside phone, but the light was not on. No one had tried to reach her; no one had missed her presence. She felt unwanted and, worse, un-needed.

It was too late for breakfast and too early for lunch, but coffee and pastries were available at any hour at various self-serve counters. She dressed quickly in a western-style denim skirt, scoop-necked blouse, and sneakers, and went searching. She found a place that offered juice, fruit, and cereal, as well as coffee and pastries. She loaded a tray and carried it out to the shady side of the Lido deck.

The wind Captain Nicolletti had predicted hadn't found them yet; the sky was cloudless, the sea calm. No land or other ship was in sight. For the moment, this ship, this deck on which she walked, made up her whole world. This isolation, encapsulation, was why people took a cruise, she thought as a shadow passed between her and the sun. She looked up. It was Simon Kittridge.

"Hi. Mind if I join you?"

"I'm not going to be here long."

"I'm on duty myself in a few minutes." Kittridge was not offended. "I just wanted to tell you that I called Lewis Aldrich this morning. We met. He listened to what I had to say and he gave me a check."

It didn't surprise Gwenn. "Congratulations."

"I told him what I told you, no more, no less. He told me I was mistaken, that his daughter Diana was not on board the *Dante* Tuesday morning, that she couldn't have been, but he appreciated my cooperation. Also, he said if anything further occurred to me, I shouldn't hesitate to contact him—directly."

"And have you thought of anything?" Gwenn asked.

"No. Unfortunately." He grinned, his long, dour face lighting up, shedding the years, becoming very attractive indeed.

"Try. I'm sure you will."

He flinched. "I didn't deserve that, Miss Ramadge. I came forward with information I believed was relevant. You disagreed. I might have been wrong, but I didn't make it up. I saw what I saw. Mr. Aldrich at least gave me credit for honesty."

"I'm sorry. I shouldn't have said that. I apologize."

"Okay." He waved it off.

There was something about this man that intrigued Gwenn. If he had been younger, she might have been seriously attracted. She owed him more than an apology; she owed him the truth. "Did you know that his other daughter, Juno Chávez, supports your story?"

"No. He didn't mention it."

"He wouldn't, not if he wants you to continue thinking you made a mistake."

"Why should he want me to think that?"

"I wish I knew," Gwenn replied.

Morning visiting hours were over and Dr. Halliday was not due back in his office until four. A young woman Gwenn had not seen before was holding down the receptionist's desk. She was nice-looking, with light skin and dark hair hanging straight down her back. She was typing slowly, taking care not to make errors. The name plaque on the desk said she was Elena Nova.

"Good morning. I mean, good afternoon," Gwenn corrected herself, and grinned. "I'm running late on everything today. My name is Gwenn Ramadge. I'm here to see Miss Castel. Okay if I go straight in?" Without waiting for a reply, she passed the desk and charged down the corridor to Nancy's room with the receptionist chasing after her. At the sight of the open door, she stopped abruptly; the nurse-receptionist almost ran into her.

Gwenn whirled around. "Where is she?"

"I don't know."

"What do you mean you don't know?"

The staid young woman flushed and looked down at her feet in their Nike walking shoes. "When I looked in this morning, the patient was up and getting dressed. I was appalled. I told her to get back in bed, but she wouldn't. She insisted she felt fine and was going back on duty."

"How could she? My God, after what she'd been through, how could you let her? You should have stopped her."

"I tried. I asked her to wait at least until the doctor examined her. She agreed. She actually started to get shaky and wobbled on her legs. I put her in a chair and went to make the call."

Gwenn groaned. "And when you got back, she was gone. She tricked you."

"Well, she can't get far, can she?" Miss Nova sought reassurance.

Gwenn couldn't bring herself to give it.

The first thing to do was to check Nancy's cabin.

On her way, Gwenn passed through the DaVinci lounge, where a class in low-impact aerobics was in full swing. An assortment of participants of various ages, some fit and some not so fit, hopped, skipped, and jumped in imitation of their teacher, an energetic, attractive young woman under thirty.

Farther on, an ice-carving demonstration had attracted a large group consisting predominantly of seniors. In the card room, bridge was being played at four tables. The casino opened two hours early and offered instruction in the various games in which one could lose money. Taking the stairs to B deck, Gwenn located the door to the crew section; Nancy's cabin was nearby. She knocked, but received no answer. She knocked again several times before accepting that Nancy wasn't inside. Then fear clutched her heart.

Surely she wasn't back at work? She was fit neither to work nor to be seen by the public, but it would be embarrassing to demand access to the cabin and then find out that Nancy was somehow serving drinks at the Miramar. The only thing to do was to go back and see for herself.

As soon as she approached the service bar, the staff gathered around her.

"I am Carlo Costa, Miss Ramadge." The bartender was their spokesman. "May I help you?"

"I'm looking for Nancy Castel."

"Have you tried the infirmary? She had an accident."

"She's not there anymore. She walked out."

The group tightened around Gwenn.

"I understood her injuries were serious," Costa said.

"They were." Gwenn looked around. Sofia was clearing tables on the far side of the dance floor. In the harsh light of day she looked older, more tired, sadder. "Do you mind if I speak to Miss Rossi?"

"Please." He gestured for her to go ahead.

"Where's Nancy?" Gwenn asked when she was within earshot.

Sofia turned around, surprised at both Gwenn's presence and the question. "I thought she was in the infirmary."

"She walked out."

"They let her?"

"She didn't ask permission. She just put her clothes on and walked out."

"I suppose you tried the cabin."

"First place I went. I knocked, but there was no answer. I knocked several times."

"She's a heavy sleeper," Rossi answered. "Maybe she didn't hear you. She was under sedation."

"We have to find her," Gwenn almost pleaded.

"Has it occurred to you that perhaps she doesn't want to talk to you?"

"I want to help her."

"Could it be she doesn't want your help?"

"I'll have to hear that from her," Gwenn retorted, and walked away.

Sofia threw a quick glance at Carlo Costa and hurried after her.

It was Sofia Rossi who knocked at the cabin door; she who called out, but got no answer; she who unlocked the door.

Nancy lay on her back on the lower bunk bed, dressed in her uniform, wearing shoes and stockings; her hair was combed and neatly arranged on the pillow. The damage to her face was artfully masked by makeup. A wave of relief swept over Gwenn.

"Nancy?" Gwenn murmured.

She didn't stir. The vicious bruises that discolored her pretty face had healed remarkably; but considerable swelling remained. "Nancy?" Gwenn repeated, then put a hand on her shoulder and shook her gently. No reaction. "Nancy!" she called out, and matched it with a smart slap.

Sofia gasped. But there was no reaction from Nancy.

Gwenn put her ear close to Nancy's mouth and listened. She lifted one eyelid, then the other . . . On the nightstand there was a small cylindrical plastic container, the kind pharmacists use for prescription medicines. The label identified it as Valium, and it was empty.

"Help me," Gwenn ordered Sofia. "We've got to get her on her feet and moving."

"Isn't there some kind of antidote?"

"Probably. I don't know. A stomach pump would be the most effective tool, I suppose." There was so much she didn't know, Gwenn thought. "I don't think we can afford to wait to find out if there's one available. Come on."

Between them, they dragged the unconscious girl to a sitting position, then hoisted her to her feet.

"Come on, Nancy, move!" Gwenn urged. "Walk. Come on, girl, help us." They dragged her back and forth in the limited space between the bunk bed and the bureau. "This is no good; let's get her outside."

Crew members came running. Someone brought steaming black coffee. Gwenn held Nancy while it was poured into her mouth. She gasped and opened her eyes. She gagged, and when the cup was raised again to her lips, she fended it off.

"A couple more sips, come on, it's good for you," Gwenn urged, and pried open her mouth to get the bitter brew into her. Nancy started to retch and heave, and then, with a shudder that coursed through her whole body, she vomited. It was the best thing that could have happened.

"No more," she gasped, white and shaking.

"Okay. No more coffee," Gwenn agreed. "Let's walk."

And the ordeal began anew. As word of what was happening spread, more of the crew and staff came down to B deck to volunteer assistance, among them Simon Kittridge.

"You're in almost as bad shape as she is," he told Gwenn. "It'll be a while before she's in any condition to make sense. Why don't you go back to your cabin and rest? I'll call you when she's better."

"I don't want her to be alone." It wasn't necessary to be more specific.

He understood. "I'll see to it. I promise."

"Don't trust anybody," Gwenn warned.

"How about the roommate?" They both looked to Sofia, who sat apart, obviously shaken and spent. "How much do we know about her? Can we trust her?"

"We have to."

"Why don't we put Nancy back in the infirmary? I'll stay with her."

Once again Gwenn was faced with a situation that could be interpreted in one of several ways. Had Nancy taken the Valium of her own free will, intending only to get some rest, and then forgotten how much she had taken or that she had taken any at all? That could easily have resulted in an accidental overdose. It happened often enough to be a recognized danger. Or she might have been forced to take it. A demonstration that that was possible had just taken place.

"All right. But you'll have to watch her."

Somehow, without intending it, Gwenn had placed herself in the position of trusting Simon Kittridge. She was close to putting Nancy Castel's life in his hands. And her own too, for that matter, because if he wanted to get rid of Nancy, then he couldn't afford to leave her around. Actually, he'd have to get rid of her first. Gwenn shuddered.

From the beginning, when they watched the departure of the *Dante* from the Sky deck, Gwenn had taken a liking to Simon Kittridge. Despite his fitting so smoothly into her image of the elegant gentleman burglar, the con man who flattered rich ladies, wined and dined them till they were tipsy, and then stole their jewels, she was charmed by him. He remained the prime suspect, in fact the only suspect with regard to the thefts. She could not, however, bring herself to believe that he was responsible for what had happened to Nancy. It was Kittridge who had steered Gwenn to the waitress in the first place. Would he have done that if he had anything to fear from her? There—she was doing it again, relying on instinct. Ray would not be pleased. He kept telling her, over and over, hunches were for amateurs. At this point, Gwenn thought, it looked like she'd stay an amateur forever.

Gwenn had intended to stop at her office, but suddenly, she was tired. Simon Kittridge was right, she needed rest. She was also emotionally drained, and any conclusion she might reach under these conditions would be flawed. So she continued on to her cabin. As soon as she was inside, she kicked off her shoes and flopped on the bed. Then she committed the one unforgivable sin: she turned off her telephone.

"She still doesn't answer." Paul Racine put the phone down hard, indicating his considerable annoyance.

"Why are we making such a big deal of this?" Diana Aldrich asked her stepfather. "Why don't we just pay her off?"

"Because she wouldn't take the money," Lewis Aldrich replied.

"She's one of those people who think their special mission on earth is to see justice done," Racine added.

They were gathered, along with Juno Chávez, in the sitting room of the suite booked for the sisters. Drinks had been ordered and were being consumed. They would have dinner served there also. The family of Minerva Aldrich continued to keep to themselves. The solitude, though self-imposed, was beginning to grate.

"Whatever possessed you to tell her I was on board?" Diana asked her sister.

"I didn't see anything wrong with telling her. I only repeated what Minnie told me." Juno's lower lip trembled.

"That doesn't make it true!" Diana snapped. "Lewis," she appealed to Aldrich, "I don't mean to speak ill of the dead and we all loved Minnie, but we also know how she was."

He looked at her from beneath lowering brows. "How was she?"

"When necessary, she lied."

"Why should she lie about your being on board?"

Sensing that their stepfather was veering to her side, Juno broke in. "The first few days of the cruise we were together constantly and Minnie poured out her feelings. She considered Diana incompetent to run the company. She was particularly opposed to Paul as CEO. She had already turned down Diana's request for money and she was annoyed that Diana had come down to make another request. Once Minnie made up her mind, she never reversed a decision; it was a matter of principle. We all know that."

"You as well as any," Diana pointed out.

Juno flushed. She had to admit Diana's charge was true. Her husband, Vicente, had applied to Minnie for a loan after the failure of his crops when he was near to losing his ranch. Minnie took no interest in his heritage; she only studied the bottom line. She saw no way to turn the ranch around. She would be throwing her money away, she told him. She was *forced* to deny his request.

"It so happens that this time, Minnie broke her own rules." Diana drew herself up erect and proud. "She changed her mind and agreed to let me have the money I needed to save the company."

A gasp, then a murmur of surprise verging on disbelief passed through the group. Diana acknowledged it. "Not for my sake. She didn't do it for me. Don't feel bad, Juno," she told her sister. "She did it for Mama. For Mama's sake, she couldn't let Goddess go under. I needed her check with her signature right away. I flew down to get it."

"You never let me know how bad things were at the company. You should have told me. I would have managed to get you what you needed . . . somehow," Lewis put in.

"Minnie asked me not to."

He frowned for a moment as though analyzing what the reason for that might be, then turned to Juno. "And you should have come to me about your doubts and uncertainties, instead of letting me hear it from a stranger."

"I didn't think you'd believe me. You seem to have more confidence in this private investigator you hired than in any of us."

Aldrich bowed his head. Avoiding eye contact, they sat in silence. After a while, Racine lit a cigarette, took a deep drag, and exhaled.

"I think we should get rid of Miss Ramadge. But first, since Juno is the one who spilled the beans to her—"

"I didn't spill any beans!"

"She should be the one to straighten Miss Ramadge out. She should admit Diana did come to see Minnie and that everything was amicably resolved between them—which, in fact, it was. Then we'll pay her off."

"No we won't. Not till we find out who killed Minnie." Aldrich indicated the telephone. "Try again."

Racine dialed. He let it ring seven times before hanging up.

CHAPTER

13

Christine Fleming sat at the dressing table of the luxe stateroom on the Upper Promenade deck and studied herself in the mirror. Within the past month there had been a tremendous change in her appearance: her face sagged; her jaw was slack; her color had become an ugly jaundiced yellow. Up to now she had worn her sixty-one years lightly, with patrician elegance. She was now bowed under them.

She was chronically fatigued. The slightest exertion wore her out. She was depressed. She had come on the cruise with high hopes, and had been told she would be contacted when they were at sea. That should have been the second day out. She had sat up most of that night, waiting. But nothing had happened. The next morning she heard that one of the passengers, a Mrs. Sturgess from a retirement community in Florida, had reported the disappearance of a valuable piece of jewelry. The rumor spread and speculation abounded. Other mysterious losses had occurred on the *Dante* on previous crossings and Tri-Color Lines were concerned enough to have hired a private investigator to look into the matter. She was now on board. Even more titillating was the news that the antique brooch had been either lost or mislaid and Mrs. Sturgess was claiming it was stolen in order to collect the insurance.

Everyone watched everyone else, particularly the crew. It was no wonder that the person who was to have contacted her had not come forward, Christine thought. The agitation would subside, she reasoned. She had only to be calm and wait.

On the fifth day, Minerva Aldrich drowned in the ship's pool. The suspicion that it had been no accident raced through the ship like wildfire. Would it drive her contact farther under cover? Christine Fleming was desperate. What could she do to reassure him? What could she do to coax him out?

A light tap at the stateroom door made her jump, but it was only the cabin steward with the extra towels she'd requested.

Tonight was the Captain's Gala Dinner and Ball, the most important social event of the cruise. Christine had no interest in it; she'd intended to skip it and have her meal in the stateroom. Suddenly, she changed her mind: No! She must make one final attempt to draw her contact out of his hole. She would not only attend the affair, she would make an appearance! It was possible that making her wait was a ploy to intensify her need. They could be manipulating her. All right. Let them see she could afford to pay.

She soaked in a hot bath, then wrapped herself in a thick terry cloth robe and returned to her dressing table to work on her makeup. The result fell short of what she was aiming for. Maybe a glass of sherry would relax her and provide the needed glow. She unlocked the liquor cabinet and opened the panel door. A split of champagne with a slender tulip glass beside it was prominently placed on the middle shelf. The label read: *Flor Blanco de México.* The accompanying card read: "Compliments," no more.

But it was all Christine Fleming needed. The blood rushed to her head. Her eyes sparkled. She opened the walk-in closet and surveyed the assortment of clothes she'd brought with her. She chose a long, black, matte jersey gown, somber until she added the jewels Percy had given her for their various anniversaries: a diamond and ruby necklace for their twenty-fifth; teardrop earrings for the thirty-fifth; a matching diamond and ruby bracelet for their fortieth. There were no more after that: her beloved Percy was dead. She seldom wore the pieces; the memories were too painful. But tonight she put them all on. That should do it, Christine thought, taking one final look before going up to show herself off. Who would be the one to approach her? Simon Kittridge? He was her favorite of the hosts. He had devoted a great deal of time to her; she hoped it wasn't he. He was much too nice for this sort of thing.

Suppose nothing happened? But it would. It must. Who could resist what she offered?

Gwenn had slept right through into the next morning. She woke feeling groggy but she knew that would pass. She had fallen asleep thinking about the jewel thefts and, as sometimes happens, her subconscious had served her and suggested a different way to proceed in her effort to solve them. Up to this point, she had concentrated on events after the crimes were committed. How about trying to anticipate the crime? How about staking out the victim before the deed? Great! If you knew ahead of time who the victim was going to be. How could she find out? Could she *select* the victim in the same way the perpetrator did?

Gwenn dressed in a simple white lace shift, adorning it with a discreet gold chain and gold bangle bracelets—fourteen-karat but not worth this thief's time, she thought as she left her cabin and took the escalator up to the festivities.

Everyone was turned out in his or her best. The women glittered. Gwenn assessed them not for style but for the value of what they wore, as the prospective thief would. Since only a fraction of the value would be recovered when he fenced his loot, it helped narrow the field of candidates. She posted herself at the entrance to the formal Michelangelo dining room, with its scarlet velvet–draped walls and massive windows and panoramic view of the sea. She watched as the diners entered and took their assigned places to the accompaniment of the same string ensemble that had played at teatime. Of all those Gwenn observed, there was one outstanding. Christine Fleming.

With the exception of the loss of Mrs. Sturgess's brooch, the pattern of the other thefts was always the same. The items had been taken without the owner's knowledge, while she was out of the stateroom or at least sound asleep. In the latter case, the perp would have made sure she was sleeping heavily as a result of too much partying. He might even have slipped a sedative into her drink. So, Gwenn thought, nothing was going to happen to Mrs. Fleming's magnificent jewels until she retired. Meanwhile, the lady presided at her usual table for six on the main level. Gracious as a queen, she conversed with her dining companions, turning this way and that, always in such a way that the splendid jewels were displayed to the diners at nearby tables as well. After dinner, Mrs. Fleming strolled along the Arcade looking into the shops. She visited every lounge and bar. She meandered through the casino, where she bought five hundred dollars' worth of chips and tossed it away at the roulette table in a short fifteen minutes. She stayed awhile longer as a spectator, then made her way to the DaVinci lounge in time for the second show; she sat with a group other than the one she'd sat with at dinner. As the houselights went down and the stage lights came up—in that brief hiatus of darkness—the jewels around her neck, at her ears, and on her wrist flashed iridescent as a cascade of fireworks against a moonless and starless sky.

Mrs. Fleming was conducting herself just as Gwenn would have advised if she'd had the opportunity to discuss strategy with her. What was she after? Gwenn wondered. The answer seemed to be the man who now approached her, who raised her hand to his lips and lightly brushed the back of it. He was not Simon Kittridge, but he was very much like him and he was also one of the hosts. He whispered something to the lady. She immediately got to her feet and followed him out. Several heads turned, but the curtain was going up; the show was about to begin.

Gwenn followed, tripping over feet in the darkness and landing in someone's warm and comfortable lap. By the time she apologized, untangled herself, and reached the main aisle, the subject and her escort were gone.

"Damn!" Gwenn muttered.

Why had Mrs. Fleming left so precipitously? And where could she be going? Obviously, she had gone willingly. Maybe it had nothing to do with the jewels. It wasn't likely the jewels would be snatched from her person in public. The perpetrator had no reason to change a successful MO, so there was no reason to change her own plan, Gwenn thought. She had lost Mrs. Fleming, but only temporarily; the lady must ultimately return to her stateroom. Gwenn reached it just in time to see Sofia Rossi, carrying a tray with a bottle of wine and a glass, let herself in.

Gwenn waited for her to come out, but she didn't. Time passed. Very intriguing, Gwenn thought. There was nothing to do but wait some more.

By now, Gwenn was familiar enough with the ship's design to know there was a service bay for each section. It was little more than a closet containing linens, towels, and cleaning supplies and equipment. There was a step stool for reaching the upper shelves. Gwenn entered the bay, turned out the light, and cracked the door just enough so that she could see Mrs. Fleming's door. Then she sat on the stool.

Time dragged. When she checked her watch, she saw that only seven and a half minutes had passed. Patience was a prerequisite of the job, Gwenn reminded herself; that and a strong stomach. A stakeout could mean days of junk food at odd hours, or no food at all. Either way it resulted in a ravenous appetite, leading to binges of peanut butter by the spoonful, sardine sandwiches, sour apples— and devastating stomachaches. On this case, however, she was not only eating regularly but feasting on gourmet fare. In spite of that, her stomach was in revolt. Could she absent herself just long enough to go to the bathroom? No, because at that very moment Mrs. Fleming appeared. The ease with which she entered her stateroom suggested Sofia had left the door unlocked.

Gwenn waited, and still Sofia didn't come out. What was going on? Further speculation was useless. Gwenn emerged from her hiding place and crossed over to Mrs. Fleming's door. It opened at her touch.

"Never leave the door unlocked behind you, Mrs. Fleming," she said. "Anybody could walk in."

The two women stood transfixed.

"Good evening, Sofia."

Sofia Rossi picked up the tray. "Is there anything else, Mrs. Fleming?" she asked.

"Don't be in such a hurry," Gwenn chided. "I need to ask you some questions. And you too, Mrs. Fleming."

Christine Fleming stiffened. "What kind of questions?"

"I want to know what's going on between you two."

"I beg your pardon?"

"What were you doing alone in here?" Gwenn asked the waitress.

Her hesitation was barely discernible. "Mrs. Fleming ordered wine. I served it."

It was a quick answer, but not good enough. "You were here before she was. How do you account for that?"

"Mrs. Fleming placed the order earlier this evening. She wanted it served in the stateroom before she retired."

She was resourceful, but so was Gwenn. "May I see the chit?"

Sofia's lips trembled but she was not dismayed. "The wine steward has it."

Gwenn studied the girl. She and Nancy were similar in their looks and attitudes. Both were slim and seemingly fragile. Both were soft-spoken, suggesting they would bend easily to another's will. Appearances could be misleading.

"I'll check," Gwenn told her.

"Do what you want!" Sofia snapped. "What business is it of yours?"

"I'd like to hear your answer, Miss Ramadge," Christine Fleming said. She was still wearing the long black gown, but the glory of the costume was gone. She no longer wore the diamond and ruby necklace and the accompanying pieces. Sparkling eyes and an inner glow took their place. She waved Gwenn to a comfortable chair and sat opposite her. "You may leave, Sofia."

"I prefer that she stay," Gwenn said.

"It's her choice."

"I'll stay." Sofia wasn't happy about it.

"Now, can we please get on with it? What's this all about?" Christine Fleming asked.

"You must know that there have been a spate of burglaries aboard the *Dante* on recent crossings."

"Everybody on the ship knows it." Mrs. Fleming kept her eyes on Gwenn and off Sofia.

"I need to confirm certain information."

"I'll help if I can, naturally, but I don't know anything."

"Earlier this evening you ordered a drink to be served here in your stateroom."

"What Sofia said was correct. When I went in to dinner, I was informed by the wine steward that I had received a gift of a bottle of the wine of my choice from my travel agent. The wine steward wanted to know my selection and if he should serve it at table. I said I preferred to have it delivered to my stateroom at about ten—which was when I expected to turn in. Why do you want to know?"

"As I said, I saw Miss Rossi enter this stateroom. Something about her manner suggested to me that she knew it was empty before entering." Gwenn paused. She had a mental image of Sofia at the door. *She hadn't knocked.* Her subconscious had caught it and its implication. "It made me curious. I decided to wait and see what would happen. After a while, you arrived and went in. You didn't use your pass card."

"You didn't *see* me use it."

"When you came in and found a stranger in your cabin, you made no outcry."

"I knew who she was and what she was doing here."

"What was she doing here, and why did she stay so long?" Gwenn asked. It was the key question.

Christine Fleming shrugged it off. "I asked her to."

It took Gwenn aback. "Why?"

"There was a bottle of champagne in the liquor cabinet. I decided to have it rather than the wine and I asked Sofia to open it for me. She had trouble uncorking it." Suddenly, the elegant woman threw her head back and laughed. Composed of both relief and amusement, it was almost a guffaw. She stepped aside so that Gwenn could see the bottle resting in the ice bucket and the cork lying beside the single, partially full tulip glass. "These corks are part of the mystique, but they're also a nuisance."

"One doesn't usually drink champagne alone. Are you celebrating something?"

"Yes, as a matter of fact, I am. I'm celebrating becoming a grandmother for the third time."

Gwenn gasped. She had not expected such a logical answer.

"I got the call from my son-in-law just this evening. The baby was premature, but mother and daughter are doing well."

"Congratulations." So that was the reason for the precipitous departure from the DaVinci lounge, Gwenn thought. She had no doubt that it would check out—Mrs. Fleming was too smart to lie about a thing like that—but at the same time, the feeling persisted that the meeting with Sofia was prearranged. "May I?" Gwenn reached for the bottle and lifted it out of the bucket. "*Flor Blanco.* I'm not familiar with the brand."

"Neither am I," Mrs. Fleming responded. "Someone at the table mentioned it, so I thought I'd give it a try. Will you join me?"

"No, thank you. I need to ask you one more question, Mrs. Fleming, please. Where are your jewels? Those magnificent diamonds and rubies you displayed so proudly all around the ship tonight, where are they?"

"I am proud of my jewels. I enjoy showing them off."

"I'm not criticizing you, Mrs. Fleming, but times have changed. Nowadays, people who have gems like yours don't flaunt them. They keep them under lock and key."

"They're mine. I can do with them as I please."

"Of course. But where are they now? Where do you keep them when you're not wearing them? In the cabin safe?"

"Yes."

"It would be a treat to see them close up."

"I suppose it's easier to show them than to argue about it." Mrs. Fleming opened the top drawer of the bureau and took out a leather wallet. She unzipped the center partition and drew from it a card which she then inserted into the slot of the safety deposit box located on the top shelf of the closet. She twirled the knob once to the right and then to the left, and the door swung open. Reaching inside, she brought out a dark maroon velvet case, opened it, and held it out to Gwenn. The hard glitter of the diamonds was intensified by the dark throbbing of the rubies. Gwenn could only sigh.

"You're very casual with them. A great many people got a look at these jewels tonight. I think you should put them in the main vault and make sure you're seen doing it. Be as ostentatious as you were in displaying them. We'll all sleep a lot better."

Gwenn escorted Mrs. Fleming and her jewels to the main office and saw them safely stowed in the vault. Mrs. Fleming thanked Gwenn politely for her advice and assistance, and Gwenn responded in kind. In fact, Mrs. Fleming did seem more relaxed now that the jewels were put away, Gwenn thought, and at last headed for her own small office. As she entered, her phone started to ring. She snatched it up. "Hello?"

"Miss Ramadge? You have a call from New York. A Sergeant Dixon."

"Put him on, please."

"We have your party, sir," the operator said.

After several clicks and beeps, he came on. "Gwenn?"

"Ray?"

"Go ahead," they both said simultaneously, then both paused.

"I hope I'm not calling too late," Ray managed.

"Are you kidding? The ship is jumping."

"So you're enjoying yourself?"

"How could I help it? What've you got?"

"It's not police information," he warned, "but I assume you're not getting the latest news out there in the middle of the Pacific."

"We get a daily *Times* fax, but that's it."

"Exactly. So I thought you'd be interested in the latest developments according to the media."

"You bet I'm interested."

"Rumor has it, and I repeat it's only rumor, that Diana Aldrich will inherit enough from Minerva Aldrich to save Goddess Designs."

"Ah . . ." Gwenn sighed.

"There'll be enough to buy back the stock still outstanding and those board members who oppose Diana."

"Anything about Paul Racine? Any proviso?"

"None that I've heard of."

Gwenn sighed again. So Minerva had not carried her hostility to the grave. She was glad to know that. "How about Juno and her father? Did she leave them anything?"

"To Juno nothing. To Lewis Aldrich enough to bail him out of his quagmire of debts."

"Lewis Aldrich is in financial difficulty?" Gwenn exclaimed.

"Horse racing is an expensive hobby," Ray pointed out. "As a business, it's nothing if not risky. You want me to check him out? You are working for the guy, aren't you?"

"You're right. I'll ask him straight out."

"In that case, you'd better have something more than a gossip column to go on."

Gwenn gasped. Ray didn't read the gossip columns. She heard him clear his throat. She could almost see him blush.

"Marge called me. She read it in 'Sara Lou On the Town.' She wanted to know if I expected to be talking to you, and if so, would I verify it and pass it on."

Gwenn smiled to herself. So Marge was trying to validate the information and promote the romance between Gwenn and Ray at the same time. "So, what did you find out? Is it true? Is Lewis Aldrich in financial trouble?"

"Give me a break! She only called half an hour ago. I suppose you want anything I can get on Juno Chávez, too."

"Naturally." She started to hang up. "Oh, and one more thing, Ray. Don't worry about waking me; I don't expect to get to bed tonight." That was teasing, she thought. Why did she do it?

A light tap at the door prevented further soul-searching.

Paul Racine strode in.

"You're a hard woman to get hold of, Miss Ramadge," he said, with a smile that indicated she was well worth the trouble. His eyes rested on the phone, which was still in her hand. "Have I come at a bad time?"

"I was just hanging up." She did so. "Your timing is perfect." She leaned back in the chair. "What can I do for you?"

"Actually, it's what you can do for yourself."

"And that is . . . ?"

"I don't know what Juno told you, what kind of story she spun you, but don't put too much credence in it. The girls never did get along."

"My impression was that they got along very well. That they were close."

"They also had their differences. Nothing serious, nothing that would extend to murder. My God! Diana had no motive for murder."

"She needed money and Minerva refused to give it to her."

"Who told you that? Juno?" The blood rushed into Racine's face.

"She claims Minerva told her Diana came aboard on Tuesday to make a final, desperate appeal and was turned down."

"I don't suppose Juno mentioned her own desperate appeal?" Racine asked. "Things are not so great on the ranch, you know. Drought destroyed Vicente's last two crops. The cattle are dying.

The bank won't renew his loan, and the feed companies won't extend any more credit, so they're sitting out there watching the herd die and waiting for the bank to foreclose. Vicente can forget his grandiose plan to run for the Senate. Minnie was not about to finance his political ego trip with her hard-earned cash."

"You make her sound like a female version of Scrooge."

"I don't mean to. Minnie's hard shell covered a vulnerable heart. Suppose I tell you that in the end she did agree to bail Diana out?"

"With you still as CEO? I'd want proof."

Racine froze. His handsome face was pinched. A nerve twitched under his left eye. "You were hired to find out what happened to Minerva Aldrich—how she died—not to open old wounds and stir dissension."

"I didn't set out to do that."

"Maybe not, but that's the result of your actions."

"I followed where the trail led; it led to murder."

"And now you see a big opportunity for yourself. Suddenly, you're investigating a celebrity murder and you're on the verge of becoming a celebrity yourself."

"Oh, please. I'm not looking for notoriety."

"Then withdraw from the case. Get out. Leave us alone."

"Mr. Aldrich can fire me anytime he wants."

"He doesn't want to fire you. He's lost one daughter and he doesn't want suspicion of guilt hanging over the other two for the rest of their lives. He wants them cleared."

Their eyes met and held as each tried to read the other's intent.

"I'm not sure I understand," Gwenn admitted.

"You must have other suspects," Racine said.

"Yes. You're one."

"I mean outside the family."

"You're outside the family."

He ignored that. "You haven't really looked outside, have you, Miss Ramadge?"

"Not yet," she conceded.

"If you do discover other suspects and it turns out one of them is guilty, there will be a bonus in it for you."

Gwenn drew herself up. "I don't work like that."

"Work any way you want. Take the money or leave it, as long as you look everywhere. That's all we ask."

He wasn't even attempting to disguise the bribe. His bluntness and arrogance were an insult. Gwenn was tempted to ask: *How much?* But he wouldn't get the sarcasm. She backed off. "I don't know where to look."

He seized on what he considered an admission of weakness. "I'm confident that you will. As a sign of good faith I'm prepared to give you an advance of . . . five thousand?"

She almost laughed in his face. This was not the kind of money Lewis Aldrich dealt in. Aldrich had no part in this, she decided. But maybe she could learn something by appearing to take the bait.

"That's not much for what you're after."

Racine had a hard time masking his satisfaction. So she wasn't as pure as Lewis believed. "I'll make it ten."

"Say twenty. And if my work results in an arrest and conviction, another twenty."

"You're a tough negotiator, Miss Ramadge."

"And you're stingy with money that isn't yours," she countered.

"Where the money comes from is not your concern, and your attitude doesn't make for a good working relationship."

"Nor does your constant evasiveness. I need cooperation from all of you. Will I have it?"

"Of course."

"Good. I'll start with you. Give me your version of what happened on Tuesday morning between—"

"Version? You won't get far with a confrontational approach."

"Tell me what happened, as you know it," Gwenn amended. "Actually, let's go back a little farther to the morning you boarded the *Dante* at George Town. You weren't expected. I was with Minerva at the time and it was clear she wasn't pleased to see you. Why did you join the cruise so late, Mr. Racine?"

"As you know, the sisters intended to take the trip together. At the last minute, because of trouble at Goddess, Diana couldn't get away. Lewis arranged for me to go in her place and look after Minnie and Juno. It was short notice and I made it as soon as I could. Maybe Minnie thought I meant to keep dunning her. I don't know."

"I suggest that you did pressure Minerva, but it was no use. So then you contacted your fiancée and urged her to come down and make one more try herself. She did and suffered Minerva's displeasure."

Racine groaned. "All right. Diana did come," he admitted, "and Minerva changed her mind. She agreed to help get Goddess back on its feet. She did it for her mother's sake. She didn't want her mother's company to be wiped out."

"All right, I can accept that. Minerva was known for taking over sick companies and rehabilitating them. In the case of Goddess, she would have kept Diana on as president, but as a mere figurehead. You would have been removed without any attempt to gloss over the circumstances. You would have been just plain fired."

"To tell you the truth, Miss Ramadge, I've been planning to resign and start my own shop, but I didn't want to seem to abandon Diana."

"Really? Who are your backers?"

"You don't need to know that."

They stared at each other.

"You have no backers," Gwenn concluded. "Only one person believes in you—Diana. Diana flew down on Tuesday in response to your plea. The three of you met. Minerva laid down her final terms for the bailout and Diana flew back to New York to consider them. You were desperate. Minerva would not yield; Diana might. You had to take matters into your own hands and you had to do it fast before Diana lost control of Goddess or acceded to her sister's demands."

Racine shook his head.

"How about an alibi?" Gwenn asked. "Where were you between two and two-thirty Wednesday morning?"

"I was in my cabin—in bed and asleep."

"I don't suppose you can prove that?"

The casino was still going strong. The Karaoke buffs were still at it in the Eagle's Nest, but most of the bars were shut down or in the process of calling it a night. Gwenn decided to do the same. Things were happening fast. She needed time to review and evaluate. It was like preparing to fit together an elaborate jigsaw puzzle; she was in possession of the facts but they were in a jumbled pile. She needed to sort them into smaller, more organized piles. In a puzzle you could go by color—blue could indicate sky or water; brown and green could be earth or foliage, or a garden and the path leading through it. She could apply that system to the case.

But she would leave it till morning. Let the subconscious work during the night.

DAY 10
PUERTO QUETZAL

Gwenn didn't remember undressing or crawling into the twin bed nearest the wall. She didn't remember turning out the lights, but the cabin was pitch-black. She told herself that even if the cabin had a porthole, it would be sealed shut, and anyway, there was nothing out there but the limitless, featureless ocean. Nevertheless, she could feel the familiar panic gathering force like an oncoming storm. She felt trapped. She had trouble breathing. She inhaled deeply and closed her eyes.

She had no idea how long she'd slept or why she awakened. She was about to turn over to look at her alarm clock when some instinct told her not to move.

She lay very still. Someone was in the cabin. Whoever it was wasn't moving either. Like Gwenn, the intruder was listening.

She tried to control her breathing, to keep it light and steady, to simulate sleep. She didn't dare open her eyes to more than slits. After what seemed a very long time, her eyes grew accustomed to the darkness and she could distinguish the various masses of the furniture. By the line of light under the door, she could make out a silhouette. Whether it was a man or a woman, she couldn't tell— but it was moving toward her.

She assessed her chances of escape. The space between the beds was too narrow for her to get by the intruder. Suppose she got up on the bed on her knees and threw herself at him screaming? How soundproof were these walls? If he had a gun, he'd shoot, and at point-blank range he wouldn't miss, even in the dark. If he had no gun, he'd flee and get away before anyone came to investigate. So it was a gamble.

While she was still assessing the situation, the intruder made his way into the narrow space between the beds. He held something in his hands. By its shape and density and the amount of the faint light it reflected, she knew it was a pillow.

He meant to smother her! She wanted to scream, but it was too late for that. As the pillow brushed her face, she took a deep breath, rolled sideways out from under, and tumbled to the floor.

At that moment, the telephone rang.

It paralyzed them both.

Gwenn recovered first. She pulled herself to her knees and lunged, tackling him at his ankles. He tried to kick her off as he would a snapping dog. Gwenn hung on and gathered her strength for one more major effort.

The phone continued to ring.

In an attempt to get a better grip, Gwenn wrapped her arms

around his legs. She tugged, but failed to bring him down. She tried again, grunting with the effort, and felt something rip. Fabric. He gasped, reared back, and delivered a vicious slap. She let go. Lurching to the door, he fled.

Gwenn remained on her knees too stunned to move. She recalled the slimness of the ankles she had grasped, the slipperiness of the nylon-encased legs, and the pointed toes of the shoes. The fabric she had torn had been that of a skirt, not pants. The *he* was a *she*. The intruder was a woman.

After a while, Gwenn pulled herself up, sat on the side of the bed, and turned on the light.

The phone had stopped ringing.

What had all that been about? Looking around now, Gwenn saw that the only thing that had been disturbed was the pillow from the other bed. There was no sign of the brief but intense struggle. What was the purpose of the break-in? Both Lewis Aldrich and Paul Racine had tried to buy her off. Was a third party, a woman, now trying to scare her off the same way she'd tried to scare Nancy Castel off? That would connect this latest incident to the jewel thefts rather than to the murder. If she hadn't awakened, would the intruder have held the pillow over her face until she stopped breathing, or would she have left off just short of that? One thing was sure, Gwenn was not inclined to sacrifice her body for either case. She didn't consider getting beat up or shot at as part of the job. She wasn't that kind of private eye.

According to the clock, it was now six A.M. on Sunday, and the *Dante* was due to dock at seven in Puerto Quetzal. Gwenn had no interest in going ashore. What she wanted and needed was more sleep. There was no point in raising the alarm. Nothing had happened. There was nothing to report. It was ironic that having made such a point to the ladies, Sturgess and Fleming, about securing their doors at night, she had failed to lock hers. Careless. She turned out the light and crawled back under the covers; her eyes were already shut when her head hit the pillow. They flew open. But she *had* locked her door, she was sure of it. She remembered getting out of bed to do it. So someone had the equivalent of a passkey and was entering cabins at will. Tomorrow she would make a list.

The phone rang.

She picked it up.

"Sorry to wake you."

It was Marge. "Did you call a few minutes ago?"

"That's right. You did say to call anytime."

"I'm glad you did. You don't know how glad. What's up?"

Marge paused, took a deep breath, and plunged. "You remember that reporter on the *Post* who did such a good job covering the Trent case?"

"Michael O'Ryan. Sure."

"He also covers racing in the East. He's real keen on the sport. Rides himself."

"So?"

"So, I needed to verify the item in 'Sara Lou On the Town' about Lewis Aldrich? I called O'Ryan. Seems Sara Lou is right on the money about Aldrich. He hasn't had a winner since '92. That year he won ninety stakes and banked close to sixteen million. Then, all of a sudden, everything went bad. His daughter, the real one, Minerva, staked him for a while, but she gave up. He borrowed what he could, and finally ended up selling his first Derby winner, the star of his Southern Pines stable, Prince Bator. After that, the slide became an avalanche. He sold the stables at Hollywood Park and put his Saratoga holdings on the market. According to O'Ryan, he's being carried by the Mob."

Gwenn sat up straight. "What kind of a deal did you make with O'Ryan?"

"No deal. He wanted an exclusive on anything we find out. I told him we couldn't promise that. I pointed out that what he'd given us so far was general information but because he'd saved us time and considerable legwork, he could count on us to be fair."

"Good work, Marge." She was learning fast, Gwenn thought. "And he's satisfied?"

"Said if we needed any more information about Aldrich or the track, just give him a call. So I guess he must be."

"All right! We might just do that. Tell him thanks. And if you get anything further, just fax it out to me."

It was the cue that the conversation was over, but Marge Pratt ignored it. "She was dying though, wasn't she? Minerva, that is. So Aldrich would have gotten the money anyway, wouldn't he?"

"Maybe he couldn't afford to wait any longer."

"But . . . Minerva was his real daughter, not a stepchild. He wouldn't kill his real daughter, would he?" Marge was shocked.

Gwenn recalled Aldrich's reaction when he saw the drowned body of his child. "I don't think so. But the men to whom he owed money, they wouldn't have cared whose daughter she was."

CHAPTER

15

"Ask O'Ryan who Aldrich borrowed from and how deep in he is," Gwenn instructed Marge before hanging up.

The information Marge had procured changed one whole aspect of the case and provided answers to certain questions that had been nagging at Gwenn.

First of all, why had Aldrich hired her to investigate what appeared to be an accident? He seemed to be steering her toward a verdict of murder, yet at the same time he kept putting obstacles in her path to turn her away from it. She realized now that he was diverting her from implicating the family and pointing her instead to the mobsters to whom he was in debt. He couldn't tell her flat out who they were—he probably didn't know himself; loan sharks don't advertise. The money must have passed through several hands before it reached Aldrich. The decision that Minerva had to die so they could get it back would have been made by consensus and the job would have been contracted out. If he talked, Aldrich risked his life. He wouldn't take that risk until he was sure it was the Mob who had ordered Minerva's death.

Tonight's incident at the cabin clearly demonstrated Gwenn's vulnerability. Perhaps next time she wouldn't be able to escape so easily. She should take Racine's advice and quit. But she didn't want to quit; she couldn't.

She remembered how she and young Humphrey Taggart had dragged Minerva out of the pool and laid her on the deck to administer CPR. Putting her mouth to the victim's in order to clear her air passage, Gwenn had tasted blood. A lot of blood. She had nearly gagged on it. She'd fought the nausea and labored to force the breath from her lungs into Minerva's. She hadn't given up until Dr. Halliday had arrived and declared Minerva dead.

She wasn't going to give up now either until the presence of all that blood was explained. Once again, that would be up to Dr. Halliday. She went looking for him.

"I'm not accusing you of drowning your daughter, Mr. Aldrich, not for a minute. But I'm very much afraid you know who did it."

After her talk with the doctor, Gwenn wasted no time contacting Lewis Aldrich. She told him she had to see him right away. She didn't ask permission; she informed him she was on her way and that was at six when the day had just begun to break. She pulled on jeans and a pullover and went directly to the suite. He must have been standing right at the door, because he opened it almost as soon as she knocked. He was wearing pajamas, a robe, and slippers. She could see past him into the master bedroom. The bed was rumpled, but she was sure he hadn't been sleeping when she'd called.

Gwenn stood right there and faced him with what she had learned about his financial situation, and challenged him to deny it.

"My God!" Every muscle in Aldrich's wiry frame twitched. The color drained from his lean face. The dark shadows under his eyes looked like bruises. Parallel frown lines were etched deep and looked as though blood had dried in the channels.

He sank into the nearest chair. "I had no idea. I swear to God." Huddled in the leather tub chair, right shoulder raised and chin tucked under it, Lewis Aldrich looked like a boxer shielding himself. She pressed him no farther. He wasn't going anywhere; there was nowhere for him to go. For that matter, there was nowhere for any of them to go.

Six years ago Brian Bates, the ship's photographer, had signed a one-year contract with Tri-Color Cruise Lines. His father had died of a stroke and left enough money for Brian and his mother to live in the comfortable manner to which they were accustomed, but the inheritance didn't include enough to cover tuition at Dartmouth. Brian was a good student, but not outstanding, certainly not brilliant enough to win a scholarship. He had planned to go into the securities business and he knew that to achieve any kind of success he needed a degree, preferably a master's. He decided to take a year off in which to raise the tuition. In a year on the ship, he figured, he could make enough to see him through. He soon found out that he had miscalculated. The salary wasn't that good and the tips weren't as generous or as plentiful as he'd been led to believe. Most of all, he resented having to drop out even for a short period, and envied his classmates who were going ahead without him.

The work was not challenging. He felt superior to his crewmates and to the passengers who had money to squander. Most of them laughed too loudly and drank too much. His attitude came through in his dealings with the passengers. He was given a warning by the hotel director.

He seethed. Photography was his hobby, had been since high school. He had won contests. To be criticized by someone who knew nothing about it, someone who couldn't even load a camera—Graf had once asked Brian to do that for him—was demeaning.

"The passengers are your subjects," Graf told Brian. "They are not interested in the fine points of your technique, or the artistic merits of the picture. What they want is a memento of the trip, of their good time, of the fun they had. At the same time, they want to look good—if at all possible."

"I'm not doing studio portraits and I'm not a plastic surgeon."

"We hired you because of your skill and your good background in photography, but the bottom line, Brian, is—the customers aren't buying."

Even now these six years later, when he thought of it, Brian Bates felt a flood of embarrassment. He recalled shutting himself in his tiny office and taking a batch of photographs at random to study. Then he compared them to those in an album containing only his prize-winning shots. The hotel director was right; there was no empathy between him and the ship's passengers, as there had been between him and the subjects or situations of his winning photographs.

Since that interview, Brian Bates had taken untold thousands of photographs. There were between sixteen hundred and two thousand passengers on every crossing and he photographed them all several times over—embarking and disembarking, in the dining room, at the various bars, playing shipboard games, relaxing beside the pool.

"How can you expect me to remember any one individual?" he asked Gwenn Ramadge.

She had caught up with him as he was pinning up last night's pictures for display.

"These are pictures you'll never forget."

No further description was necessary. It hadn't seemed right to file them with the ordinary shipboard shots, so he had ended up putting them in a sturdy envelope in the top drawer of his desk. He knew exactly where they were.

He had photographed the body of Minerva Aldrich from every angle, her long blond hair still dripping with water, palazzo pants sodden, eyes staring. He had also recorded the crime scene from several angles. He had shot from a distance and close up. He knew nothing of the rules of evidence, but instinct guided him. When asked if he had a photograph of the area around the pool, specifically the tables and lounge chairs, he produced several. Then Gwenn asked if he recalled any drinks or food being on any of the tables.

He didn't, but he had a roll which he'd shot using the existing lighting as an experiment. As evidence, it was flawed, but it conveyed an impression of mystery and horror. He had not included these in the batch he'd turned over to the captain and Eric Graf. Riffling through them quickly, Brian pulled one out and handed it to Gwenn. It showed a small table at poolside and on it the familiar setup: champagne bottle and ice bucket with a single tulip glass beside it. The bottle was tilted in such a way that the label was visible. As an added feature, so was the chit on the tray.

"Could you blow this up so we could read the label?" Gwenn asked.

"No problem. I can also bring up the number on the chit, if you want. And the signature. The number will tell you who served the drink and the signature to whose account it was charged."

Gwenn was impressed. "You're very talented, Mr. Bates. Very artistic. Have you ever thought about doing media work?"

"Sure. But it's not an easy field to break into. And I have to earn a living."

"We all do."

Gwenn had intended to check with the billing department. She assumed the original chits were preserved at least until the end of the cruise in case of error and to respond if a passenger challenged the accuracy of a bill.

"That blowup would be great," Gwenn said to Brian. You could never have too much confirmation for a piece of evidence, she thought.

She was not surprised when the number 3304 turned out to be the same number she had noticed on the tray with the *Flor Blanco* Sofia Rossi had served Mrs. Fleming in her stateroom. Obviously, the girl had served both women. Coincidence? It was not beyond possibility that both women should develop a taste for a little-known wine or that the same waitress should serve each one, but it was unexpected and shocking to find when Gwenn asked for a look at the chits that no such number as 3304 existed.

Was *Flor Blanco* reserved as a code for those who wanted the drug? In that case, it made sense that the chits were not processed through the accounting department in the normal way.

Just how much traffic was there in this *Flor Blanco*? Was any of it legitimate? How much of it was sold on the *Dante*?

"Sorry, Miss Ramadge, we're not open yet," the bartender at the Miramar told her.

"I know. I wanted to ask about this *Flor Blanco* champagne. I've never heard of it. Is it very popular?"

"The demand is growing. In fact, we've run out of it."

"Is that so?"

"We may pick some up in Puerto Quetzal. Shall I put some aside for you?"

"Yes. That would be nice. Thank you."

They smiled at each other and Gwenn walked away. She felt uneasy. What exactly had transpired? There was a way to find out.

The food manager was in his office just off the kitchen. He was a serious man in his early forties, already stooped from peering over bills and cargo lists.

"What can I do for you, miss?"

"I wondered if I could put in an order for that *Flor Blanco* champagne I've heard so much about? Is that possible?"

"It would be if we carried it."

"You don't carry it? I was told it's so popular that you ran out."

The food manager shook his head. "*Flor Blanco*, you said? Possibly you got the name wrong?"

"Possibly I did."

"I can check my suppliers. It may be something new. If it's available, I'd be glad to get it for you."

"Oh, that's all right. It was just a whim."

The bartender had recognized the name, Gwenn thought; the food manager had not, or so he said. One of them was lying and was in on the scheme. What exactly was the scheme? Drugs, obviously. There was a drug ring operating on the Dante, and one of the men to whom she'd just spoken, as well as Sofia Rossi, was involved. Minerva Aldrich and Christine Fleming were among the customers.

By now passengers bound for shore excursions had left the ship. Somehow, Gwenn did not expect that Christine Fleming was one of them. She knew her way around well enough now to find her way to the luxe stateroom without having to ask. She knocked lightly.

"It's Gwenn Ramadge. May I speak with you?"

"This is not a good time. I'm sorry."

"Oh? When would be a good time?" Gwenn asked.

"I'm just having my breakfast."

Gwenn checked her watch: eleven-thirty. She could use some breakfast herself. "Why don't I come back in . . . say, half an hour? Would that be all right?"

There was a considerable pause; then Gwenn heard the rattle of a chain and the click of the lock and the hard snap of the bolt; evidently Mrs. Fleming had taken Gwenn's suggestion to heart.

"I suppose it's important or you wouldn't be here," she observed, then turned and went back to the table set up by room service. "Would you care for coffee?"

Gwenn started to say no and changed her mind. "That would be good. Thank you."

"Help yourself. You don't mind if I finish?" Mrs. Fleming indicated the stack of pancakes on the plate in front of her.

"By all means, go ahead." Gwenn watched as the elegant lady applied herself with gusto. Syrup dripped from the corner of her lips but she caught it with the tip of her tongue. She'd be smacking her lips next, Gwenn thought. "How long have you known Sofia Rossi?"

"The waitress? I never saw her before last night."

At least she didn't play the game of pretending she didn't know what Gwenn was talking about. "You defended her staunchly."

"Only because you accused her . . . What did you accuse her of—attempted burglary? It seemed unfair."

"And that was enough for you to take her part?"

"Why are you so determined to make trouble for this girl?" Suddenly, Mrs. Fleming was not so gracious. "What have you got against her?"

"Why was Sofia here so long last night? Don't tell me it was to serve the *Flor Blanco*; she brought you drugs and didn't have time to complete the deal. *Flor Blanco* was the password, wasn't it? When you ordered *Flor Blanco*, you identified yourself as in the market to buy drugs. The person who served it was your connection. Drugs are cheap down here. You could afford to lay in a supply."

"You don't know what you're talking about. If you weren't so far off course, I'd laugh."

"I don't think you've got much to laugh about, Mrs. Fleming."

"I'm going to report you to the captain."

"Oh, I don't think so. That would blow the whole operation. You'd cut yourself off from your source as well as ruining the setup for Sofia and the others. By the way, how many others are there? How many besides Sofia? Where does Sofia get her supply? How is Nancy Castel involved?"

"You're meddling in matters you don't understand." Where before there had been unwavering assurance, now anxiety crept in. "I'm warning you, stay out of it!"

"Why should I?" Gwenn demanded.

"If you don't, you'll regret it."

"Is that a threat? Drugs bring death, Mrs. Fleming." Gwenn was close to pleading. "We've already had one death aboard the *Dante*."

"What are you talking about? If you mean Minerva Aldrich, that was an accident. Everybody knows it."

"Before the 'accident,' Minerva had ordered a bottle of *Flor Blanco*. It was served by Sofia Rossi."

"So?"

"There is no such brand as *Flor Blanco*. The food manager has never heard of it."

"I can show you—"

"You can show me a bottle and the label on it says *Flor Blanco*. How do you know that's not an ordinary champagne with a label pasted on it?"

"You're trying to frighten me."

"Yes, I am, Mrs. Fleming. That's exactly what I'm trying to do."

Christine Fleming's high color and exuberance vanished as she studied Gwenn. "I think you mean well, Miss Ramadge, but you don't know what's involved. There's nothing in this champagne that can harm anyone." She picked up the glass, and holding it high as one about to give a toast, she drank what was left.

No use arguing, Gwenn thought. "Don't expect to get your drugs past U.S. Customs, Mrs. Fleming. You may get them off the ship, but whatever port of entry you may choose, there'll be inspectors waiting. They will search your luggage and your person in a very thorough and very intimate manner, if you follow my meaning. And don't expect to get anyone else to carry your stuff either. Every person with whom you've had any contact on board will be subjected to similar treatment. Turn in your drugs; tell what you know. You may be charged with smuggling, but that's better than being an accessory to murder."

No matter what Gwenn said, Christine Fleming remained staunch. Stubborn loyalty to the connection was not unusual among addicts, Gwenn knew. It was self-serving. To turn in the pusher meant cutting off the addict's supply. It suddenly occurred to Gwenn that Mrs. Fleming had shown none of the traits of the addict—the twitches, spasms, compulsive sniffing. Maybe she hadn't been addicted long enough for them to develop. Could she be wrong? Gwenn asked herself. Could it be that the society woman was not a user and Sofia Rossi not a pusher?

It wasn't Mrs. Fleming's habit Gwenn was interested in, but Minerva Aldrich's. The family had hotly denied any suggestion that Minerva had been addicted. She had used drugs, yes, but only to ease the pain of her cancer. And who could blame her? Anyway, that was in the past. When she died, she was clean. An autopsy could settle that definitively. Gwenn was inclined to admit it without the formality of an autopsy, but the drug angle was a new lead and she had to follow it. Reaching the coffee bar, she reflected that by now Mrs. Fleming had likely contacted Sofia to warn her that she, Gwenn, was on the way, and what questions she was likely to ask. Would it be better not to go? To let Sofia worry and wonder why she didn't come? Meantime, why not talk to Nancy?

Nancy surely knew what was going on. If there was a drug ring operating on the *Dante Alighieri* and her roommate was a part of it, of course she knew. She might even be a part of it herself, the weak link.

Gwenn ordered a cappuccino at the counter and carried it to a quiet corner. She was beginning to form a picture of the events that occurred the night Minerva had died. Assume Minerva had slipped back into her addiction. In her condition, with the severity of her pain, no one could blame her. Nevertheless, she hadn't wanted the family to know. Somehow, she made a connection on board, or perhaps she was given Sofia's name in advance. Either way, a meeting was arranged. As Minerva shared the stateroom with her sister Juno, it couldn't be there. It certainly couldn't take place in Sofia's cabin in the crew quarters, so the pool was chosen as neutral ground. After two A.M., the various public rooms were closed and it wasn't likely anyone would go swimming at that hour. They would have the place to themselves.

Gwenn finished her cappuccino and headed for the infirmary.

Morning visiting hours were over and the door to the entire medical complex was locked, but she rang anyway. She had made it a point that Nancy was not to be left unattended, but she began to feel anxious when no one came in answer to her ring. Before she rang again, however, the door was opened by Simon Kittridge.

"Hi," he said. He smiled but he seemed very tired. He had volunteered for the job of bodyguard, but she shouldn't have let him take it on—he was too old to go without his sleep.

"I thought you'd forgotten us," he said.

"I'm sorry. A lot's been happening."

"Come on in and tell me about it." He stood to one side to let her pass.

"How's the patient?"

"See for yourself." Kittridge opened the first door they came to along the interior corridor.

It was not the same room Nancy had been in before. There was no bed here; it was an examining room. But Nancy was not being examined. She was fully dressed, seated at a small table, eating and enjoying it. When she saw Gwenn, she put her fork down and smiled. "Hello, Miss Ramadge."

"Nancy!" Gwenn exclaimed. "Go on with your lunch, please." She accepted the chair Kittridge brought around for her. "Well, this is a surprise. You're looking well, really well. You've certainly healed quickly. And the bruises have faded a lot."

"It's all thanks to you and Mr. Kittridge and Nurse Kent. I'm going back on duty tonight."

"I'm not so sure that's a good idea." Gwenn looked to Kittridge for support.

"She's got to go back sometime."

"Dr. Halliday says it's all right."

"Medically, it may be, but . . ."

"You can't keep her cooped up and under guard forever."

Gwenn sighed. "Somebody thinks that you can make a lot of trouble for him, Nancy. He thinks you know something that could hurt him. He's already warned you twice to keep your mouth shut. But talking is your only way to safety. Once you share this information, the more people you tell, the safer you'll be. Why don't you start with the two of us?"

Nancy Castel paled. She pushed her plate away.

"When you and I first met, we were concerned about a series of jewel thefts," Gwenn recalled. "Somehow, that has led us to a murder. Let's stop and face the truth before something worse happens."

"What could be worse?" Kittridge asked.

"Drugs. Drugs kill. Drugs kill indiscriminately. Let me tell you the part that I believe drugs played in Minerva Aldrich's death." Gwenn took a deep breath, looking at the elderly man and the young woman with the same penetrating gaze. "As almost everybody knows by now, Minerva Aldrich had cancer. It was believed to be terminal. She began to use drugs to ease the pain. Then she went into remission and didn't need drugs anymore, or so she thought, only to discover that she was hooked." Gwenn shook her head. "She hadn't brought any drugs with her, but this is a very big ship and it is not inconceivable that she was able to find someone able to supply her need. Your roommate, Sofia."

"No," Nancy said.

"Hear me out. The buy was set for Tuesday night after we left Cartagena, which leads me to believe Cartagena was one of the supply stations. As a means of identification, Minerva was to order a *Flor Blanco* champagne and have it served at poolside."

Feeling the eyes of both Simon Kittridge and Nancy Castel on her, Gwenn decided to be open. "The transaction appears to have been completed without incident. But then something happened, something went wrong. I suggest it was nothing but Minerva Aldrich's built-in caution. She wanted to make sure of the quality of the merchandise. So she took a sample dose."

Nancy gasped. Kittridge gazed at Gwenn awestruck.

"I believe there was something wrong with the drug. Perhaps it was contaminated. Or, at the other end of the scale, maybe it was too pure. Another possibility is that there was nothing wrong with it at all, but that washing it down with the champagne caused a synergistic reaction. Minerva became dizzy and fell into the pool. Isn't that right, Nancy? That's what Sofia told you happened, isn't it?"

"It was an accident," Nancy pleaded.

"Yes, it was," Gwenn agreed. "Up to that point. If Sofia had tried to pull Miss Aldrich out of the water, or if she had called for help, no one could say anything but that. But she did neither. She ran away and left Minerva Aldrich to die."

"She was frightened," Nancy moaned. "I thought . . . I mean, she thought Miss Aldrich was dead so there was no use . . ."

"How did she know Miss Aldrich was dead?" Gwenn demanded. "Did she check for a pulse?"

Nancy looked bewildered. "She didn't say. I don't remember."

"Then how did she know Minerva Aldrich was dead?" Gwenn persisted.

"Well, because she wasn't breathing, I suppose."

"I see." Shocked and saddened at what she now perceived to be the truth, Gwenn had no choice but to continue. "Do you know what the presence of water in the lungs of a person presumed to have drowned indicates? It indicates that the person was alive and breathing when he went under. When there is no water in the lungs, that's an indication the person was not breathing, that he was already dead. There was water in Minerva Aldrich's lungs. She was alive when Sofia ran away and left her."

Nancy's jaw quivered. "She didn't know that. She thought Miss Aldrich was dead and it would be useless to sound the alarm. It would ruin everything. It would expose—" Suddenly, Nancy stopped.

"What would it expose? Whom would it expose? Who was Sofia protecting besides herself? You. Was she protecting you, Nancy?"

"I had nothing to do with it. I wasn't involved. I had no part in it."

"You were both in it," Gwenn said, both elated and sad as another piece of the puzzle fell into place. "The chit Minerva Aldrich signed at the poolside bar the night of her death, number 3304, was not from Sofia's order book. It wasn't from anybody's order book. It was the number used only by those trafficking in the *Flor Blanco*." Gwenn paused and fixed her eyes on the young woman. At last she understood at least a part of what had happened. "Including you. Isn't that right, Nancy? In fact, you were the one who made contact with Miss Aldrich by serving the champagne. You were the one who handed over the drug and you were the one who watched her die."

"No!"

"What was wrong with the drug?" Gwenn persisted. "Why did Minerva Aldrich collapse almost as soon as she swallowed it? For God's sake, Nancy! Don't let your friend suffer for something that wasn't her fault."

"There was nothing wrong with it. I don't know. You don't understand."

"Whenever I ask a question, that's the answer I get: 'You don't understand.' Well, make me understand!"

Nancy shook her head, cast a desperate look at Kittridge, and began to cry.

Up to that moment, Kittridge had sat to one side, attentive but not taking part in the dialogue. However, Gwenn's last appeal moved him. "We aren't doing anything bad," he told her. "We aren't hurting anybody. To the contrary."

"You're in it too," Gwenn murmured, admitting at last what she had refused to believe from the start. "Who else?"

"We're not dealing death. We're giving life."

"Explain that."

"We're supplying medicine that sick people can't get legally back home. We're giving the terminally ill a second chance, not just for remission but for a cure."

"Medicine?" Gwenn repeated. "What medicine?"

"It was originally intended to ease morning sickness in pregnancy and was hailed as a boon to women. Then it was discovered that the babies of the women who took it were being born deformed. Maybe you remember? Some were missing limbs—an arm or a leg or both. Hands were attached to shoulders. A foot might have too many toes or too few. Feet grew out of thighs."

"Thalidomide," Gwenn whispered. "The drug of infamy."

Few drugs had been so thoroughly discredited and reviled as thalidomide. From the depths of ostracism, it had slowly worked its way back to respectability, passed beyond it, and was now being hailed as a "magic bullet," a cure not only for one but for a variety of the most terrible scourges known to man. The afflicted, those who had lost all hope in standard treatments yet were not prepared to die, passed the word, and the tales of cures abounded. The drug, it was claimed, had conquered certain cancers, multiple sclerosis, Alzheimer's. The list was growing and the testimony of those who attributed a miraculous recovery to the drug was also growing. Gwenn had seen some of them on television. She had read pieces in prestigious magazines. The drug acted quickly, reversing the ravages of diseases which had previously been considered fatal. There was no way of knowing whether it would have benefited Minerva Aldrich. It was too soon to say whether the fresh glow in Christine

Fleming's cheeks was a sign of a beneficent reaction or of excitement. Clearly, Mrs. Fleming believed she was being cured.

"What's your part in this?" Gwenn asked Kittridge.

"I supply the medicine."

His matter-of-fact attitude made Gwenn angry. "Where do you get it?"

"The drug is legal in many countries, Argentina for one. There, I'm sorry to say, poor pregnant women continue to use it because it's available and cheap. And they suffer the tragic consequences with which you're familiar. I think I told you that I recently went on a world cruise. One of my dance partners was very sick. She had Huntington's disease. She'd heard about the drug. As a last resort—she was dying anyway—she went ashore at Buenos Aires and picked some up at a pharmacy—no prescription necessary. The results were miraculous, and almost instantaneous. The word spread. Other ladies wanted the drug either for themselves or for someone in the family, or for a friend, but either they didn't speak the language or they were afraid that if they brought it back themselves, news of what they'd done would somehow get out and customs authorities would be waiting to arrest them. More importantly, they might confiscate the drug. So they came to me and asked me to buy it for them."

Kittridge paused. He looked straight at Gwenn, his light gray eyes steady. "I was happy to do it."

"Well, I can see that. As a onetime transaction, yes. It would be hard to refuse. But to set up an operation, to go into business . . ."

"I don't go looking for clients; they come to me. I don't introduce them to the drug; they already know about it."

"This ship doesn't go to Argentina," Gwenn observed.

"I have contacts at various ports who acquire the substance for me."

Still no trace of remorse, Gwenn thought. In fact, Kittridge seemed to feel he should be commended.

"People come to us as a last resort. We are their last hope. If they came to you, would you turn them down?"

She had no ready answer; it would take considerable soul-searching to provide one. "How do you rationalize what happened to Minerva Aldrich?"

"A tragic accident."

At least, Gwenn thought, and Minerva was not the only victim. "What about Nancy and Sofia? What's going to happen to them?"

"They didn't do anything wrong."

"They acted as couriers."

"They delivered medicine and received payment for it. I remind you that the medicine is legal in the country in which it was bought."

"Nancy stood by while Minerva Aldrich died."

"You don't really know that, do you?" the host asked gently. "It is possible that Miss Aldrich didn't take the medicine till Nancy left and she was alone."

From the moment they met on the sky deck on the afternoon of departure, Gwenn had taken a liking to Simon Kittridge. She had observed him with the lonely ladies he was paid to dance with. Yet she could not ignore the fact that he had turned innocent young women into drug couriers. She looked at Nancy. "You must have known that what you were doing was wrong."

"Mr. Kittridge said we weren't breaking the law."

"But morally . . ." Gwenn stopped. It was the same ground all over again. "How did you come to select Nancy and Sofia?" she asked Kittridge.

"I was attracted to Nancy first. I was struck by her demeanor; she was shy, withdrawn, no one would suspect her. Next, I checked her background. She came from a poor family in Naples. When I say poor, I mean at a level you and I can hardly picture—the kind of poor who live in a shack without running water or electricity."

"So she was not difficult to convince."

Nancy flushed.

"She has three children to support," the host reminded Gwenn.

"How about Sofia?"

"As Nancy's roommate, she had to be included. Also, Sofia has a younger brother who's constantly in trouble with the police and has to be bailed out."

"All right. I'm willing to accept all this, but how could you physically abuse Nancy the way you did?"

"It wasn't me. I never touched her. I swear."

"Who then?"

"I have no idea. You wanted to talk to somebody about Mrs. Sturgess and the stolen brooch. I steered you to Nancy. If I had any fear she might talk about the operation, why would I do that?"

"Because you'd rather have me talk to someone you could control."

"Why ask the question if you're going to supply the answer?" Kittridge snapped, angry for the first time. "How about it, Nancy? Was it me that hit you from behind and went on hitting you after you were down?"

Gwenn's eyes flashed. "You know she can't answer that."

"Excuse me," the girl interposed. "I think I would have known if it was Mr. Kittridge."

"How?" Gwenn asked.

"I would have sensed it."

Further efforts to shake her would only serve to make her more stubborn in her denial, Gwenn thought. "Let's talk about the Valium then. Did you take it or any other sedative of your own accord?"

Nancy Castel started to say no, then changed her mind. "They gave me some at the infirmary in case the pain got bad. It did, so I took two. That's all, just two."

"With what? A glass of water?"

"No, I washed them down with some hot cocoa. Sofia and I usually have a cup before going to bed. We use the powdered kind in individual packets. All you need to do is add the water."

"Someone could easily have doctored the packets—slit the envelope, pounded the Valium into a powder, added it, and resealed the whole thing."

"It did have a strange taste," Nancy recalled.

"Are you sure you only took two tablets?"

"I did have a second cup of cocoa, I remember that."

The perp could not have known Nancy would take some of the drug on her own. Once again it appeared her reaction was more severe than he intended.

Kittridge was following Gwenn's line of reasoning. "Whoever is responsible for these attacks doesn't seem to be very well organized, but he is cold-blooded and ruthless. You can't believe I'm either of those things."

"I don't want to believe it," Gwenn replied.

"Then don't. Trust your instincts," Kittridge urged. "At least, don't report the girls. You can't prove any of this and if you tell the captain or Graf, you'll ruin their lives."

"I can't just forget about it."

"Then wait. We have two more days at sea before we reach Acapulco. A lot can happen."

Gwenn frowned. "Will you stop trafficking in illegal medicines?"

"If I say yes, will you believe me?"

She hesitated.

"I will not dispense any more thalidomide till we put ashore on this trip," Kittridge conceded.

It was an ending without a conclusion, Gwenn thought, and left the infirmary.

A wave of depression washed over Gwenn Ramadge. She had the feeling that she'd been manipulated from the very first moment she set foot on the *Dante Alighieri*. She no longer had any doubt that when Simon Kittridge started that seemingly innocent conversation, he knew who she was and what she was doing there. At least Lewis Aldrich had frankly stated he had hired Gwenn so he would know what was going on in the investigation of Minerva's death. He did seem genuinely shocked when she suggested that the Mob bosses to whom he owed money might somehow be responsible. If it turned out they were, then Minerva's death and the thalidomide trafficking were unrelated after all.

Trust your instincts, Kittridge had said, and she always had. She could continue to do so, Gwenn thought, and returned to her cabin.

It was three in the afternoon. She set her alarm for five, kicked off her shoes, and lay down for a couple of hours.

She slept soundly. The alarm rang a considerable time before she woke, but when she did, she was instantly alert. Something, a new piece of evidence or a fresh interpretation of old evidence released during sleep, now lurked at the edge of her consciousness. Ray would have called it a hunch and played it down. Gwenn admitted it was a hunch, but did not denigrate it. Nor did she try to force it to reveal itself. It would come in its own time. She stripped and got under the shower. She ran it lukewarm while she shampooed her hair and lathered her body with the fragrant soap the ship provided. For the final rinse, she turned the water to stinging hot and then invigorating cold.

She dried herself with a thick towel, twisted another towel around her head like a turban, and snuggled into the terry cloth robe also provided by the *Dante*.

In every investigation there came a time when the most useful thing Gwenn could do was sit down quietly, alone, not merely to think or to review the facts and make sure there were no inconsistencies—she did that regularly—but to go one step higher and let her mind float free without conscious direction . . . to meditate. This was that time.

Relaxed and also eager, Gwenn made herself comfortable at the small desk, opened the file she had compiled on Minerva Aldrich's drowning, and spread out the photographs Brian Bates had supplied. She was more impressed than ever by the sensitivity with which he had treated his subject. He had managed somehow to be factual and at the same time impart a sense of compassion. In the photograph of the champagne bottle in its bucket with the single, nearly empty tulip glass beside it, he had managed to convey loneliness. The longer Gwenn looked at it, the more certain she became that something was missing.

Money! Minerva Aldrich had gone to the meeting with the intent to buy. So she must have brought money. What had she carried it in? A purse? Where was it? Gwenn couldn't remember seeing it. Say she hadn't brought it in a purse but in an envelope which she handed over to the courier, and the courier took it away; where were the drugs she got in exchange? Gwenn believed she knew the answer, but she needed facts to support it. Being neat by nature and having learned to be organized, Gwenn put the papers and photos away in the bottom drawer and dressed quickly. Dabbing some gel on her fingertips, she ran them through her damp, tousled hair, shaping a cap of sculptured curls. She was tanned enough not to need much makeup—only a light brown liner for her eyes and lipstick labeled "tangerine" completed the job. She put on a pants outfit of aqua silk and added the gold hoop earrings that were fast becoming her trademark. The whole job had taken five minutes. She looked in the mirror: not bad, under the circumstances.

Leaving her cabin, Gwenn hesitated. The family was taking meals in the suite originally occupied by Minerva and Juno, now used by Lewis and Diana. By now, their self-imposed solitude might have become wearing. Gwenn decided to take a look in the Michelangelo dining room first. Entering by way of the top tier of the handsome room, she had a good view of all the diners. Off to the right of the lower level, she saw them. As the maitre d' scurried over to her with the intention of seating her, Gwenn waved him off and left. While the Aldriches dined, the suite would be empty. Luck was running her way.

Of course, she still had to get into the suite, but there should be no great difficulty. She found the cabin steward for the section and identified herself. She explained that she had visited the Aldriches earlier and had forgotten her sunglasses. Would he be kind enough to let her in to look for them?

Aldo—his name plaque was pinned to the breast pocket of his midnight-blue uniform—had seen her with members of the Aldrich family. Even better, he knew who she was and what position she had in the ship's hierarchy, so he admitted her readily. However, he was cautious enough not to leave her in the suite alone. How was she going to get rid of him?

"I don't see them," Gwenn said, with a look that swept the sitting room. She couldn't think of an excuse to go opening drawers and peering into closets. She shrugged. "I must have left them somewhere else."

"Maybe they were turned in?" the cabin steward suggested, studying her thoughtfully.

"I hope so. I just bought them and they were expensive. If by any chance they turn up, you'll let me know?"

"Of course, Miss Ramadge." Aldo hesitated.

He was short and slim and his right hand was twitching. It struck Gwenn that she had seen no overweight crew or staff members. Either it was a tribute to their self-discipline or they were being served a different menu from that of the passengers. Also, Aldo was older than most of the crew and the hand he held at his side wouldn't stop twitching. At this moment he had something more important than a missing pair of sunglasses to worry about.

"Will you be crossing back to Fort Lauderdale with us, Miss Ramadge?" he asked.

"No, I'll be leaving the *Dante* in Acapulco."

He cleared his throat. "I was wondering . . . Is Mr. Aldrich's offer of a reward still open?"

"As far as I know, it will be until the truth about Miss Minerva's death is known," Gwenn said, careful not to appear too anxious or to discourage him. "Do you think you have new information?"

He nodded and plunged. "I saw Miss Minerva leave the suite on the night she was drowned. It was two A.M."

"And?"

"She was followed."

"What do you mean? Who followed her? Her sister?"

"No. A man."

Gwenn shook her head as she tried to fit in this new and startling revelation.

"Where did this man come from?"

"The other bedroom."

"Of this same suite?" She wanted to make sure she wasn't making a mistake.

"That's right." He was patient as though with a slow child.

"And the man who came out of this other bedroom followed Miss Minerva how closely? On her heels?"

"Well . . . almost."

"Where did he go?"

"Toward the escalators."

"You didn't follow, of course. Why should you? You had no reason to." Gwenn was thinking aloud. "Had you ever seen this man before? Had he ever visited the Aldrich ladies before?"

"I can't say."

"Would you recognize him if you saw him again?"

"Oh yes."

"Describe him."

"He was big, robust, with a dark beard."

The beard could be a disguise, she thought, but the build . . . The build eliminated Paul Racine at least.

"Why have you waited so long with this information? You should have come forward right away. Why didn't you?"

"Mrs. Chávez asked me not to."

Another bombshell. "How did she know about it?"

"I told her. News of the drowning was all over the ship that morning. Everybody had a version of how it happened. The most popular was that Miss Minerva was sick and her sister was supposed to keep an eye on her. But Miss Minerva waited till Mrs. Chávez fell asleep and got away. While wandering around, she got dizzy and fell into the pool."

Remarkably close, Gwenn thought. "You knew it wasn't that simple, yet instead of reporting it to the captain, you went to Mrs. Chávez. Why?" She held up a hand, forestalling his answer. "Because you wanted money. Mr. Aldrich hadn't come aboard yet; no reward had yet been offered, so you went to Mrs. Chávez. Unfortunately, she had no money, but she promised to get it."

The little man sighed.

So did Gwenn. "Did she try to explain the presence of this strange man in the suite the night her sister died?"

"She said he was somebody Miss Minerva had . . . picked up." Aldo flushed, embarrassed. "She said he was not the first one, or the only one. She asked me not to say anything. She wanted to protect her sister's reputation and her memory."

Gwenn thought it over. "According to Mrs. Chávez, she and her sister shared the master stateroom, and the other room, intended for Miss Diana, was unoccupied. Why should I believe you rather than her? I think you're tired of waiting for Mrs. Chávez to pay you, so you're trying to get money from Mr. Aldrich. I can tell you that he's not going to be anxious to buy information that implicates one daughter in the death of another. You'll have to convince me that what you say is true so that I can convince him."

"How can I do that?"

"Details, Aldo, details. The more details you can supply, the more credible your charge will be."

Whereas before he had been withdrawn, now, within reach of

what could be the biggest windfall of his life, Aldo broke out in a cold sweat.

"Yes," he agreed. He rubbed his hands. "What kind of details?"

"For example, something more about this man who was supposed to be having a fling with Minerva Aldrich, more than that he was big and had a beard. How was he dressed?"

"I don't remember."

"Was it a formal night? No. So probably he wasn't wearing a tux. How about slacks and a blazer?"

"I don't know. I wasn't paying attention to his clothes." He scowled. "All right, all right. He had linen slacks and an embroidered shirt like you can buy in any of the ports of call. The cuffs were unbuttoned and the tails weren't tucked in all around."

"Like he'd gotten dressed in a hurry?"

"Yes. He was disheveled."

"Would you be uncomfortable if I took a look around to see . . . well, what there is to see? Traces of this stranger?"

Aldo wanted only to extricate himself from what had become for him a no-win situation.

"I am still working for Mr. Aldrich," she reminded him. "And you're still in the game."

Gwenn knew the room had long since been cleaned and made up. Also, it was presently being used by Lewis Aldrich, but there was always the possibility that this other man, if he existed, might have left something behind. If he had, Gwenn might not find it, but it was an excuse to move on to the sisters' quarters. By now Aldo was committed, so that when Gwenn came upon the plastic container, made her mark, and handed him a receipt, he accepted it without protest.

Returning to her office, Gwenn settled down to making some calls. The first person she needed to talk to was Ray Dixon at Internal Affairs in Brooklyn. The call went through as smoothly as any call on shore.

"Sergeant Dixon isn't available just now, ma'am," the detective who picked up told her. "May I help you?"

"No, I don't think so."

"Would you care to leave a message?"

She considered. "No, thank you. I need to talk to him. Maybe he left a number where he can be reached? This is Gwenn Ramadge."

"Gwenn! Sure." The atmosphere warmed considerably. "He did leave a number in case you should call. Let's see . . . Where did I put it? Ah. Here it is!"

A woman answered.

"I'm trying to get in touch with Sergeant Ray Dixon and I was given this number," Gwenn explained. "Is he there? May I speak with him?"

"Who's calling?"

"Gwenn Ramadge. And you are . . . ?"

"Patty Dixon," the woman replied. "I'm so sorry, you just missed him. Is there anything I can do for you? Would you like to leave a message?"

Gwenn's voice broke twice as she struggled to recover. "No, that's all right. I'll get in touch with him later." She hung up quickly, before embarrassing herself.

Ray's divorce was final. There were no children to tie Ray Dixon and his wife. All property problems had long since been resolved. There was no reason Gwenn knew of for them to be seeing each other. If Patty Foley—or Patty Dixon, as she was apparently continuing to call herself—was in some kind of trouble and needed help, it was natural that she should appeal to Ray and that Ray would respond right away. But Patty hadn't sounded like a woman in distress. On the contrary, she had sounded like a woman sitting on top of the world.

What most annoyed Gwenn was Patty's condescension.

For the time being, Gwenn gave up trying to reach Ray and

called Marge instead. At this hour in New York, Marge should be at home with her son, she thought, and was pleased when Marge answered promptly. As usual, Marge was eager to take on the assignment.

"And you have someone to stay with Brucie?" Gwenn asked.

Again Marge assured her that any of several neighbors would consider it a privilege to look after the boy while she ran down the information Gwenn needed. How long it would take was another matter. Time was running out. Soon the *Dante* would dock in Acapulco, and once the passengers left the ship, it would be very difficult to reassemble the suspects. So she had to proceed on the assumption that Marge's research would support her theories. She couldn't do it alone though. Who would be willing to help? Whom could she trust? Ironically, only one name came to mind.

Simon Kittridge.

He was skeptical. "Suppose she calls your bluff?"

"It's not a bluff. I have the evidence."

"You conducted an illegal search and you found some pills you think are thalidomide among Mrs. Chávez's effects. Even if it turns out you're right and that's what they are, it doesn't prove they're the same ones Minerva bought."

"Can't you identify them?"

"You don't honestly expect me to? And if I did, how could it help?"

"It would put Juno Chávez at the scene of the crime. That first."

"Drop it. For the sake of the girls, drop it."

"It's for their sakes that I can't drop it. And for yours, too, Simon. Minerva Aldrich was murdered. Don't you want to know if the blame is on you and the girls?"

Kittridge broke out in a cold sweat. "You should have been a lawyer. All right. What do you want me to do?"

She explained her plan which was, perforce, loose.

He pointed that out.

"I'm open to suggestion."

"I have only one. Watch your back."

Gwenn telephoned Mrs. Chávez.

"I know how your sister died and why," she said. "I can tell your stepfather or Captain Nicolletti, who will then pass on the information to the authorities when we dock in Acapulco. Ultimately, they'll have to turn you over to Interpol or the FBI, but meantime, you'll spend a while in a Mexican prison. Not a pleasant experience. Or I can tell you what I know and leave the matter in your hands."

She paused, but Juno Chávez did not take the bait.

"It's true that, as you pointed out, I have no official standing," Gwenn continued. "I could make a citizen's arrest, I suppose, but I don't really want to and I'm not so sure it would be valid. Also, to be honest, there'd be nothing in it for me. Captain Nicolletti might thank me, but that wouldn't help my bank account, and I don't think your stepfather would be inclined to be generous either. So, you're my best bet. I think we can make a deal."

For Juno Chávez, this had to be the moment of truth, Gwenn thought. Relying on the absence of hard evidence against her, she could simply refuse to deal, or she could ante up and see what cards Gwenn held. Gwenn literally held her breath.

"We need to talk," Juno said.

And Gwenn could breathe again.

They agreed to meet on the Sky deck, starboard side, near the paddle courts.

CHAPTER

18

Gwenn laid out her equipment on the bed and examined it meticulously to make sure it was in working order: the first rule of the game. She had changed into dark, snug-fitting knit pants which would facilitate movement, and a dark, loose jacket to camouflage the gun in its shoulder holster. She looked herself over in the mirror—the piece didn't show, but could she get at it fast? She practiced a couple of quick draws. Good enough.

Next, she considered the camera, small as a cigarette lighter. Would she need it? Probably not, but she slipped it into a pocket just in case. Finally, she picked up the intricate spray brooch in which the mini-transmitter was cunningly nestled. A state-of-the-art device, it could transmit the drop of a pin to a receiver fifty yards away. Simon Kittridge was equipped with the receiver. Satisfied, Gwenn headed for the Sky deck.

A stiff breeze swept across the open expanse. It was warm and moist and laden with the scent of the tropics. The rising moon was as yet only a silver disk in a lavender sky. It shone on the paddle courts, the putting practice alley, and the various housings lined up like chessmen across the deck. Fighting the wind, Gwenn made it to the railing and hung on. After a while she got used to the conditions. Gaining confidence in her ability to deal with them, she prepared herself to wait for Juno's arrival. She knew she'd have to wait—it was standard in such situations. As time passed, however, Gwenn began to wonder if Juno would come at all.

The moon grew brighter. Clouds chased each other across the sky. Peering into the shifting shadows, Gwenn thought she saw someone lurking. Then the next gust of wind swept the illusion away. There was nobody there. She broke out into a cold sweat: if she couldn't trust her own eyes, what could she trust? At that moment, Gwenn wished herself anywhere but here on this lonely, windswept deck. She didn't need this. She needed lights and people.

Suddenly, a door opened. "What's this all about, Miss Ramadge?"

Instinctively, Gwenn turned toward the voice.

"Don't move, Miss Ramadge. Stay right where you are. I have a gun."

Gwenn froze. She should have anticipated something like this, she thought; Juno Chávez had been much too accommodating. Even while she was making her preparations, so was Juno, and now Gwenn found herself facing what, in the uncertain glimmers of moonlight, looked like a toy.

"Speak up, Miss Ramadge. I'm getting impatient."

Impatient and afraid someone might come by and wonder what was going on, Gwenn thought. "In your initial statement to Captain Nicolletti on the night your sister died, you said that the two of you turned in early, about eleven, as usual. You slept in twin beds in the same room. You dropped off right away and didn't hear your sister get up."

"That's correct."

"You suggested that your sister probably took her clothes into the sitting room and dressed there in order not to disturb you."

"Minerva was very considerate."

"You must be a heavy sleeper," Gwenn suggested.

"I was very tired."

"You slept right through till Eric Graf woke you at around three A.M. with the news that your sister had had an accident."

"We've been over this before, Miss Ramadge. I wish you'd get to the point, if there is one."

"The point is—you lied, Mrs. Chávez. Minerva was seen leaving the suite and you were seen following after."

"Seen? By whom?"

Gwenn chose to ignore the question, for now. "Careful as she was, Minerva did wake you when she got up, didn't she? You pretended to be asleep, but when she went into the sitting room to get dressed, you dressed too. When she went out, you were right behind her. You followed her." Gwenn paused. She had regained control. "Any comment, Mrs. Chávez?"

"I'll wait till you're finished."

"You followed your sister but kept at a distance. She headed for the pool and when she got there settled herself in a lounge chair, obviously prepared to wait a while. Using a nearby companionway, you climbed to the Upper Promenade and chose a spot where you could watch her without being seen. Not long after, a waitress appeared carrying a tray with a bottle of champagne in a bucket and a glass. Your sister signed for it. The waitress opened the bottle and poured. There was some conversation, which I assume you couldn't hear, and then there was an exchange—the pills for the money. Your sister examined the pills. She took one and put it in her mouth. Raising her glass, she washed it down with the champagne. She'd barely had time to set the glass down when she started to convulse. She clasped her throat, made a gurgling sound, and keeled over.

"You were stunned. You couldn't move. You could only watch as Minerva tried to get to her feet, almost succeeded, then slipped and fell again, this time into the pool.

"You watched as the waitress tried to pull her out, but she wasn't strong enough. You could have gone down to help her, but you didn't. Between the two of you, you might have been able to save Minerva, but you stayed where you were, and she panicked and fled. You each had your reasons." Gwenn paused.

Juno's pallid face was set like that of a stubborn child caught in a lie. Once again, Gwenn offered her a chance to clear herself. She could admit her first statement had been a lie and go with Gwenn's version of her sister's death. If she did, she might get away with a charge of fleeing the scene of a crime. However, the law does not allow anyone to profit from a crime if involved in any way, so she would lose her inheritance.

"I didn't see Minerva till Mr. Graf escorted me to the pool."

So she was going for the win! Juno had dubbed Diana a gambler, but it appeared to be a family trait.

Gwenn shifted the attack. "What do you think your sister was doing drinking champagne poolside at that hour of the night? Alone."

"Waiting to buy drugs, I suppose."

"No, she wasn't buying drugs. She didn't need drugs anymore. She'd found a new medicine that she believed would cure her. She was waiting for it to be delivered."

"She was in remission. I don't know anything about any new medicine."

"Sure you do. She told you. She announced it with joy: She had found a cure! Another victory for Minerva. She had beaten the big C. You didn't believe it, but you had to allow for the possibility that it might be true. You, along with everyone else in the family, needed money and expected to get it by inheriting a part of Minerva's estate. But Minerva wasn't ready to die. She wasn't going to do you the favor of lying down quietly and dying for your convenience. It seemed you would have to assist her. You called for a family council.

"Paul Racine arrived first. Though he was not officially family, he counted himself and was counted as such. He joined the ship Sunday in George Town. As you recall, I was sitting with Minerva when you brought him over, and Minerva was clearly not pleased to see him. Diana joined you in Cartagena on Tuesday."

Gwenn paused for a moment to collect her thoughts. "I don't know what plan you had concocted, but on that Tuesday night, Minerva played into your hands. She waited till she thought you were asleep, then dressed quietly and sneaked out to meet her connection who delivered the new medicine she believed would save her life.

"You witnessed the transaction, though I don't think you quite knew what was happening at the time. All you knew then was that suddenly your sister was having some kind of seizure. A panorama of the benefits you would enjoy from your share of the estate passed through your mind. There would be more than enough money for your husband to pay off the mortgage, enough even to finance his political ambitions. According to my associate in New York, Vicente Chávez was planning a run for the Senate but had to withdraw due to lack of funds. You shrank back in the shadows and watched in fascinated horror as the waitress tried vainly to raise your sister, gave up, and fled. Not till she was long gone did you leave your shelter and go down the stairs to the promenade deck and over to the pool for one last look at your sister, who was floating faceup. That was when you got your second shock of the night.

"She moved. Minerva moved!"

Juno tried to speak, but the words refused to leave her mouth.

"The sea was rough; the ship was rolling, causing the water in the pool to undulate. Could that have made it seem that Minerva moved? No. No. Imagination could not make her arm rise up out of the water and reach for the pool ladder.

"Minerva was alive," Gwenn repeated.

"That brief image of a future in which Vicente would be a respected figure on the national scene shimmered before you like a mirage. You saw yourself at his side, entertaining brilliantly, inspiring him to ever greater achievements, in the company of world leaders. You would be as much a celebrity as Diana and Minerva." Gwenn had a sudden inspiration. "You would be as much admired as your mother. All those dreams would be destroyed by that arm rising out of the water and reaching for you." Gwenn stopped. It was Juno's turn.

"Well! You certainly know how to tell a story, Miss Ramadge. It's like you were there and saw the whole thing. Were you?"

"No."

The aspect of the night had changed. From soft and balmy it had become angry and threatening. Thunder was distant but ominous. Lightning lit sea and sky to the horizon. Gwenn worried about how Simon Kittridge was doing. Was he getting any of this? Would the delicate equipment he was using be affected by the electrical surges?

"Your imagination is remarkable, but nobody's going to believe you, not without some sort of evidence. Real evidence, Miss Ramadge. Otherwise, forget it."

"While you were at dinner, your stateroom was searched. Captain's orders," Gwenn put in quickly, though it wasn't true. "A generous supply of thalidomide was found in a bureau drawer." That part was true. "Obviously, Minerva didn't put it there, so it had to be you. A mistake, Mrs. Chávez. You should have left it at the pool, but you were greedy."

"Have you forgotten I'm not occupying the same stateroom anymore? Those aren't my things you went through. They're my sister's."

"But she wasn't aboard when Minerva received the drugs. You were."

"You can't prove they're the same drugs Minerva bought."

She parried every thrust, Gwenn marveled. Each time she thought she had Juno cornered, she managed to wriggle free.

"There was an identifying mark on the package put there by the person who made the delivery."

Juno's eyes narrowed. "She could be lying."

Gwenn pounced. "How do you know it was a woman?"

"You indicated it."

And so she had. Gwenn sighed. "When you moved out of the suite on the night of the drowning, you were in a hurry; you left most of your things behind."

"So you found the drugs you say belonged to Minerva among my things. They could have been planted—by anybody. You, for instance."

Her audacity was stunning, Gwenn thought as a sudden pitch of the ship almost caused her to lose her balance. But Juno Chávez was scarcely affected. A storm was coming, but she seemed unaware of it. It was time to bring the confrontation to an end. It hadn't gone as Gwenn had hoped. Instead of breaking Juno down, she had shored up her resistance. Gwenn decided to make one more try.

"There's also the matter of the fingerprints on the container."

"You almost make me laugh, Miss Ramadge. You think I don't know that identifying fingerprints is a long and complicated process and that you haven't had nearly enough time to accomplish it?" She gestured with the gun. "Let's go."

"I hope you're not foolish enough to use that," Gwenn said.

"I'm smart enough to get rid of it after I use it."

Her mental agility continued to surprise. Under that stolid, sluggish exterior, it was unexpected. "Where did you get the gun? Isn't it light for the job?"

"I own several guns and I'm a good shot too. I'm good at a lot of things. You'd be surprised."

"I understand you're also a very good skier, much better than either of your sisters."

"I used to be expert. World-class." Her eyes lit up and her face glowed.

Ah! Gwenn thought, this was what Juno Chávez craved—praise. She had lived in the shadow of her famous mother and her glamorous sisters. Her real father was a hero, but he was dead and she hardly remembered him. Her stepfather was the American equivalent of an aristocrat. She herself had neither looks nor talent. She was, by any standard, ordinary. She was starved for reassurance of her own worth.

"You were a candidate for the Olympic ski team, but on the final practice run before leaving for the Games, you fell and broke your leg. It must have been a terrible disappointment." All of this had been on the most recent fax from Marge. When she first scanned it, Gwenn had not realized its significance. She was just beginning to.

"It was," Juno affirmed. Though her gaze was on Gwenn, she was looking into the past.

Without any indication of what she intended to do, Gwenn suddenly lobbed her small evening purse up high over Juno's head.

Juno reacted automatically. She pivoted, aimed, and shot, hitting the purse as it reached the top of the arc before starting down. It was like trapshooting and the purse was the clay bird. She hadn't taken her eyes or the gun off Gwenn for more than three seconds when she turned back again.

"Convinced?" Juno Chávez asked, raising her voice over the howl of the wind and the slap of the waves against the ship's side.

"And impressed." Gwenn shouted too. The .22, smothered by

nature's turmoil, had sounded puny. The ploy had been intended to attract Kittridge's attention in case his transmitter had failed. But Gwenn had little hope that he'd heard the shot. She knew what was coming: Juno would force her forward to the prow and shoot her where the wind would sweep her off the deck into that turbulent sea below, with almost no effort on Juno's part. She would never be found. No one would ever know what had happened to her. *Forget Kittridge,* she thought. *Don't look for help from anyone but yourself.*

Dear God, she prayed. *Lord Jesus, come to my aid.*

Then, planting her feet squarely to withstand the ship's rolling, she raised her voice and shouted: "I'm not going anywhere!"

Juno Chávez shrugged. "It's your choice."

"I thought we were here to make a deal," Gwenn argued, buying time.

"You have nothing to offer, Miss Ramadge. You've concocted a story out of ifs and buts. You have no evidence. Nobody's going to believe you."

"I believe her."

Juno Chávez winced as Simon Kittridge came up from behind and with his strong hand grasped her wrist and twisted it until the pain made her drop the gun. Gwenn ducked and retrieved it.

"Let her go!"

Another voice came out of the darkness.

Juno recognized it. "Lewis! Oh, thank God you're here. She was trying to blackmail me."

"Don't say any more," Aldrich cautioned.

"You can't believe that silly story? You can't! You know I loved Minnie. I would never hurt her. There was no plot, no conspiracy. This 'council of war' she talks about, that's an invention too. Ask Diana. Ask Paul." She paused and finished lamely. "Ask them."

A 'family council' was what Gwenn had dubbed the meeting in Cartagena. Juno referred to it as a 'council of war.'

A Freudian slip?

Lights came on on the deck below. The ship's full orchestra struck a chord. Colored spotlights played their beams into the sky as the passengers assembled for the night's entertainment.

They repaired quickly to the Aldrich suite and waited in gloomy silence while the others—Diana Aldrich and her fiancé, as well as the two waitresses—were summoned and joined them. Since they had been alerted to the possibility that they might be wanted, they came quickly and now all waited silently for what Lewis Aldrich had to say. Kittridge sat to one side with the girls, Gwenn by herself on the other side.

Aldrich positioned himself at the front of the room, facing them as though he were about to address a corporate meeting. Gwenn was glad for him to take over; there were still questions for which she didn't have answers.

Aldrich looked haggard. It seemed to Gwenn he stayed on his feet by sheer will. She sensed he would have liked to walk away from the whole affair, to leave things as they were, but an inner force would not allow it.

Forgoing introductions, Aldrich began with Nancy Castel and

went straight to the point. "You admit to supplying my daughter Minerva with thalidomide?"

Nancy was pale but firm. "Yes."

"And what happened when she ingested some of it?"

"She went into a convulsion and fell into the pool. I tried to pull her out, but she was too heavy for me."

"Why didn't you call for help?"

"I thought she was dead."

"There was always the possibility that she could be revived. You should have called for help."

Nancy threw an imploring glance at Kittridge.

"She was afraid she'd be accused—"

"Let the girl speak for herself." Aldrich cut him off. "Go on," he said to Nancy. "No one is going to accuse you if you tell the truth."

"I was afraid the drug had killed her. I thought if it appeared that she had died accidentally, by drowning, that would be the end of it—nothing would be said or done. Once it was learned that there was an illegal drug involved . . . well, we would all be in trouble."

Aldrich's sigh rose from the very depths of his sorrow. "You let my daughter die to protect a smuggling operation." It was not an accusation, rather an acceptance of the way things were. He bowed his head.

"She thought Miss Aldrich was dead." Once again Kittridge tried to soothe the bereaved man.

"The drug killed her!" Aldrich cried out. "You're the one who supplied the drug."

"I supplied the medicine I believed might save your daughter's life. I did it at her request."

"What he says is true, Lewis." Diana broke into the exchange. "Minnie was determined to take the drug. She couldn't wait. She had a bad reaction to it and it killed her."

"I swear to you, Lewis, that I had nothing to do with Minnie's death," Juno Chávez pleaded. "I didn't hear Minnie get up in the middle of the night. I didn't see her leave the stateroom. I didn't follow her. The first I knew of it was when the phone rang and Eric Graf told me there'd been an accident."

Aldrich turned to Gwenn expectantly. It was time for her to make her case. Gwenn began by addressing Diana.

"Would you care to explain why, in the midst of your grievous problems in New York, you dropped everything, rented a charter, and flew down to Cartagena and came aboard the *Dante* on Tuesday morning?"

"It should be obvious," the eldest sister replied. "Mr. Racine joined the cruise on Sunday in George Town to serve as an escort for Minnie and Juno. When he found out that Minnie was taking, or planning to take, thalidomide, he was very upset. He couldn't reason with Minnie, so he called me to come down and try to talk some sense into her. We wanted, if possible, to dissuade her from taking the drug at all, or at the least to make sure she wasn't doing any harm to herself by taking it. It is, of course, a very dangerous substance with a terrible history."

And she had offered an eminently plausible explanation for her presence on the ship, Gwenn thought.

Apparently Lewis Aldrich did too. Slowly, he walked over to the cellarette and fixed himself a Scotch on the rocks. "I don't think we need detain you and the young ladies any longer," he told Kittridge. "I'll contact you before we dock in the morning."

It was a direct dismissal; nevertheless, Kittridge sought Gwenn's eye before accepting it. Gwenn herself made no move to leave. The affair was far from ended.

"We won't keep you any longer either, Miss Ramadge. If you'll send your bill—"

"You told me that your wife died two years ago while skiiing in what also appeared to be an accident," she interrupted. "You said that doubt about her death has haunted you. You didn't want there to be any uncertainty this time. You wanted the truth, whatever it might be. That's why you hired me, to get the truth."

Aldrich stared into his glass.

"My associate in New York has sent me several accounts of Mrs. Aldrich's death. I also read the testimony of various witnesses at the coroner's inquest. All of them saw Mrs. Aldrich on the beginner's slope that morning. The area is open, well frequented, and well patrolled. She appeared to be skiing in good control, but had she fallen and injured herself, there was plenty of help available."

"I know all this. It's very painful to have it rehashed. Besides, I didn't authorize you to—"

"I'm afraid you'll have to bear it."

That shocked everyone. No one spoke to Lewis Aldrich like that, certainly not a "hired hand." They waited for the thunder, but Aldrich didn't say a word.

Gwenn continued. "According to Mrs. Chávez's testimony, her mother, who excelled in everything she undertook, was bored and impatient to graduate to more challenging terrain. She wanted Mrs. Chávez to take her down the Whip, a narrow, twisting trail cut into the face of the mountain. Its danger lay both in the vertical drop and in the series of tight, corkscrew turns. Missing one meant flying out to crash in the chasm below. Of course, Mrs. Chávez refused, told her mother she wasn't ready. Her mother was angry and said she'd do it on her own."

Juno Chávez sighed. "I never thought she'd try it."

"Witnesses saw Mrs. Aldrich at the top of the trail and she seemed to be surveying the terrain."

"Do we really have to go through this?" Aldrich asked.

"If you want the truth."

Aldrich groaned and poured more Scotch over the dregs in his glass.

"Your wife and her daughters, Diana and Juno, were spending a long weekend at the house in Vermont. If I'm correct, Mrs. Chávez, you weren't married yet."

"No, I wasn't."

"You, Mr. Aldrich, and your daughter, Minerva, were spending the weekend at the North Carolina stables." Seeing that he was once more about to break in, she hurried on. "It's important to establish everyone's whereabouts. Vicente was with you, wasn't he, Mrs. Chávez?"

"Both he and Paul made up the party, yes. My mother wasn't too happy about it, but there wasn't much she could do."

"She could have asked them to leave," Gwenn pointed out.

"Diana and I would have left with them. She knew that."

"She could have stopped your allowances. Cut you out of her will. She threatened it often enough that gossip about it got into one of the columns." "Sara Lou On the Town" again, Gwenn thought.

"But she didn't," Juno pointed out. "And she never would have. She thought Vicente and Paul were playboys, that they didn't really love us and were only after our money. She didn't understand that they worked just as hard as she did, in their own way. In time, she would have accepted them."

Gwenn didn't challenge that. It might even be true, but at this point it was irrelevant.

"On the morning in question, the weather report predicted a light snowfall of one to three inches. You had breakfast together and then went your separate ways to your favorite runs. You agreed to meet for lunch back at the lodge at noon. You all showed up except Mrs. Aldrich. While waiting for her, you had a drink at the bar. After about half an hour, you decided to go into the dining room and order. You weren't worried. You thought that Mrs. Aldrich probably was in bad humor because Juno hadn't given in to her, and that she was keeping everyone waiting as punishment.

"In the meantime, what had been predicted as a light-to-average snowfall was turning into a blizzard. While you sat at the table, it intensified. Visibility was poor; the snow, wind-driven, was reaching whiteout conditions. In your testimony at the inquest you all claimed to be worrying about Mrs. Aldrich, yet not one of you did anything about it."

Both Diana and Juno kept their eyes downcast, looking neither at each other nor at Gwenn.

Paul Racine spoke up. "We did go to the ski patrol and report her missing."

"By then it was too late. The mountain was closed and the search had to wait till the storm passed."

"Are you implying that we waited deliberately?" Racine demanded. His indignation lacked conviction.

"You're all experienced skiers and you knew very well what could happen to someone caught in such a storm, particularly a beginner. Any one of you could have left the table and put in a call to the ski patrol to advise them that Mrs. Aldrich hadn't returned and that you feared she was still out there—somewhere." Gwenn took a deep breath. "But you waited till you finished lunch."

"You make it sound like . . ."

"Like what, Mr. Racine?"

"Like we did it on purpose."

Gwenn sighed. "The fact remains that while you sat in front of a blazing fire in the lodge, Valerie Horvath Aldrich lay alone on the mountain waiting and watching for someone to come and get her. Did she finally realize that no one was coming? That the girls she loved so much didn't love her? That they were greedy and selfish and obsessed with greedy and worthless men? I think she did, and in that moment she gave up the fight against the cold and the loneliness. In that moment, she died."

Tears coursed down Lewis Aldrich's ravaged cheeks. "Why, Juno? Why, Diana? She was your mother."

Juno answered. "She didn't love us—not Diana, and not me. She loved Minnie."

"She loved you all equally."

"She gave Minnie whatever she wanted. We had to work for what we got."

"She wanted to teach you the value of money. She had worked so hard for what she would ultimately turn over to you. She was afraid you would turn it over to Vicente and Paul and they would squander it. Which is exactly what has happened."

"You're not exactly an example of fiscal acuity," Juno snapped.

Aldrich winced. The color drained from his face, but he didn't retaliate. "Where is this leading, Miss Ramadge?"

"We're nearly there."

Juno stood up. "I've heard enough. I've got better things to do than listen to the figments of this woman's overactive imagination," she declared, but made no move to leave.

Gwenn continued relentlessly. "Any one of you might have saved Valerie Aldrich's life simply by reporting her absence, but you didn't. Failure to act bound you together. The money you inherited as a result of that failure also bound you. Inertia, you learned, could be a powerful weapon. Now, once again in need of money, you thought you could get it the same way—by doing nothing.

"Your sister Minerva was sick. Terminal. You thought all you had to do was wait for her to die. You couldn't have been very happy when she announced she had found a cure."

"You're wrong," Diana told her. "We were thrilled, but we couldn't be sure the drug would really work. It had a terrible reputation. We feared it might do her more harm than good."

"I said you called for a family council. Mrs. Chávez referred to it as a council of war."

Juno shrugged. "What's the difference?"

"One suggests consultation; the other, action. Probably they both apply. When the ship docked in Cartagena, the four of you met to decide what to do about Minerva; that would be Mrs. Chávez, Miss Diana, and Mr. Racine. There was the fourth?"

"There was no fourth," Racine replied. "You're mistaken."

"As he had taken no part in the decision to abandon Valerie Aldrich, Lewis Aldrich was not included in the plot against his own, natural daughter."

"There was no fourth and there was no plot against anybody." Diana's declaration had a touch of panic.

"There was a fourth person at lunch with you when your mother died on the mountain," Gwenn stated firmly. "I realize now, this same fourth person came aboard the *Dante* in Cartagena. We have a witness who saw him. He doesn't know the person's name, but it was a man. The witness describes him as big, about six foot four, robust, heavily bearded. It can only have been your husband, Mrs. Chávez. It can only have been Vicente."

"Vicente is home at the ranch hundreds of miles away. Check it out."

"You were about to make a life-and-death decision. It was important that you all participate, that you all share in the responsibility. It couldn't be done by long distance or by proxy. Vicente was summoned and he came."

"He did not," Juno protested.

Gwenn rolled right over her. "The decision had to be shared by all, but only one could do the deed. For that you drew lots and the responsibility fell to Vicente."

In spite of herself, Gwenn shuddered.

"The council broke up. Diana returned to New York and the litigation which so consumed her. Mr. Chávez remained aboard—unofficially. It wasn't difficult. On a ship this size an extra passenger can easily lose himself. As for accommodations, he stayed right here. The suite consists of two large staterooms in addition to this sitting room. The larger of the staterooms was shared by the sisters and the other was vacant. It has its own separate entrance and suited

Mr. Chávez's needs perfectly. He could come and go as he pleased and also keep an eye on the intended victim."

Gwenn paused to collect herself. She had reached the point where she would be threading her way between what she knew for fact and what she inferred.

The others were too stunned to offer objections. Even Juno was too numb to speak.

"So when Minerva left her bed Tuesday night, she didn't wake you, Mrs. Chávez. You spoke the truth about that and I apologize for accusing you of lying. She didn't wake you, but she did wake your husband in the other room." Gwenn paused for a moment, looking toward the closed door. The others followed her gaze, then turned back to her.

"So it wasn't you but Vicente who followed Minerva to her rendezvous with Nancy Castel. Watching from the Upper Promenade, he saw the transaction and understood what it was all about. He saw his sister-in-law put some of the drug she had just purchased into the champagne glass, wait a moment, raise her glass in a salute, and drink. He saw her collapse and fall into the pool. He made no move at all while Nancy struggled desperately to pull her out. He waited till she gave up and went away. Then and only then did he leave his hiding place and go down, not to help Minerva, but to make sure she was beyond help. If she was dead, then he was home free. But she was still breathing, so he had to finish her off and quickly before anyone happened by. Vicente Chávez is a big man, strong, athletic. Minerva was frail, already weakened by illness and drugs and barely conscious. It was no match."

While she explained to them, Gwenn clarified for herself what had happened. She paused for a moment so that the picture she was drawing would be fixed in their minds as it was in hers; so they could feel the horror in full measure as she did. Then she resumed.

"Skin scrapings under the fingernails would have indicated a struggle. We know from Dr. Halliday's examination that there weren't any. There was, however, blood in her mouth. I know; I tasted it. I prevailed on Dr. Halliday to test it. It was not Minerva's blood."

There was a long, uneasy sigh and an uneasy stir; this next would be critical.

"Whose blood was it then? It could only be the assailant's. How did it get into Minerva's mouth?

"I noticed that one section of the deck, close to the pool, was wet. It was logical to assume the assailant was dressed, and it wasn't likely he would get into the water with his clothes on, or that he would take the time to strip. He must have knelt at the edge of the pool and reached out for her and pulled her over. Then when he had her close, he put a hand on each shoulder and pushed her under and held her there.

"In the last few moments of clarity before dying, Minerva realized that resistance was futile and that the end was near. Lungs filling, heart pounding, the last of her strength oozing out of her, Minerva was determined to mark her killer. She stopped struggling and went limp in the hope that he would think she had expired and let her go. At last she felt the pressure ease. As she shot to the surface, she took one final gulp of air and then sank her teeth into his hand. She bit down as hard as she could and held on." Gwenn paused. "Bite marks are as individual as fingerprints and can last for years."

There was a shocked silence.

"Would you mind showing me your hands?"

As in a trance, one by one, they submitted to the inspection. All were clean.

"Thank you. Only Vicente bears the brand, but you are all guilty."

Not one of those present offered a defense.

"The pain shot from his hand right up Vicente Chávez's arm, but he didn't cry out. He wanted to, but he was still rational enough to be aware that he might be heard. Instead, he translated what in other circumstances might have been a shriek into retaliation; he pushed her under harder than ever and held her there longer than ever and when he let go—she came up again. Rage blotted out any shred of sanity that remained. He grabbed her by her long blond hair and dragged her along the side of the pool to the deep end until he came to one of the outtake grills. He wove strands of her hair through it till he was sure she would not come loose. He got to his feet slowly, but at the sound of voices he ran.

"Vicente was in trouble. If he came back here to the suite, he ran the risk of being discovered. He couldn't get off the ship because we were just about to enter the canal. Mrs. Chávez solved the problem for him. Claiming she was too upset to come back here to the room she had shared with her sister, she requested other accommodations. The truth was, she wanted a place for her husband to hide, and unwittingly, it was provided." *By me,* Gwenn thought ruefully. "So, by day, while the cabins were being cleaned and serviced, Vicente Chávez roamed the ship, but at night he slept with his wife. At last we docked in Puerto Caldera and he was able to leave the *Dante.* By now, I'm sure, he's back in Colorado. Inevitably, however, he had been seen and recognized by one of the stewards he had tried so hard to avoid."

"How can you recognize someone you don't know?" Juno demanded.

It was remarkable how assertive she could be in defense of her man, Gwenn thought.

"The same way the police do," she replied. "It's called a picture lineup. One of my contacts faxed me a photograph of Mr. Chávez which appeared recently in *The Cattleman.* It was mixed in with several similar portraits provided by our ship's photographers." Gwenn laid out a row of four-by-five glossies on the coffee table and with a gesture invited each person to step forward.

"Can you pick out Vicente Chávez?"

Juno began to cry.

"While we are at sea, the captain represents the law. I will turn my report in to him," Gwenn told Lewis Aldrich. "The rest is in your hands."

CHAPTER

20

Since the *Dante* was still two days out from her final destination, Captain Nicolletti was faced with a dilemma. He couldn't arrest all the suspects, particularly as the actual perpetrator was no longer on board. One sister, Juno Chávez, would probably be charged with conspiracy to commit murder. The other sister, Diana, and her fiancé were at least accessories, but it was not up to him to make that judgment. Should he turn around and go back to Puerto Quetzal and put these troublesome persons ashore? Or should he continue making all possible speed to Acapulco? His solution finally was to place Juno Chávez in protective custody, and continue on. He acceded gladly to the wishes of her stepfather and ordered her held in protective custody in the relative comfort of the infirmary. Then he returned to the bridge with strict instructions that he was not to be distracted from the business of running his ship except in dire crisis.

Lewis Aldrich was torn between the desire to avenge the deaths of his natural daughter and his wife and the obligation to ensure his stepdaughter the best possible defense. He accompanied Juno to her quarters and made sure she would be under constant observation through the night till the ship docked in Acapulco the next morning and the local authorities took her off his hands. *Suicide watch,* Gwenn thought sadly, pitying both stepfather and stepdaughter. Though she had not actually committed the crime, Juno was inextricably joined to it.

In Gwenn's experience with homicide cases, once the crime was solved and the perpetrator apprehended, it was over—at least her part in it was. Once the suspect was absorbed into the justice system, he was automatically processed. Not this time. There were complications Gwenn had never encountered before. For one, she had never seen or spoken to the perp. He was, in fact, yet to be apprehended.

Gwenn had no doubt that her final reconstruction of the crime was the right one. The obvious motive of the conspirators was the same—greed. But she was beginning to see that it was more complex. Juno had been obsessed by her desire for Vicente and frustrated by her mother's disapproval of him. She was jealous of her half sister. It was possible that deep down she resented Lewis Aldrich for taking the place of her real father, even that she felt her mother had betrayed her real father by marrying a second time. Left alone tonight, locked up with these conflicting emotions, Juno might try to do herself harm.

All Gwenn could do was to offer to help keep watch, and her offer was accepted.

What was left of the night was divided into six one-hour shifts, of which Gwenn drew the first and the last. Lewis Aldrich sat at the desk in the reception area of the medical suite and was within shouting distance throughout. Most of the time, he was on the telephone making arrangements for the defense of both stepdaughters. By daybreak, Aldrich had lined up a local Mexican attorney to meet them dockside, prepared to take care of Juno's and Diana's interests while they were in Mexican jurisdiction and through the extradition process. There was no way of knowing how long that would take, but Lewis Aldrich intended to stand by his girls. He had also secured the services of one of the top criminal lawyers in the United States, who would be waiting for them as soon as they set foot in the country.

In a rare moment of repose between calls, Aldrich felt Gwenn's eyes on him.

"It's what *she* would have wanted. It's what my Valerie would have done."

Gwenn nodded. She had to respect him for that. At the same time, she pitied him.

It was expected that when Juno was turned over to U.S. authorities, she would return in custody via a commercial aircraft. Aldrich had chartered a plane to stand by so that the family could fly back at the same time as escort.

"I don't know when we'll be leaving, Miss Ramadge. It might be a day or a week or more, but if you're still here, you're welcome to fly back with us. There's plenty of space."

"Thank you, but I've decided to return with the ship. I have some unfinished business." He didn't ask what it was and she didn't tell him. She had another question. "What about Vicente?"

"The local police should be ringing his doorbell"—he consulted his watch—"just about now."

There was nothing more to be said.

They continued to watch over Juno in shifts for the last dreary days of the trip. She slept most of the time. Gwenn and Aldrich exchanged glances only when there seemed to be a change in her condition. At last they reached Acapulco.

DAY 13
DEBARKATION

The MS *Dante Alighieri* docked in Acapulco at 6:55 A.M. on Wednesday, January 25. Five minutes later, the Mexican police came aboard and were escorted to sick bay, where they took Juno Chávez into custody and escorted her ashore. The lawyer Lewis Aldrich had engaged during the night was there to protect her rights, and her family followed her off the ship like a cortege.

At seven-thirty, Mexican Immigration boarded the *Dante* and set up a processing center in the Vasco da Gama Room in order to examine those few passengers who were not U.S. citizens. There were a dozen or so Canadians, about the same number of South Americans, two Australian couples who were going around the world. They presented no problem, and the ship was cleared. At eight, as passengers began to go ashore, Gwenn took breakfast in the main dining room. That was where Simon Kittridge found her.

"Hi." He stood across the table and looked over at her. She was wearing white slacks and a bright red shirt, its tails tied at her bare midriff. Her toenails, visible in open sandals, were lacquered to match. Not a costume for traveling. "I hear you're going back with the ship."

Gwenn nodded. "I'm going to make one more try at nabbing the jewel thief. How about you?" At this very moment Kittridge should have been either in the lounge giving debarkation instructions or at one of the gangplanks bidding the passengers goodbye. "Aren't you on duty?"

"I've been fired."

He said it lightly, but he was dejected. Though meticulously turned out as usual, today Kittridge didn't seem to fill his clothes. He appeared shrunken, his spirit and energy depleted. He was an old man, Gwenn reminded herself, very old, but she couldn't commiserate with him.

"Actually, they're being easy on me. They could have turned me in to customs. Then I would have been on the suspect list and I'd be harassed every time I went in and out of the country."

"Did they give you any salary in lieu of notice?"

"Are you kidding?"

"How about your passage back to Fort Lauderdale?"

"Mr. Aldrich offered me a seat on his charter—whenever it goes. I turned it down. I also gave him back his check."

"You didn't need to do that."

"I know." He stood a little taller.

It was time to say goodbye, but neither one knew how to do it.

"Well . . ." Kittridge shuffled awkwardly. "I brought back your equipment." He set the small canvas bag he'd been carrying on the chair beside Gwenn.

"Thanks." She'd almost forgotten about it. "How much of what passed between me and Juno Chávez did you get?"

"Practically nothing. When I checked out the area earlier, I noticed the weather starting to deteriorate. I wondered how bad it would get and whether your equipment could handle the electrical fluctuations. I decided not to leave it to chance. I went to Mr. Aldrich and told him the plan to record was in large part for his benefit, but that conditions were not favorable. I told him if he was sincere in wanting to learn the truth, he would come with me."

"You didn't give him much choice. Thanks. I owe you."

"Forget it. When I come up to New York sometime, you'll buy me a drink."

"You bet." She couldn't summon much enthusiasm. "What about the girls?"

"They're fired too, but the company is paying their way home. They'll be all right. They're young, attractive, eager. There'll be other jobs. For my part, I was already retired when I signed on. The odd job now and then will suffice for me. I could be your man in Florida." He tried a smile.

She didn't respond. "Whose idea was it for Nancy to get beat up?"

"They cooked it up between them."

"I don't believe that."

"Nancy was traumatized by what happened to Minerva Aldrich and her part in it. She was practically hysterical by the time she got back to the cabin. Sofia tried to comfort her but she was inconsolable. She felt she was somehow to blame and she was afraid of being charged and arrested. They called me, but nothing I said helped."

Kittridge sighed. "I mentioned that if it could be made to appear that Nancy herself was being victimized she would probably avoid coming under suspicion."

"Sofia hit her friend?" Gwenn groaned. "She knocked Nancy on the back of the head and then punched and kicked her when she was down? And you let her?"

"She didn't ask my permission."

"How about sneaking into my cabin in the middle of the night? That was Sofia, too?" Working for room service, Sofia could have gotten into any cabin she wanted, Gwenn thought. "You didn't know about that either, I suppose."

"She wouldn't have done you any harm. Believe me. She only meant to—"

"Scare me half to death! Yes, I know, and she just about succeeded." Gwenn shook her head. "And the Valium? Was that really necessary?"

"That was an accident, I swear."

"Do you realize what a close call it was? How close to the edge Nancy came? We nearly lost her."

"You can't put the blame for that on me," he began hotly, but modified his tone at the look in Gwenn's eyes. "But you do, don't you? You consider me responsible for everything that's happened."

"I do. The fact that supplying thalidomide wasn't illegal doesn't make it all right. Two wrongs don't make a right. Everything that's happened on this ship originated with your dealing."

"I don't see it like that."

"Just because you haven't been arrested doesn't mean you've been exonerated!" Gwenn's temper flared.

"You shouldn't try to impose your standards on everyone." Kittridge's voice rose to match.

"Is this a private argument, or can anyone get in?"

Gwenn and Kittridge stopped and looked around.

"Ray!" Gwenn exclaimed. "Ray!" Pushing her chair back, she rose and threw her arms around Ray Dixon.

They held each other. He bent down and kissed her energetically. She responded with enthusiasm. When he let her go, they continued to look into each other's eyes, oblivious of Kittridge and various diners who were openly watching.

"How are you? What are you doing here?" Not having seen Ray for what seemed like weeks but was only days, Gwenn now regarded him with clearer vision. She was struck anew by his quiet good looks and by the way he carried himself. He was dignified without being overly assertive. She saw too that he was tired and shifting from foot to foot, indicating that he was nervous—very uncharacteristic. Before she'd talked to his ex-wife, Patty, Gwenn would have attributed all this to his new assignment at IA. Now she wasn't so sure.

"I'm fine," he told her. "How are you? You look great—all tanned and healthy and relaxed."

So much for appearances, Gwenn thought. "Oh, excuse me. This is my friend Simon Kittridge. Simon is . . . was . . . on the cruise. Simon, this is Sergeant Ray Dixon. I've told you about him."

"Many times." The two shook hands. Simon regarded Ray with some awe. "You people sure move fast."

Ray frowned. "How do you mean?"

"No, no, no," Gwenn put in hastily. "Ray has nothing to do with the case." Then she frowned. "What *are* you doing here?"

"What case?"

"I'll tell you later. After you tell me why you're here."

"I came to see you. Patty told me you called. I called back, but you weren't in your cabin and they couldn't locate you."

"It's a big ship."

"It sure is," Ray agreed. "Anyway, I decided to fly down and surprise you."

"You did that, all right."

"I have a few days off and I thought we could spend them together."

"You mean we should stay over, here in Acapulco?"

"Sure. I thought you'd be all for it. You're always saying we should get away . . . together."

Slowly, Gwenn sank back into her chair. "What about Patty? What's she going to say?"

"It's none of her business."

"It isn't?"

"No. Anyway, she's getting married again."

Kittridge squirmed. He was beginning to feel very much out of place. "If you'll excuse me, I have to be going," he said. "They'll be calling my number to board the bus. . . . Gwenn? Sergeant?" *Oh hell!* he thought. *Neither one is listening.* He turned and walked away.

Gwenn gaped at Ray. "Who's she going to marry?"

He shrugged. "Someone she met at a wedding. She wanted me to meet him, so I went over there to her place. Seems like a nice enough guy. Has a good job. Steady. Nine to five, five days a week."

"Okay, if that's what you want."

"That's what Patty's always wanted."

Suddenly Gwenn became aware that Kittridge was gone. "Where's Simon? He left without saying goodbye."

"Don't feel bad. He was too old for you."

"Are you serious?" She grinned. "I've always enjoyed the company of older men."

Ray pulled out a chair and sat beside her. "So, what do you say? Should we stay over for a couple of days?"

"That would be wonderful!" Then her green eyes dimmed. "I can't. I'm sorry. I'm really very sorry, Ray. I've agreed to take passage with the ship for another shot at getting that jewel thief."

"And you couldn't possibly break a commitment like that, could you?"

"You should have called me and let me know in advance . . ."

"You're the great advocate of spontaneity!" he charged. "Hell, Gwenn! We might never get a chance like this again."

"Probably not," she agreed. "So why don't you sail back with me?"

"Really? You mean it? Would you really like me to?"

"I wouldn't have suggested it otherwise."

"Thirteen days . . . I don't know. I had to mortgage Christmas and Labor Day to get this four-day weekend. I suppose it could be arranged."

Just when she thought he was going to agree, he backed off.

"You're probably going to spend the whole time running around the ship chasing clues."

"No I'm not. Once the case is solved . . ."

"You haven't made any headway so far, have you? What makes you think you're going to do better anytime soon?"

"I'll have you to help me." She grinned.

He almost relented. "No you won't. Look, you told me there are close to thirteen hundred passengers and six hundred crew on this ship, right?"

"Right."

"And not a lead among them."

"We've narrowed it down. The thefts were committed on the *Dante* on three separate and consecutive trips. The same passenger wouldn't risk being identified."

"How do you know? Maybe he's a master of disguise and enjoys the challenge. Or he thinks he can outsmart everybody. So far, he's right."

"It would be so much easier to hit a different ship each time." She had used these arguments before at the head office and with Captain Nicolletti and Eric Graf. They were no more impressive now than they had been then. "We've got to start somewhere," she finished lamely.

"True enough." Ray Dixon helped himself to rolls and butter still on the table from Gwenn's breakfast. He felt the coffee pot, and finding it warm, poured himself a cup. His mind was far away.

"Okay. Let's say for the moment that your theory is correct and we eliminate the passengers. The public areas of the ship and the crew quarters were thoroughly searched, but nothing was found. The loot could have been thrown overboard, but somehow I doubt that."

"Of course it wasn't thrown overboard!" Gwenn was indignant at the idea. "It wasn't passed to an accomplice who was going ashore either, for the same reason we eliminated a passenger being the thief."

"Well then, whoever conducted the search didn't look in the right places," Ray concluded.

"They searched everywhere," Gwenn insisted.

"Couldn't have."

"They did."

"Hm," Dixon grunted. "Did they search the captain's quarters?"

Gwenn was stunned. "The captain's quarters? Are you mad? Captain Nicolletti's private quarters? He is the commander of this ship. He is the supreme and sole authority. His word is law. He controls everyone and everything." Gwenn spread out her arms as though embracing the entire ship. "You think Captain Nicolletti is a common thief?"

"In other words, his room wasn't searched."

"I didn't ask. I couldn't."

"That's answer enough. How about the chief officer?"

"The hotel director, Graf? He was in charge of the search and oversaw the searchers."

"Ah . . ."

"Don't say 'Ah' like that," she mimicked. "You don't know the esteem and respect these men are held in, the prestige of their positions. They would never risk—"

"Who else was exempt? The doctor? Was a priest or minister aboard?"

"I don't know. For God's sake—"

A light flashed and then another in a far corner where Brian Bates captured the merriment of an early luncheon party.

"How about the photographer? Was his place searched?" Ray asked. "Did anyone go into his darkroom? Examine his equipment? Open his cameras and expose his film?"

Gwenn jumped to her feet. "Someone is about to do that right now."

Ray reached out a hand and stopped her. "It's not even a hunch," he warned.

"It's all we've got." Gwenn indicated an empty alcove. "Wait. I'll be right back."

She was gone less than five minutes, and when she returned, she waved for Bates to join them. Shaking hands with Gwenn, he was all geniality. When she introduced Ray as Sergeant Dixon of the NYPD, he cooled off.

"What can I do for you, Miss Ramadge?"

"Sergeant Dixon is interesed in cameras. I thought you wouldn't mind showing him how yours works."

He gasped. His pale blue eyes bulged. The rush of blood to his face washed away the freckles. He managed, with great effort, to get hold of himself. "Some other time, Miss Ramadge. The next group of passengers is just about to board. I'm on my way down to the dock right now to document the momentous event." He tried a laugh that sounded as though he were choking and made him redder than ever. "You'll have to excuse me."

He tried to go around them, but Ray stepped in his way.

"What do you want?" Bates cringed like a trapped animal.

"We want to look at your cameras and your equipment," Gwenn said. "If we don't find what we expect to find, Captain Nicolletti will turn you over to the Mexican authorities and let them . . . interrogate you. If we do find the items we're looking for, or you tell us where they are, Captain Nicolletti will hold you for the U.S. authorities. Take your choice."

It didn't take long for Bates to decide. "I don't have them anymore. I got rid of them. I sold them. Naturally. What would you expect?" He shrugged, tried to be casual once more. "I got rid of them as soon as I could."

"Too bad. That's really too bad. I think the ladies from whom you stole the jewels might have been convinced to drop charges if you made restitution. The jewels had sentimental value."

He carried two cameras and an equipment case slung over his shoulder. He selected one, opened it, and handed it to Gwenn. Behind the lens, where the film should have been, cotton had been stuffed. Picking at the cotton, Gwenn removed the missing gems: the emerald pendant, the diamond earrings, the diamond bracelet.

"Why in the world did you keep them all this time?" she demanded.

"I couldn't get rid of them! Nobody would pay anything like what they're worth." His pale face was twisted with rage and frustration. "All I wanted was a nest egg so I could get off this damn ship and start a normal life. But I wasn't about to give the damn things away!"

DAY I
ACAPULCO
DEPARTURE

Lifeboat drill over, orange life vests returned to the cabin, Gwenn Ramadge and Ray Dixon stood at the rail watching the land glide by. The sun was sinking. Twilight would come fast and the night even faster. It was a magic moment. Simon Kittridge had said that and it was true. Ray put an arm around Gwenn, tilted her chin up, and kissed her.

"Mind if I ask you something?"

"No, go ahead."

"When did you set up the deal for Bates with the captain? You weren't gone from the table all that long."

"Long enough. I couldn't reach the captain. There was no deal."

Ray groaned. "I might have known."

"The captain's a decent man. I figured he'd go for it."

"And you're a decent and compassionate woman." He kissed her again with enthusiasm.

A door opened behind them and they separated. The music of the Lombardo Strings wafted out.

"Shall we have a drink before dinner?" Gwenn suggested.

"Or after dinner?" Ray asked.

New York Post
November 4, 1995

Horror drug is back—as a cure for AIDS

by PAUL THARP

Thalidomide, the morning-sickness pill that caused a generation of deformed babies worldwide, is going into mass production here as a possible treatment for AIDS.

Celgene Corp., a biotechnology firm in Warren, N.J., obtained a patent for thalidomide, restricted for use on AIDS sufferers in ongoing tests with Rockefeller University.